THE FRONTIERSMAN
DAMNATION
VALLEY

Look for these exciting Western series from bestselling authors
WILLIAM W. JOHNSTONE
and J. A. JOHNSTONE

The Mountain Man

Preacher: The First Mountain Man

Luke Jensen, Bounty Hunter

Those Jensen Boys!

The Jensen Brand

MacCallister

Flintlock

Perley Gates

The Kerrigans: A Texas Dynasty

Sixkiller, U.S. Marshal

Texas John Slaughter

Will Tanner, U.S. Deputy Marshal

The Frontiersman

Savage Texas

The Trail West

The Chuckwagon Trail

Rattlesnake Wells, Wyoming

AVAILABLE FROM PINNACLE BOOKS

THE FRONTIERSMAN
DAMNATION VALLEY

William W. Johnstone

with J. A. Johnstone

PINNACLE BOOKS
Kensington Publishing Corp.
www.kensingtonbooks.com

PINNACLE BOOKS are published by

Kensington Publishing Corp.
119 West 40th Street
New York, NY 10018

PUBLISHER'S NOTE
Following the death of William W. Johnstone, the Johnstone family is working with a carefully selected writer to organize and complete Mr. Johnstone's outlines and many unfinished manuscripts to create additional novels in all of his series like The Last Gunfighter, Mountain Man, and Eagles, among others. This novel was inspired by Mr. Johnstone's superb storytelling.

All Kensington titles, imprints, and distributed lines are available at special quantity discounts for bulk purchases for sales promotions, premiums, fund-raising, educational, or institutional use. Special book excerpts or customized printings can also be created to fit specific needs. For details, write or phone the office of the Kensington sales manager: Kensington Publishing Corp., 119 West 40th Street, New York, NY 10018, attn: Sales Department; phone 1-800-221-2647.

PINNACLE BOOKS, the Pinnacle logo, and the WWJ steer head logo are Reg. U.S. Pat. & TM Off.

ISBN-13: 978-0-7860-4038-4
ISBN-10: 0-7860-4038-6

First printing: July 2018

10 9 8 7 6 5 4 3 2 1

Printed in the United States of America

First electronic edition: July 2018

ISBN-13: 978-0-7860-4039-1
ISBN-10: 0-7860-4039-4

Chapter 1

Breckinridge Wallace held on to the tomahawk with his thumb and flexed his other fingers. He had been waiting for a while to kill a man, and he didn't want his hand to get stiff.

As Breckinridge gripped the tomahawk firmly again, he lifted his head a little and listened. His hearing was keen, but the sound he thought he had just heard was so faint, he wasn't sure but whether it was his imagination.

He wasn't really the sort to be gripped by flights of fancy, though, so he pressed his back harder against the tree trunk, looked over at Morgan Baxter, who was crouched behind a boulder, and nodded.

Their quarry was coming.

Earlier, the two men had pulled their canoe ashore on a gravel bank next to the Yellowstone River. Breckinridge thought he had spotted shadowy figures darting through the trees and underbrush alongside the stream, following their course, and the logical assumption was that somebody was trailing them and planned to ambush them.

Morgan hadn't seen the men stalking them, but he and Breckinridge had been partners for a while, and he had learned to trust Breck's instincts.

"What do you want to do?" he had asked in a voice quiet enough not to be heard over the bubbling of the river.

"First good place we come to, we'll go ashore and head off into the woods. That'll lure 'em after us, and then we can jump 'em, whoever they are."

"If they're thieves, won't they just steal the canoe and the supplies in it?"

Breckinridge hadn't thought about that. He was a young man who believed in direct action, and sometimes the subtleties of strategy escaped him.

"We'll take the packs with us," he'd decided.

That was just what they did.

Breckinridge shouldered the heaviest packs, since he was a foot taller and weighed seventy or eighty pounds more than Morgan. Morgan had an added disadvantage because his right leg ended just below the knee. A stout wooden peg took its place. An evil man named Jud Carnahan was responsible for that mutilation. It had taken some time for Morgan to recover from the injury that had almost killed him, but he had regained most of his strength and learned how to get around on the peg without too much trouble.

Breckinridge intended to settle the score for what had happened to his best friend, as well as for all the other terrible things Carnahan had done, and this journey they were on was the first step in that quest.

They had tramped into the woods bordering the

Yellowstone for about half a mile before stopping. A clump of boulders provided a place for Morgan to take cover, while Breckinridge waited behind a thick-trunked pine. Morgan had pulled a brace of flintlock pistols from behind the leather sash around his waist and held them with his thumbs on the hammers, ready to cock and fire the weapons. Breck preferred the tomahawk for close work.

They were going to feel mighty foolish if whoever was following them turned out not to be a threat, Breckinridge told himself. But out here in the Rockies, hundreds of miles from civilization, it paid not to take any unnecessary chances.

Of course, in his experience, civilization had never been all that safe, either. Back home, he'd had to worry about a murder charge that wasn't true hanging over his head, and he'd gotten in trouble any number of times in St. Louis. Anywhere there were people, a good number of 'em were going to be sorry sons, and that was just the way of the world.

Not far away, a footstep whispered on the soft duff under the trees. Breckinridge raised the tomahawk a little. A man stepped into view between him and the rocks where Morgan was hidden. The man wore buckskins, and his reddish-bronze face was painted for battle. Breck recognized him right away as a Blackfoot and knew his instincts had been right. The Blackfeet hated all white men and killed every one they came across.

Breckinridge raised the tomahawk and tensed to leap at the warrior. As he did, he heard a tiny crack somewhere behind him. Instantly, he knew that was a twig snapping under the foot of someone else.

"Behind us!" he shouted to Morgan as he leaped from behind the tree. "It's a trick!"

He heard a flutter and then a thud, and knew without looking back that an arrow had just embedded itself in the tree trunk. If he'd moved a split second later, the wickedly sharp flint arrowhead would be buried in his flesh.

The warrior who had served as the decoy whirled toward Breckinridge and slashed at him with a knife. Breck twisted enough that the blade stirred the fringe on the sleeve of his buckskin shirt but didn't cut him. He brought the tomahawk down on the warrior's wrist and heard the sharp crack of bone breaking. The man's fingers opened and he dropped the knife.

The Blackfoot had a tomahawk, too. He tried to yank it from the loop at his waist where he carried it, but Breckinridge didn't give him enough time to do that. Breck swung his 'hawk in a backhand that shattered the warrior's jaw. A swift, looping overhand swing cleaved the Blackfoot's skull to the eyes.

While that was happening, both of Morgan's pistols boomed. As the reports echoed through the forest, Breckinridge bent at the waist and twisted, kicked the dead Blackfoot away from him, and spotted another warrior charging at him. He dived for the man's knees and upended him. They wound up in a tangle on the forest floor.

The Blackfoot was lean and wiry, but his muscles were like thick cables. He thrust a knife at Breckinridge's throat, but Breck caught the man's wrist while the point was just shy of its target. The Blackfoot was strong, but the strength of the massive young man sometimes called Flamehair was legendary on the frontier. Breck squeezed the warrior's wrist until bones ground together. The Blackfoot let out an involuntary gasp as he dropped the knife.

His other hand had hold of Breckinridge's wrist. For the time being, he was keeping Breck from dashing his brains out with the tomahawk. Breck knew he could overcome his opponent eventually, but he didn't want to take the time to do that. He needed to see how Morgan was faring with the other attackers.

Breckinridge lowered his head and butted the top of it into the warrior's face. He felt the hot spurt of blood from the man's crushed nose. The stunning impact made the warrior's grip slip. Breck yanked his arm loose and slammed the tomahawk down. More blood flew as the Blackfoot died.

Breckinridge surged up, saw Morgan a few yards away, wrestling with another warrior. A fourth Blackfoot lay sprawled on his back nearby, a dark hole in his forehead where the heavy ball from one of Morgan's pistols had smashed into him. A pool of blood spread around the back of his head.

Morgan was putting up a good fight, but he appeared to be getting the worst of it. The warrior was on top of him, hands wrapped around his throat, choking the life out of him.

Breckinridge reached them in two swift strides, gripped the tomahawk with both hands, and swung it with all his strength. The 'hawk's keen, blood-smeared head struck the warrior on the side of the neck, cut all the way to bone, and then sheared through the Blackfoot's spine as well. The blow knocked the man off Morgan. He landed with his almost-detached head flopping grotesquely.

"You cut his head off!" Morgan gasped.

"Not quite," Breckinridge said. "Are there any more of 'em?"

Morgan sat up, rubbed his throat under the close-cropped brown beard where the Indian had been strangling him, and looked around.

"I don't think so. I didn't see any others."

"Must've been just the four of 'em. The way they're painted, they were lookin' for trouble. Reckon they're scouts from a bigger war party?"

"I don't know," Morgan said. "I'm no authority on such matters, but isn't this a little far south for Blackfeet to be roaming around? They *are* Blackfeet, aren't they?"

"Yep. And you're right, they're a little out of their usual stompin' grounds. But we've seen how they like to come down here and raid the Crow villages in these parts."

A bleak look settled over Breckinridge's rugged, clean-shaven face. His words reminded him of how Jud Carnahan, among the man's other crimes, had formed an alliance with the brutal Blackfoot war chief Machitehew in order to wreak bloody havoc on the Crow Indians who had befriended Breck. One of the Crow, the beautiful young woman Dawn Wind, had been more than a friend . . .

But that was all in the past now. All that was left from those days were bitter memories and a hunger for vengeance.

Breckinridge helped Morgan stand up. Morgan looked around at the scattered bodies and said, "You killed three of them and I did for one. That's usually about how it turns out."

"I don't keep count," Breckinridge said. "They were

clever varmints. Must've figured we might be onto them, so three of 'em circled around while the fourth one walked right up on us. Came close to workin'." Breck bent and used the shirt on one of the dead men to wipe away the blood and brains smeared on his tomahawk. "Out here, though, close ain't good enough most of the time."

Morgan sat on one of the rocks while he reloaded his pistols. He said, "We'd better get back to the others. If there really is a Blackfoot war party in the area, they might run into trouble. We don't want to lose those furs." He paused for a second, then added, "And of course, we don't want anything to happen to our friends."

That brief delay was explained by the fact that Morgan's father had been a successful businessman, and Morgan had been raised to take over that business someday. Sometimes he just naturally thought in terms of profit and loss, instead of human considerations. But he had a good heart and was the best friend Breckinridge had ever had, other than his brothers. In some ways, Morgan was closer to him than his brothers. They had shared a lot more dangers, that was for sure.

They hefted the packs and started back toward the river, leaving the dead Blackfoot warriors where they had fallen. The canoe was where they had left it, and as they were loading the packs back into the craft, another canoe came around a bend upstream, being paddled by two men. Two more canoes followed it into sight.

The lightweight canoes rode low in the water because they were packed with bundles of furs, mostly beaver. Breckinridge and Morgan had trapped some

of those furs themselves, but many of them came from
the stronghold where Carnahan's band of thieves had
hidden. Breck had recovered them after the final
battle in which all of Carnahan's gang, except for the
leader himself, had been slain. There was no way of
knowing who had taken those pelts originally, so after
thinking about it, Breck had decided the best thing to
do with them was to use them to finance his pursuit of
Carnahan.

The men in the canoes spotted Breckinridge and
Morgan on the bank and paddled toward them. They
were a rough-looking bunch, most with beards and
long hair, dressed in an assortment of buckskins,
canvas and wool trousers, and linsey-woolsey shirts.
Some sported coonskin caps while others wore the
broad-brimmed, round-crowned felt hats common
among mountain men. One man named Richmond
even had a beaver hat like the ones the swells wore
back East.

The nominal leader of the group was Charlie Moss.
He had been in charge of the dozen men Morgan had
hired back in St. Louis to bring him back to the
mountains while he was still recuperating. He had set
out to find Breckinridge and deliver the news that Jud
Carnahan was still alive. Morgan had spotted him in
the city and discovered that Carnahan was preparing
to head back to the Rockies, no doubt bent on more
treachery and evil.

After locating Breckinridge, who was still at the
Crow village where he had spent the winter, half of
the party had elected to set out on their own and do
some trapping. Moss, Richmond, and the others had
accepted Morgan's offer of a job helping track down
Carnahan. A large, well-armed group would have

more of a chance of success than two men—even when one of those men was Breckinridge Wallace.

"I thought you fellas were scouting for a good place for us to camp tonight," Moss said as the men grounded the canoes.

"We were," Morgan said, "but we realized we were being stalked by a small party of Blackfoot warriors and had to deal with them."

Moss's eyebrows rose as he said, "Blackfeet? Where are they?"

Breckinridge jerked a thumb over his shoulder and said, "Back yonder a ways. They won't give us any trouble."

Moss grunted and shook his head.

"Somehow that don't surprise me, Wallace. You reckon there are any more of them around?"

"We don't know," Morgan said. "So we're going to push on and try to reach Absalom Garwood's trading post as soon as possible. We ought to be there tomorrow. Then we can sell these furs and be one step closer to finding Carnahan."

Breckinridge thought about everything Carnahan had cost him and then, as a vision of him smashing the man into bloody bits with his tomahawk filled his head, he said, "Can't be too soon to suit me."

Chapter 2

Breckinridge had figured they would have to take the furs all the way back downriver to St. Louis to sell them, but Morgan had brought news of more than Jud Carnahan's survival.

"A man named Garwood has built a trading post on the Yellowstone, about fifty miles from here. Evidently he arrived last fall, built a cabin for shelter, and then expanded it into a larger building over the winter. We stopped there on the way up, and he said that if we had any pelts later, he would be in the market for them."

"He built the place and is runnin' it by himself?" Breckinridge had asked as he and Morgan sat cross-legged on buffalo robes in one of the lodges in the Crow village.

"No, he had some helpers. His sons, I suppose, since he called them his young 'uns. I didn't see them, though. We weren't there long, since I was eager to get on out here and find you."

"From what I hear, independent traders don't pay

as much as what you'd get from the fur companies back in St. Louis."

"Probably not," Morgan had said, "but Garwood's place is hundreds of miles closer than St. Louis. It would take us weeks to go all the way downriver and back. Weeks that Carnahan could use to disappear even deeper into the mountains."

That comment had brought a scornful grunt from Breckinridge.

"We'll be able to find him. Wherever he is, he'll be up to such no good that we'll hear about it."

"You may be right about that. But I still think it would be better to take that pile of furs you have and sell them to Garwood."

Breckinridge couldn't argue with his friend's logic. They had struck a deal with the six men who were going to accompany them, promising partial payment once the pelts were sold and the rest of the money when Carnahan had been brought to justice.

They had loaded the pelts in three canoes, the supplies they would be taking with them into another that would be paddled by Breckinridge and Morgan, and then the whole party had set off, paddling down the creek on which the Crow village was located until it merged with the Yellowstone. They had been traveling downstream for a couple of days on the river, making good progress since they didn't have to fight the current.

They paddled several more miles downriver from the site of the battle with the Blackfoot warriors before making camp. The flames of a campfire were dancing merrily in the clearing where the men had spread their bedrolls when a voice hailed them from the river about fifty yards away.

"Hello, the camp! All right to come on in?"

Breckinridge had leaned his long-barreled flintlock rifle against a log. He picked it up as he came to his feet. His thumb rested on the rifle's hammer.

Morgan and the other men were instantly alert, too. They weren't expecting trouble, but out here a man always had to be prepared for it.

Breckinridge said, "You boys stay here. I'll go talk to those fellas."

"I'll come with you," Charlie Moss said. "If they're lookin' to start a fight, you'll need somebody sidin' you."

That wasn't necessarily true—Breckinridge had waded into plenty of ruckuses where he was outnumbered and still emerged triumphant—but he didn't see any reason to hurt Moss's feelings by saying so. He just nodded his agreement and let his long legs carry him toward the river. Moss had to hurry to keep up.

When they reached the bank, in the fading light Breckinridge saw two canoes floating a short distance offshore. There was only one man in each canoe. With four-to-one odds against them, they didn't constitute any sort of threat, Breck supposed. He called, "Howdy, fellas. You by yourselves?"

"Just the two of us," one of the men answered. "Name's Roy Deming. This is my partner Fred Kane."

"Howdy," Kane said. "We saw your fire and thought you might be willing to have some company for the night. We can share some coffee."

"Come on in," Breckinridge told them. He still had his rifle cradled in his left arm in case of trouble, but he used his right hand to wave the men toward shore.

Deming and Kane dragged their canoes up onto the bank. Kane got a bag of coffee out of their supplies and carried it with him as he and Deming walked toward the fire with Breckinridge and Moss. As they entered the circle of yellow light cast by the flames, Breck studied the two newcomers.

Deming was tall and thin, with a shock of dark hair under a pushed-back hat. Kane was shorter and stockier without being fat. His brown hair fell to his shoulders, and he had a rather bushy beard to match. Both men wore new-looking buckskins.

"First time trapping out here?" Breckinridge asked.

Deming laughed. "Do we look that much like greenhorns?"

"Don't worry about it. Spendin' time in the mountains seasons a man pretty quick-like."

Moss added, "At least you knew to call out when you came close to our camp. Taking a fella by surprise is a good way to get yourself shot."

"That's just common sense, isn't it?" Kane asked.

"Yeah, but sometimes that's in short supply, even out here," Breckinridge told him.

They reached the fire, and the two men introduced themselves to Morgan and the others in Breckinridge's party. Kane said, "I see you've already got a pot of coffee going, so we can use this I brought in the morning."

"Help yourselves to some salt pork and beans," Richmond offered. He'd been in charge of rustling up tonight's supper.

As they were eating, Deming asked, "Any trouble with the Indians hereabouts?"

"We were told that the Crow usually get along pretty well with white men," Kane added.

Breckinridge nodded and said, "That's true. All the tribes in these parts will generally leave you alone if you leave them alone. Except the Blackfeet."

The two newcomers exchanged a worried glance. Deming said, "I didn't know this is Blackfoot country."

"They figure anywhere they happen to be is Blackfoot country, and they're mighty touchy about it, too." Breckinridge paused. "We ran into a few of 'em earlier today."

"What happened?" Kane asked, his eyes wide.

"You don't have to worry about those particular Indians," Morgan said drily. "They won't bother you."

Kane and Deming looked at each other again, and Deming said, "Oh."

"But they could have friends," Breckinridge said, "so keep your eyes open. If you see any Indians, you'd do well to steer clear of 'em, just on general principles."

"We'll remember that," said Kane.

Deming frowned and added, "Mr. Garwood didn't say anything about there being Blackfeet around here."

"Could be he doesn't know about it," Breckinridge said. "You stopped at Garwood's trading post?"

"We sure did," Kane said. An enthusiastic note had entered his voice. "I'm looking forward to going back there, too."

"Why's that?" Morgan asked.

"Why, the girls, of course."

Breckinridge, Morgan, and all the other men gathered around the fire sat forward a little.

"Girls?" Morgan repeated.

"Garwood's daughters," Deming said. "What was it he called them, Fred?"

"His young 'uns," Kane replied. "Or do you mean their

names? Let me see if I can remember . . . Desdemona, Ophelia, and . . . Eugenia, that's it. Isn't that right?"

Deming nodded and said, "Yeah, I think it is."

Charlie Moss looked at Morgan and said, "I don't remember seein' any girls around that place when we stopped there a while back."

"Yeah, but we didn't go inside," Morgan pointed out. "Garwood mentioned his children, but I just assumed they were boys—"

Kane laughed and said, "If you'd ever laid eyes on those three, Mr. Baxter, you wouldn't ever take them for boys!"

"I think he likes to sort of keep them hidden away," Deming said. "Can't really blame him, them being probably the only white women in a hundred miles or more, and mighty nice to look at, to boot. I reckon he doesn't want a bunch of scruffy fur trappers getting ideas in their heads . . . no offense meant."

"Especially since *we're* scruffy fur trappers, too," Kane added with a laugh. He nodded toward the river. "I saw the bundles of pelts in your canoes. You boys have been *really* lucky so far this season, if you've taken that many furs."

"Yeah, we have," Breckinridge said. He didn't want to have to explain the circumstances, so he didn't mention that many of those pelts had been taken the previous summer and fall by other trappers whose identities were unknown to him.

The thought put a frown on his face. He hadn't really considered it before, because all he really cared about was finding Jud Carnahan and settling the score with him, but what he was doing wasn't really honest. Those furs weren't his, by rights, and yet he was going to sell them and use the money. That wasn't as bad as what Carnahan and his gang had done—they had murdered as well as robbed their victims—but it wasn't exactly proper, either. Despite his numerous past brushes with the law, Breckinridge considered himself an honest man.

Maybe, once this was all over, he would try to find out the names of some of the men Carnahan had stolen from and killed. If he could track down their families, he could see to it that they got some of the money from the furs.

That would have to wait, though. Avenging those men, and all the others Carnahan had killed, had to come first.

The night passed quietly, and after breakfast the next morning the two groups parted, Deming and Kane heading on upstream to try their luck at trapping while Breckinridge and his companions paddled on down the Yellowstone toward the trading post.

Around midday they followed a narrow, winding valley between two high ridges until they reached a point where the valley widened out into a grassy meadow perhaps a mile wide. Set back a hundred yards on the northern bank of the stream was a large, rambling log building with a pole corral behind it and a log barn on the other side of the corral. A smaller, sturdy-looking building sat off to one side. A number of trees around the place had been cleared off, leaving stumps, and a stockade wall enclosed the compound. The double gates in the wall were open, so Breckinridge was able to look through them and see the buildings inside.

"Pretty impressive place," he commented to Morgan as they beached their canoe.

"Garwood told me he was building to last," Morgan replied. "I think he hopes to have an actual town here one of these days . . . with himself as the biggest, richest businessman in it, of course."

"Of course," Breckinridge said. He had never fully understood such vaulting ambition, since it didn't come naturally to him, but he recognized it in other men.

As for himself, he was content simply to live his life on his own terms, free to roam the wild, to see and do things other men had never done. The snow-capped mountains, the blue sky with an eagle soaring through it, the music of a cold, clear stream as it raced along over a rocky bed . . . those were the things that were the stuff of life for him.

At least, he would have been content to live like that if Jud Carnahan hadn't come along and stained the wilderness with blood that had to be avenged. Breckinridge hoped that once he had settled the score, he could go back to such an easy, uncluttered existence.

By the time the men had pulled all four of the canoes onto the shore, a man was walking through the gates of the trading post toward them. Despite the frontier surroundings, he dressed like a successful merchant from St. Louis or even Philadelphia, in a sober black suit, a shirt with pearl fasteners, and a silk cravat. He had a salt-and-pepper beard and a shock of curly dark hair. A jeweled ring sparkled on one of his fingers.

"Gentlemen," he greeted them, "welcome to Fort Garwood." He smiled as he recognized Morgan. "Ah, Mr. Baxter! So good to see you again. You said you hoped to be coming back my way soon." He turned to Breckinridge and looked him up and down. "And this young Goliath must be the friend you sought. Wallace, isn't it?"

"Breck Wallace," Breckinridge said as he stuck out his hand. "Pleased to meet you, sir."

They shook, Breckinridge's big paw practically swallowing Garwood's hand as they did so, and then, with widening eyes, Garwood looked at the cargo in the canoes.

"My word," he said. "Are those all beaver pelts?"

"Mostly beaver. There are a few other animals mixed in."

"And you've come to sell them to me?"

Morgan said, "That's right, sir. I'm sure you'll give us a good price."

"A fair price," Garwood said. "Some of you men will have to bring them in." He nodded to Breckinridge and Morgan. "While they're doing that, we'll go in and have a drink and talk business."

Breckinridge said, "Morgan, you can handle that part of it. I can do more good unloadin' these pelts."

He grasped the rawhide straps lashed around two of the bundles, lifted and swung them out of the canoe as if they weighed hardly anything at all. None of the other men attempted to carry more than one bundle at a time.

Breckinridge followed Morgan and Garwood toward the gates. They were just passing through the opening when, without warning, a shot blasted from the trading post and a rifle ball smacked into the gatepost right beside Breck.

Chapter 3

As splinters flew from the gatepost, Breckinridge acted without thinking. He dropped the bundles of furs, grabbed Morgan with his left hand, and half shoved, half threw his friend back outside the gates and to one side where the stockade wall would protect him from any more shots.

Then Breckinridge hauled one of the pistols from behind his belt and dropped to one knee, leveling the weapon at the trading post as he searched for a target. A number of crates were stacked in front of the building, and he thought the shot had come from behind them. A haze of powder smoke floating in the air above the crates confirmed his guess.

But before Breckinridge could find anything to aim at, Absalom Garwood jumped in front of him, waving his arms and shouting, "Wait! Hold your fire, hold your fire!"

"Get out of the way," Breckinridge snapped. "We don't know how many ambushers are up there."

"There are no ambushers," Garwood insisted. "Just my daughters."

A frown creased Breckinridge's forehead.

"Why in blazes would your gals be shootin' at us?" he asked. "You're right here with us. They ought to know we ain't lookin' for trouble."

"I don't know why." Garwood twisted his head around to look at the trading post. "Girls, no shooting! These are friends!"

A slight figure in buckskins and a coonskin cap stood up from behind the crates and waved.

"Sorry, Pa! It was an accident." The voice was definitely female, despite the garb. "Ophelia's rifle went off, but she didn't mean for it to happen."

Garwood shook his head as he looked at Breckinridge and Morgan again.

"I'm sorry, gentlemen. Not all of my children are equally proficient with firearms."

Another woman stood up, this one wearing a gray dress that clung to an unmistakably feminine figure. Blond hair fell around her heart-shaped face and on down her back. Even at this distance, Breckinridge could tell that she was very attractive.

"I didn't mean to," she called. "I just can't get the hang of this thing!"

She lifted the rifle she held, and its barrel swung toward the gate and the men standing there.

Morgan had caught himself against the outside of the stockade wall, then stepped into the opening again. He flinched a little and said, "Maybe she shouldn't be pointing that thing at us."

"Don't worry," Garwood said. "She hasn't had time to reload. She's rather slow at it, as you might expect. And Desdemona wouldn't have done it for her."

"When I was here before, you mentioned your

children, Mr. Garwood, but you didn't say anything about them being daughters."

"Well, look at them," Garwood said with a wave of his hand toward the trading post. "Would you say anything, in a country full of lonely men?"

Breckinridge could understand why the man felt that way. The other members of his party had come up to the gate, now that it was obvious they weren't going to be shot at, and when Breck glanced over his shoulder at them, he saw that they were all staring. It had been a while since they had seen any white women, he knew, and probably even longer since they'd seen any as pretty as these two.

Garwood inclined his head toward the building. "Come. I promise you're safe."

Breckinridge put away his pistol and picked up the two bundles of furs again. "I never worried overmuch about bein' shot by some girl," he said as they started walking forward again.

His naturally booming voice carried to the front of the trading post, where the young woman in buckskins—Desdemona, Garwood had called her—responded, "Maybe you should, you big ox. A rifle doesn't care who aims it and pulls the trigger."

Morgan chuckled and said, "She's got a point, Breck."

Breckinridge scowled. He was close enough now to see that Desdemona had red hair under the coonskin cap. It was a darker shade than his, but went well with her fair complexion that was lightly freckled across her nose.

He couldn't tell yet, but he was willing to bet she had green eyes, too.

He noticed such things only because he was an

observant sort, he told himself. After everything that had happened with Dawn Wind, and before that, Dulcy Harris, had left him wary of any sort of romantic entanglements. Besides, he had just laid eyes on Desdemona Garwood and hadn't even actually met her yet.

A third young woman stepped out onto the trading post's porch as the men approached. This one was as petite as Desdemona but had dark hair put up on top of her head and wore a dress like Ophelia's. She looked over the men and the bundles of furs they carried and said, "That's a lot of pelts, Papa. We'll have to pay less per pelt than we would for a smaller purchase."

"My bookkeeper," Garwood said with a smile. "That's Eugenia, gentlemen, my youngest. Then Ophelia . . ."

The blonde had laid the rifle across one of the crates. She smiled and dropped a polite curtsy.

"And young David Crockett there is Desdemona," Garwood concluded.

"I saw Davy Crockett once, when I was a little 'un," Breckinridge said. "She don't look nothin' like him."

"He's talking about the buckskins and the coonskin cap," Desdemona said. She hefted the rifle she held, which appeared to be almost as long as she was tall, although she handled it easily. "And Old Betsy here."

The self-confidence in her voice bordered on arrogance and bothered Breckinridge. He knew he had no business doing so, but he asked her in a challenging tone, "Can you actually shoot it?"

Her eyes narrowed at him. "Look at that stockade fence."

Breckinridge turned and did so. "What about it?"

"Count three posts over, to the right of the gate. You see it?"

"Yeah."

Desdemona lifted the rifle to her shoulder, eared back the hammer, paused just for a second, and then squeezed the trigger. As the rifle boomed, splinters and a bigger chunk of wood flew from the very tip-top of the post in question.

Morgan had turned to watch, too, and he let out a whistle of admiration. "That's some shooting!" he said.

"Desdemona, I've told you about shooting at the fence," Garwood said. "It's supposed to protect us from enemies outside, not serve as target practice inside."

"I know, Papa," she said as she lowered the rifle, grounded the butt, and started reloading. "I just wanted to show Mr.—What *is* your name, anyway?"

"Breckinridge Wallace," he introduced himself. "My friends call me Breck."

"I just wanted to show *Mr. Wallace* that I can shoot just fine," Desdemona said as she slid the ramrod down the rifle's barrel and tamped the load in place.

"Maybe we'll have to have us a turkey shoot one o' these days and find out who's better."

"Anytime," she said.

Grinning, Morgan clapped a hand on Breckinridge's back and said, "Don't just stand there holding those pelts, Breck. Let's go on inside and *talk* turkey."

They came to a suitable arrangement with Garwood for the purchase price of the pelts, but not before Morgan did some spirited haggling with Eugenia.

Breckinridge thought both of them seemed to enjoy it, though.

Once the furs had been carried in so they could be examined and a deal settled on, Charlie Moss, Richmond, and the other men lined up at the bar on the left side of the trading post's main room. It was made from wide, rough-hewn planks laid across the tops of barrels, but it served its purpose just fine. Ophelia Garwood and a stout Indian woman stood behind the bar and handled the chore of filling tankards with beer for the thirsty men.

Absalom Garwood sat at a table with Breckinridge, who stretched his long legs out in front of him and crossed them at the ankles. Morgan and Eugenia stood at a long table where the furs were piled, finalizing the details of the arrangement.

"When I first came out here," Garwood mused, "I hid my girls away, not wanting anyone to know there were women here. I thought it would just cause trouble and put them in danger. I have several Mandan men and women who came out with us to work for me, like Rose behind the bar there."

"Rose?" Breckinridge said.

"It's not her real name, of course," Garwood said with a shrug, "but it's certainly easier for me to say and remember. At any rate, I worried that I should have left the girls back in St. Louis instead of bringing them with me, but their mother passed away, God rest her soul, and we had no other family there to look after them. Besides, I wanted to keep them with me."

"Reckon I can understand that," Breckinridge said. "You're not hidin' them now, though."

"Desdemona convinced me that I wouldn't be able to keep their existence a secret forever. I must say, she really took to the frontier life. She altered a pair of buckskin trousers and a shirt belonging to one of the Mandan braves so that she could wear them, and she claimed one of the rifles she brought out here as part of my trade stock."

Breckinridge nodded. "Old Betsy."

"She doesn't really call it that. She was just having a bit of sport with you. She'd read about Colonel Crockett's pet name for his rifle, I suppose."

Morgan came over to join them at the table while Eugenia went into a room at the back of the trading post. He held out a hand and said, "It's a pleasure doing business with you, Mr. Garwood . . . and with your daughter."

"Eugenia has a sharp mind and sometimes a sharp tongue, as well. I trust she didn't take advantage of you, Mr. Baxter?"

"No, I think we're both satisfied with the deal."

"Sit." Garwood waved a hand at one of the empty chairs. "I'll have Ophelia bring us some ale."

He signaled to the blonde, and a minute later she carried over a tray with three mugs on it. When she bent over to place the tray on the table, the square neckline of her dress sagged enough to draw Morgan's eyes to the upper swells of her ample bosom that showed above it. Breckinridge saw his friend looking and hoped Garwood wouldn't notice, too, and take offense.

He didn't appear to, not even when Morgan's gaze followed the sway of Ophelia's shapely body as she walked away.

"To your health, my friends," Garwood said as he lifted his tankard of ale. After they all drank, he went on, "Now that you've sold those pelts, what are your plans? Are you going to head back deeper into the mountains and trap more beaver?"

"Actually, we're looking for someone," Morgan said. "A man named Jud Carnahan."

Garwood frowned in thought, pushed out his lips, and shook his head. "The name means nothing to me, I'm afraid."

Breckinridge sat forward and wrapped both big hands around the mug. "Then he hasn't been here?"

"I can't say that conclusively. A great many trappers have passed through this valley on their way farther west. Some told me their names, and some didn't. This man Carnahan may have been one of the ones who didn't."

"That makes sense, I reckon," Breckinridge said. He was vaguely disappointed. He had hoped to be able to pick up Carnahan's trail here. According to Morgan, Carnahan and the other men he had recruited for another trapping expedition—which probably meant another murder and robbery expedition—had left St. Louis first. They should have come through here before Morgan stopped at the trading post the first time. He hadn't asked Garwood about Carnahan then because at that point he didn't know if he would be able to find Breck—or even if Breck was still alive.

"This Carnahan . . . he's a friend of yours?"

Breckinridge grunted. "Not hardly."

"Then you're not looking to renew an old acquaintance with him," Garwood said with a shrewd look.

"I suppose you could call it that," Morgan said, "if renewing an old acquaintance includes killing the no-good skunk."

Garwood cocked a bushy eyebrow in surprise. "He must have done something terrible to make you feel that way. You don't strike me as a normally vindictive young man."

Breckinridge said, "Carnahan did plenty of things. Whatever happens to him, he's got it comin'. I was hopin' he'd been here and you could tell us which way he went."

Garwood took another drink of ale and then licked his lips. "You see, there's the problem," he said. "I have a strict rule about not involving myself in any feuds or disagreements among my customers. As long as they conduct themselves peacefully while here at Fort Garwood, their behavior elsewhere is no business of mine."

"You might not feel that way if you knew everything he's done," Morgan said with a note of anger in his voice. He reached down to slap the wooden peg that took the place of his lower right leg. "Carnahan's responsible for this."

"Then I can see why you bear a grudge against him. But it's not *my* grudge."

Morgan leaned forward in his chair, and Breckinridge could tell that his friend was about to make some other heated comment. Before he could say anything, though, all three of them turned toward the bar, where loud, angry voices had just been raised.

Chapter 4

Two of the men standing at the bar were jawing back and forth at each other. One was a rawboned, straw-haired man Breckinridge knew only as Cabe. He had never given an indication whether that was his first or last name. The other was a stocky gent named George Donnelly, whose broad face always seemed to be sunburned. They were upset with each other about something, and it didn't take Breck long to figure out what that was.

"You need to apologize to the lady!" Donnelly yelled at Cabe.

"What for? I didn't say nothin' I'm sorry about."

"You did the next thing to callin' her a whore!"

"I never did," Cabe insisted, "and you're the one makin' the gal blush now."

Donnelly turned to the bar and jerked a curt nod to Ophelia. "Beggin' your pardon, miss. I was too plainspoken. This no-good bas—this no-good varmint has got me seein' red, that's all."

Ophelia looked upset about the men arguing in front of her, but Breckinridge thought she didn't

seem too worried about it, as if that was just the way
she thought she ought to react.

"Please," she said, "there doesn't need to be any
trouble here."

"There won't be none if he just says he's sorry for
bein' rude to you," Donnelly insisted.

Cabe shook his head. "I done told you, I ain't sorry.
I just asked if she ever went for a walk with the fellas
who stop here at her pa's tradin' post."

"Yeah, a walk in the *moonlight*," Donnelly said with
a sneer.

Cabe turned toward the bar again. "I'm done
arguin' with you, you thickheaded skunk."

Breckinridge wasn't surprised by what happened
next. He was already starting to get up when Donnelly
grabbed Cabe by the shoulder, yanked him around,
and smashed a fist into his face.

The blow sent Cabe flying backward. He crashed
into Charlie Moss and one of the other men, Ben Pentecost, and would have fallen to the puncheon floor if
they hadn't caught him.

"Hold on just a minute—" Moss began.

Cabe wasn't in any mood to hold on. As soon as he
got his balance, he charged at Donnelly, roaring in
anger. Donnelly tried to block the left that Cabe
hooked at his belly, but he wasn't quite fast enough.
Cabe's fist sunk into his midsection, and as he started
to double over from the punch, Cabe brought his
right up in an uppercut that landed under Donnelly's
chin and lifted the man off his feet.

Richmond and the other member of the group,
John Rocklin, caught him. Donnelly shook his head
like a dazed bull, reached up to grasp his jaw and work

it back and forth, and then tackled Cabe. Both of them went down this time.

By now, Breckinridge, Morgan, and Garwood were up and moving toward the bar. Garwood shouted, "Take it outside, you men! I won't have you busting up my place!"

Cabe and Donnelly ignored him, of course, as they rolled around slugging, kneeing, and kicking at each other. They crashed into Pentecost's legs and knocked him down. He yelled as he toppled over, and when he landed he lashed out at both combatants.

Breckinridge had seen things like this plenty of times before. Even though the men all seemed to get along most of the time, a full-fledged brawl was on the verge of breaking out. And not surprisingly, a pretty girl was the cause of it. Nothing else caused men to lose the ability to think straight so quickly and completely.

His long legs carried him across the room in only a few steps. He bent down, intending to grab hold of the two men, haul them upright, and shove them away from each other. That would leave the third man on the floor with nobody to fight, and maybe this fracas would be over before it got too bad.

Instead, a wildly flailing leg came up and a boot heel planted itself in the middle of Breckinridge's belly. Breck was bigger than all the other men, but that didn't mean they were lightweights. The kick had plenty of force behind it. With the air driven out of his lungs, Breck doubled over, gasping for breath.

Whoever had kicked him hadn't meant to, and Breckinridge knew that. But instinct still told him to strike back, and as soon as he had enough air back in his body, he yelled angrily and grabbed the man who happened to be at the top of the struggling knot at the moment. Breck didn't shove him away. He *threw* the man along the area in front of the bar.

Which knocked Richmond flying like a pin in a game of ninepins.

Breckinridge swung around to give the same treatment to one of the others, but he turned just in time to catch a fist in the face. The punch rocked his head back and made a red haze drop over his vision. He roared again and struck out at the man in front of him, not knowing or caring who it was.

Vaguely, he heard somebody shout his name—maybe Morgan—but he ignored it and waded into the melee, bellowing and lashing out at anybody within reach of his long arms and bruising fists. The fray surged back and forth, and although Breckinridge was too caught up in the heat of battle to realize it at the time, the fight soon turned into an effort by the other men to bring the rampaging beast he had turned into under control.

Men hung on his arms, trying to hold them down. He shook them off like a giant grizzly bear shaking off tormenting wolves. Someone else jumped on his back. Breckinridge reached behind him, caught hold of the man, and heaved him up and over his head in an amazing display of raw strength. Breck slammed him down on top of the bar.

Another man tackled him from behind, getting hold of his legs around the knees. At the same time, two opponents rushed him from the front, lowering their shoulders and barreling into him. That was finally enough to take Breckinridge off his feet. All of them landed in a welter of arms and legs. The others piled on in an effort to keep him down.

Breckinridge climbed out of the pile, flinging men right and left. Everything that had happened to him in the past few years . . . all the danger, disappointments, and despair . . . had formed into a great festering boil inside him, and now that boil had burst, filling him with blinding, white-hot rage. He couldn't think straight. Didn't want to think straight. He just wanted to lash out.

Someone was there in front of him. He grabbed the figure in both hands, lifted it off the floor, poised to throw whoever it was across the room.

A voice that was cool and controlled but tight enough to show some strain said, "You'd better not do it, mister, or you'll be sorry."

His chest heaving from both exertion and anger, Breckinridge stood there spraddle-legged and tried to push aside the red curtains of fury in his head. Gradually he became aware of Morgan and the others yelling at him. As his vision cleared, he realized, with a shock that rattled him to his core, his hands were wrapped around Desdemona Garwood's upper arms and he was holding her with her feet dangling almost a foot off the floor.

He had to look past the barrel of the flintlock pistol she was pointing at him in order to see her pale, furious, freckled face. With the weapon's muzzle only inches from *his* face, the barrel looked about as big around as a cannon.

"Are you going to put me down, you big lunatic?" she asked. "Or am I going to have to blow your head off?"

Breckinridge suppressed the impulse to just open

his hands and drop her. He was still pretty far gone, but he was thinking straight enough to realize if he did that, the jolt might cause the gun she was holding in both hands to go off. At this range, the pistol would put a good-sized hole in him.

Instead, he lowered her until the soles of her high-topped moccasins were on the floor again. Then he let go of her and took a step back.

"Miss Desdemona," he managed to croak, "I'm sorry—"

Morgan clomped up beside him on the peg and said, "Breck, what the blazes got into you? You could've hurt somebody."

Breckinridge scrubbed a big hand over his face and then looked around.

"I didn't kill nobody or break any bones, did I?"

"You didn't kill anybody. I wouldn't swear to it about the broken bones, though."

The other six men in the party were scattered around the trading post's main room, battered and bruised. Some were lying on the floor, groaning and only semiconscious. Others leaned on the bar or sat in chairs, shaking their heads groggily.

The man called Cabe sat at one of the tables, leaning forward so that his head rested on the wood. Slowly, he raised it and glared at George Donnelly.

"This is all your fault, Donnelly," Cabe said. "If you hadn't got your back up 'cause you were tryin' to impress that yaller-haired girl, none of it would've happened!"

"You didn't have to be so blasted rude to her," Donnelly shot back from where he was propped up against the bar. "Anyway, I didn't know Wallace was gonna go hog wild!"

"Both of you shut up," Morgan snapped. He turned to Breckinridge. "Are you all right now, Breck?"

"Yeah, I ain't loco anymore." Breckinridge had a few aches and pains, but he knew he could take a lot of pounding in a fight and never feel it much. His recuperative powers had always been astounding.

More important, he had control of his emotions, at least for the time being. He looked at Desdemona and told her again, "I'm sure sorry—"

She cut him off with a scornful sniff. She had lowered the hammer on her pistol, and now she set the weapon on a barrel.

"We have a barn out back if you're going to insist on acting like an animal."

Breckinridge shook his head. "No more trouble, I swear."

"I'll believe that when I see it," she said coolly. She turned and walked across the room to where her younger sister Eugenia was standing with a worried expression on her face.

Ophelia was still behind the bar. Breckinridge might have been mistaken, but he thought she wore a faint smirk, as if she were satisfied that a bunch of men had gotten into a huge brawl and she had been, at the very least, what had started it all off.

"I wouldn't blame you, Mr. Garwood, if you told us the deal was off," Morgan said later as he and Breckinridge sat with Absalom Garwood again.

"Business is business, and a deal is a deal," Garwood

replied. "Besides, there was no real damage done except to your associates." He smiled. "If there had been, I would have taken it out of the price I'm paying for the pelts, I assure you. But as it is, you're welcome to spend the night. Assuming, that is, that you meant it when you said no more trouble, Mr. Wallace."

"I meant it, all right," Breckinridge said. "I don't rightly know what came over me. I swear, I don't go crazy like that all the time."

"He's telling the truth," Morgan said. "He doesn't."

"Are you going to continue looking for the man you mentioned before? Carnahan, was it?"

Breckinridge nodded. "He's out here somewhere, and we're bound and determined to find him."

The other men had gone back outside as the day waned. Now Charlie Moss came into the trading post and said, "Cabe's gone."

Morgan frowned. "What do you mean, Charlie?"

"He left. Took his gear and walked off downriver. Said he wasn't going to have anything more to do with any of us, especially Donnelly." Moss shook his head. "I knew he was the sort to hold a grudge, but I didn't expect him to do that."

"Blast it, I paid him to come with us."

Moss took a couple of gold coins from his pocket and laid them on the table. "The stiff-necked varmint told me to give 'em back to you. He kept a little for the time he'd put in so far, but he wouldn't take the rest of it."

Morgan sighed. "Maybe he'll change his mind. He went downriver, you said?"

"That's right."

"We'll catch up to him, and if he's gotten over being

mad and wants to join us again, he'll be welcome."
Morgan looked at Breckinridge. "We *are* going downstream, aren't we, Breck? We know Carnahan isn't west
of here because we came from that direction."

"Unless he's not followin' the river and took out
across country," Breckinridge said. "More than likely,
though, he held up somewhere between here and St.
Louis, and you just didn't see him when you went past
him on your way up."

Most travelers on the frontier followed the rivers;
they were the only dependable routes. But from time
to time someone would strike out away from the
streams. Breckinridge wouldn't even try to predict
what Jud Carnahan might do, except whatever it was,
Carnahan would be ruthless about it and wouldn't
care who he hurt as long as he got what he wanted.

Eugenia came over to the table and asked, "Are you
gentlemen going to be staying for supper?"

"We have our own supplies," Breckinridge said.
"Figured we'd build a cook fire—"

"Nonsense," Morgan interrupted as he smiled up
at Eugenia. "We can't turn down such a gracious invitation, Breck."

"It wasn't exactly an invitation," Eugenia said. "You'll
be paying for it."

"Of course."

"All right, then. I'll tell Rose to make sure there's
plenty of stew." She smiled at Morgan and turned to
walk behind the counter at the back of the room. She
disappeared through a door that Breckinridge assumed led into the kitchen.

"She's a canny one, my Eugenia," Garwood said. "Never misses a chance to make a profit."

"Beauty *and* brains," Morgan said. "That's a formidable combination."

Breckinridge didn't say anything, but he saw the way Morgan was looking at the door where Eugenia had gone, clearly waiting for her to appear again. Breck had promised that he wouldn't cause any more trouble, and he meant what he said.

He suddenly wondered, though, if Morgan could make the same claim.

Chapter 5

Absalom Garwood offered to let the visitors sleep in the barn—for a price, of course, as Eugenia quickly reminded them—but the weather was pleasant and the men were accustomed to spreading their bedrolls outside and sleeping under the stars.

Breckinridge was up before dawn the next morning, stretching, yawning, and then heading down to the river to get a drink and dunk his head in the water to help him wake up. He enjoyed this time of day, when everything was quiet and the approaching sunrise was still just an arching band of pink, orange, and gold on the eastern horizon.

He was shirtless and barefooted, wearing only his buckskin trousers and carrying his rifle. Even though the trading post and its surrounding stockade fence were close by, he wasn't going to leave its protection without taking a weapon with him. He seldom went anywhere without a gun, knife, or tomahawk—preferably all three—close at hand.

As he approached the river he saw movement in the dim light and tightened his grip on the rifle. When he came closer, he could that a man was kneeling at the edge of the stream, filling a bucket. Another bucket sat on the ground beside him. When he was finished with what he was doing, he stood up, grasped the bails of both buckets, lifted them, and turned toward the trading post. A little water sloshed from the top of both vessels.

The man stopped at the sight of Breckinridge striding toward him.

"Mornin'," Breckinridge said with a nod. He hadn't seen this fellow the day before around the trading post, but it was obvious he was one of the Mandan Indians Absalom Garwood had mentioned. He was middle-aged, with deep trenches beginning to form in his coppery, pockmarked face, but his hair was still black as midnight and he stood straight, with an air of vitality.

Solemnly, the man returned Breckinridge's nod and then started to walk past.

"My name's Breck. Breckinridge Wallace."

"Edward," the man said.

"Really?"

A hint of amusement appeared on the man's face as he said, "No, but that is what Mr. Garwood calls me." His English was good. "He has given white man names to all of us who work for him. My true name, in your tongue, means Blue Feather."

"That's what I'll call you, then, while we're here. Which won't be that long, I reckon," Breckinridge added as his brawny shoulders rose and fell in a shrug, "because we'll be leavin' later this morning. Headin' on downstream."

"Most white men who come to Damnation Valley are going the other way, deeper into the mountains."

"That's where we came from," Breckinridge said, then he frowned. "Wait a minute. What did you call this place? Damnation Valley?"

He knew that most Indians had few words in their languages that could be considered curses, and although they possessed a concept of hell—wandering endlessly in the spirit world without being able to move on to the happier realms beyond—the word *damnation* didn't sound at all like something an Indian would come up with.

Blue Feather tried to move past him again. "I should not have spoken of it," he muttered.

"Now, hold on," Breckinridge said. He put out a hand to stop the Indian. "I understand why the tradin' post is called Fort Garwood. Man likes to name things after hisself, I reckon. But why Damnation Valley? Who called it that?"

With obvious reluctance, Blue Feather answered, "The other white man who was here first. He said the valley was cursed."

"What other white man?"

"An old man. Evil spirits were in him. He came here to trap beaver but fell sick. He wandered in the woods and lived like an animal. We found him soon after we arrived, but he died not long after that. My people said his body should be burned, but Mr. Garwood said he must be buried." Blue Feather set one of the buckets down and swept that hand toward the trees. "We put him deep in the woods, in the hope that the evil spirits in him would not find their way back here."

Breckinridge nodded. Setting aside what Blue Feather had said about evil spirits, it was a simple enough story. Some trapper had come along here and been laid low by sickness, probably a fever of some sort, and it had deranged him. No telling how long he had wandered up and down the valley, slowly starving to death.

"My people want nothing to do with the evil spirits that possess white men," Blue Feather went on. "They came to us on the great boat that bellows smoke—"

"You mean a steamboat?" Breckinridge interrupted.

Blue Feather nodded gravely. "That is what the white men call them. It brought their evil spirits to my people and caused a great sickness among them. Many died. The ones who survived were left like this."

He touched one of the pockmarks on his lean cheek, and with a cold feeling in the pit of his stomach, Breckinridge realized what the Mandan was talking about.

Smallpox.

He had heard about outbreaks of the disease that had taken great tolls among the Indians. Anybody with any sense feared the pox, but it was even worse when it struck among the natives. It was no wonder that Blue Feather had a grim cast to his features if he had fallen victim to it but survived. Doubtless many of his friends and loved ones hadn't made it.

"I'm sorry, Blue Feather." Something occurred to Breckinridge. "The white man who was here when you and the others came with Garwood . . . did he have the pox?"

The Mandan shrugged. "I do not believe so. But evil spirits are still evil, and who can tell what form they will take?"

He was right about that, Breckinridge thought. Maybe that explained Jud Carnahan. Maybe he was an evil spirit in human form.

A new voice made Breckinridge and Blue Feather turn toward the trading post. "Rose sent you for water a long time ago, Edward. She's wondering why you haven't come back."

Breckinridge saw Desdemona Garwood walking toward them. She wasn't wearing the coonskin cap this morning, and the thick red hair that had been tucked up under the cap the day before was loose this morning, falling around her shoulders. In the golden light of approaching dawn, it made for a pretty glorious display.

Blue Feather grunted and said quickly, "I am sorry, Miss Desdemona—"

"It's my fault," Breckinridge broke in. "I'm the one who kept pesterin' him with questions."

"Questions about what?" Desdemona wanted to know. Her gaze lingered on Breckinridge's broad, bare chest.

Breckinridge hesitated. He didn't know if Blue Feather wanted him talking about everything he had just revealed. It might be bad for Garwood's business if the story got around about how a sick man—maybe sick with the pox—had died here, but not before declaring that the valley was cursed.

"Nothing important—" Breckinridge began.

A whisper of sound, followed instantly by a thud and a gasp, interrupted him. He heard the other water bucket hit the ground. He looked around and saw Blue Feather staggering. The Mandan tried to reach behind him and grasp the shaft of the arrow protruding from his back between the shoulder blades, but he couldn't manage it.

Not that it would have mattered if he did. He pitched forward onto his face.

Breckinridge was moving before Blue Feather hit the ground. He leaped forward, grabbed Desdemona's arm, and half shoved, half threw her toward the open gates in the stockade fence.

"Run!" he told her.

He didn't know where the arrow had come from that had killed Blue Feather, but he had seen the markings well enough to recognize them as Blackfoot. Those warriors he and Morgan had killed the day before had had friends, all right, and now they had followed the white men downstream to the trading post and were out for revenge.

Desdemona raced toward the gates. Breckinridge turned, caught a glimpse of movement in the trees along the riverbank, and whipped the rifle to his shoulder. Another arrow cut through the early-morning air and whistled past his ear. He saw where it came from, drew a quick bead on the spot, and pressed the trigger. The rifle boomed and kicked against his shoulder.

He heard a shrill cry of pain and figured that was the only sign he would get that his shot had found its target. With no time to reload because arrows were still flying around him, he turned and sprinted after Desdemona. His long legs enabled him to close the gap between them in a hurry.

As he was coming up behind her, he saw three warriors running to cut them off from the gates. The Blackfeet had a good angle to do just that, and Breckinridge knew he would have to fight them to clear a path for him and Desdemona.

She was far from helpless, though. She yanked a pistol from behind her belt, cocked it, and fired on the run as one of the warriors screamed a battle cry and launched himself at her. The heavy lead ball slammed into his chest and stopped him like he had run into a wall. He twisted, stumbled, and crashed to the ground.

Breckinridge leaped to meet the second man's charge. The Blackfoot swung a tomahawk in a vicious arc aimed at Breck's head. Breck blocked it with the flintlock's barrel, then rammed the rifle's brass butt plate into the man's throat. The warrior began gagging and gasping as he tried and failed to drag air through his crushed windpipe.

The Blackfoot was mortally injured, but he wasn't dead yet. He slashed a backhanded blow with the tomahawk. The head raked across Breckinridge's chest, leaving a shallow cut. Breck hit him again with the rifle butt, this time in the face. The upward angle of the stroke crushed the Indian's nose and sent splinters of bone into his brain, killing him almost instantly. He wouldn't choke to death from the blow to his throat after all.

There was still a third Blackfoot warrior to deal with, but as Breckinridge swung toward him, another shot rang out and the warrior's head jerked as a rifle ball blew away a fist-sized chunk of his skull. Breck glanced toward the trading post and saw Morgan standing at the gates with a smoking flintlock in his hands.

He would thank his old friend later for shooting that third warrior, he thought. Right now, another arrow flashing past his head reminded him that he needed to get inside the stockade as quickly as possible. Desdemona was already at the gates, having pulled ahead of him again because he had stopped to fight the second Blackfoot.

A moment later, Breckinridge raced through the gates. Men were already in position to close them as soon as he was inside. They pushed the gates up, and Charlie Moss was there to drop the bar across it. Rifles began to roar as men took up spots along the wall and fired through loopholes cut for that purpose. Lead raked the trees along the river where the Blackfoot attackers were concealed.

Breckinridge's chest heaved as he caught his breath following the hard run and the brief hand-to-hand battle. Morgan came over to him and asked, "Are you all right, Breck? You're bleeding in a few places."

Breckinridge looked down at himself and saw that in addition to the cut across his chest from the tomahawk, his arms and shoulders had little trickles of crimson here and there on them as well.

"Reckon I got a few scratches from all them arrows flyin' around me," he said. "None of 'em hit me hard enough to stay in, though. I was a mite busy at the time and never noticed these little nicks." He paused. "I'm obliged to you for that shot, Morgan. I might've been able to handle that last varmint, but it would've slowed me down even more."

"I was already up and about, and when I heard a shot, I figured you had to be involved somehow."

"Wasn't me who fired that pistol. That was Miss Desdemona," Breckinridge said, nodding toward the young woman as she came toward them.

"You're hurt, Mr. Wallace," she said.

"Nothin' to worry about," he assured her.

"Come on inside, anyway. Those cuts need to be cleaned up. Eugenia's a fair to middling doctor when she needs to be."

"I thought maybe you'd tend to 'em," Breckinridge said.

Desdemona snorted and said, "I'm going to fetch my rifle and see if I can help the men drive off those Indians." Her fierce expression softened slightly. "I wish they hadn't killed Edward."

"So do I," Breckinridge said. "I didn't know him except for a few minutes, but he seemed like a good fella."

"He was. And he'll be avenged."

She turned and hurried toward the building to get the rifle she had mentioned. Morgan watched her go with open admiration on his face.

"That's an unusual young woman," he said, "but a very impressive one."

Breckinridge couldn't argue with that.

Chapter 6

The firing was still going on along the walls when Breckinridge came out of the trading post a short time later. Eugenia had cleaned all the cuts and scratches on his torso and arms, then rubbed a salve on them she said would keep the wounds from festering. Breck felt a little awkward while she was doing that. She was so petite that beside his massive frame, she seemed like a little girl.

He returned to the spot where he had slept, pulled on his shirt and boots, and slung his shot pouch and powder horn over his shoulder. Then he hurried to the wall and found a spot where he could thrust the flintlock's barrel through a loophole and search for a target once he had loaded the rifle.

If there was a battle going on anywhere in the vicinity, Breckinridge Wallace was bound and determined to take part in it.

Charlie Moss called over to him, "You reckon these savages are friends of that bunch we tangled with yesterday?"

"You could bet a hat on it," Breckinridge said as he

squinted over the rifle's sights. The sun still wasn't up yet, but it was getting pretty close. The light was certainly better. Breck spotted a flicker of movement in the trees. A single feather showed. Breck had the rifle cocked and ready, so all he had to do was shift his aim slightly and squeeze the trigger. The flintlock roared and spouted smoke and fire.

A second later, the limp body of a Blackfoot raider rolled out of the brush and sprawled with outflung arms. Breckinridge could see the blood leaking from the hole in the man's head.

The Blackfeet had a problem. The trees where they had taken cover were within rifle range of the stockade wall around the trading post. Their arrows, however, consistently fell a little short of the log wall. There were at least a couple of rifles among the attackers, no doubt stolen from white trappers the Blackfeet had killed, but they were notoriously bad shots. If any of their shots actually hit one of the loopholes in the wall, it would be by blind luck.

After reloading, Breckinridge caught a glimpse of another Blackfoot moving around in the trees and fired again. This time he couldn't tell if his shot scored. He got the rifle ready again and settled down to wait for another chance.

From the corner of his eye, he saw someone step up beside him. Desdemona stood there, holding her long-barreled rifle. She had a powder smudge on her freckled cheek.

"I realized I didn't say thank you," she said.

"You don't owe me any thanks," Breckinridge told her.

"I believe I do. You're the one who gave me a push toward the fort and told me to run after Edward was shot. I was so shocked I might have stood there staring at him until one of those Indians put an arrow in me."

"Have you ever been in a fight like this before?" Breckinridge asked her.

She shook her head. "No, the Indians have left us alone since we got here, and we haven't had any real trouble from the trappers passing through. I . . . I never killed anyone before."

"The way you shot that fella down while you were on the run, you'd never know he was your first." That sounded awkward to Breckinridge as soon as he said it, so he hurried, "I mean, the first fella you . . . well, shot, I reckon."

"Don't worry, Mr. Wallace, I'm not offended. My sensibilities aren't *that* delicate. I'm not going to lose any sleep over shooting that man. He would have killed us without hesitation, if he'd had the chance."

"Damn right he would have. Beggin' your pardon for the language."

Breckinridge had been keeping an eye out through the loophole while he was talking to Desdemona, and now he saw one of the Blackfeet dart out into the open. The warrior had an arrow nocked in his bow, and the end of it burned brightly. The man ran a good twenty feet while rifle balls kicked up dirt around him, then he stopped short, hauled back the bowstring, and let fly with the burning arrow. A second later, he staggered as two shots slammed into his chest.

The trading post's defenders had gotten in range, but not in time to prevent the blazing arrow from being launched.

The firebrand arched through the air, and there was nothing anybody could do to stop it. The head struck one of the upright logs and embedded itself. Breckinridge couldn't tell exactly where the arrow had hit, but he heard it land and saw smoke spiraling up on the other side of the wall.

"Somebody's got to put out the fire!" he told Desdemona. "Run and get me a blanket!"

"We can't open the gates!" she said. "They'll rush us and get through!"

"Won't have to open the gates. Just get the blanket!"

She still looked dubious, but she turned and ran toward the trading post.

Breckinridge leaned his rifle against the wall and tipped his head back to study it. The wall was approximately eight feet tall, and the end of each log forming it had been hewn down with axes until it came to a sharp point.

Morgan had seen the exchange between Breckinridge and Desdemona. He limped over and said, "I've seen that look before. What are you up to, Breck?"

"That fire's gonna burn the wall down if we don't do somethin' about it. I reckon I'm the one to take care of it."

Absalom Garwood joined them while Breckinridge was answering Morgan's question. The trading post's proprietor wasn't nattily dressed this morning. In fact, he still wore his nightshirt stuffed down into a pair of trousers. Like the others, he held a rifle.

"You can't go outside the wall," Garwood exclaimed. "Those savages will shoot you!"

"Their arrows won't reach quite that far. To get the one that was on fire all the way to the wall, that fella had to run closer. Just bad luck for us he made it far enough before somebody shot him. But all you fellas have to do is keep up a steady fire so the Blackfeet can't come out of the trees, and I'll be fine."

"I've seen some powder smoke down there, Breck," Morgan said. "They have rifles, too!"

"Not many, and they ain't any good with 'em. I'll take my chances." Breckinridge shrugged. "Not much choice in the matter."

Desdemona, clutching a woolen blanket, ran up to them. "Here," she said as she handed it to Breckinridge. "Now what are you going to do?"

"Climb over that wall," he said. He draped the blanket around his neck and shoulders. "Pour some lead into those trees!"

"You *are* a crazy man," Morgan said, but a reckless grin lit up his face. He took his place at one of the loopholes, as did Desdemona and her father. "Keep firing!" Morgan called to the other defenders. "Space your shots! Keep up the pressure!"

Breckinridge bent his knees a little, then sprang upward and grabbed the top of a log with both hands. He had climbed plenty of trees when he was a boy, and this wasn't much different. It helped that he was incredibly strong, but at the same time, his great size meant his muscles had to support and lift more weight.

He grunted with the effort as he hauled himself up. With his boot soles planted against the rough logs, he was bent almost double. When he had pulled himself high enough, he braced himself and threw a leg over, wedging it between two of the sharpened tops. Angry howls went up from the Blackfeet in the trees as he lifted himself into view.

From where he was, it wasn't too difficult to lever himself the rest of the way over the wall and drop to the ground. He landed with surprising gracefulness for a man his size. The burning arrow was stuck in the wall about twenty feet to his left. The fire had spread to a couple of the logs, but it wasn't burning too strongly yet.

Breckinridge heard more arrows humming through the air as he ran toward the blaze, bending low so he would be out of the line of fire from any of the loopholes. The arrows thudded into the ground as they reached the end of their flight, but he didn't look to see how close they were coming to him. Instead he yanked the blanket from around his neck and began beating at the flames with it.

The rifles continued to fire inside the wall. Breckinridge saw splinters leap from a log to his right and knew that shot had come from *outside*, which meant one of the Blackfeet had fired it. A grim smile tugged at his mouth. He hoped none of those varmints had been practicing too much lately. That was why most Indians were terrible shots. They didn't have enough powder and ammunition to practice with the weapons they had taken from the white men they'd killed.

The blanket was getting charred, but he was making progress putting out the fire. Another shot from the trees smacked into a log to his left. They were bracketing him, and if they kept it up, one of them might actually get lucky enough to hit him. He needed to get this fire put out so he could scramble back into the stockade.

Just as Breckinridge was beating out the last of the flames, Morgan shouted from inside, "Breck, here comes another one!"

Breckinridge's head came around on a swivel. He saw another flaming arrow headed toward the wall with only a slight flutter in its flight. His keen eye judged its path, and he sprinted to intercept it.

The warrior who had fired the arrow was already down, spasming in his death throes. Breckinridge saw that from the corner of his eye as he raced along in front of the wall. He timed his leap and reached out with his right hand. His fingers closed around the arrow's shaft and plucked it out of midair. He flung it away from him, and it landed in the dirt, where the flames quickly guttered out.

He threw on the brakes as Morgan shouted, "Back the other way!"

Blast it, Breckinridge thought as he wheeled around and spotted a third flaming arrow headed for the wall, couldn't anybody shoot one of those Blackfeet *before* the ornery son of a gun had a chance to use his bow?

At least Morgan had the sense to yell, "Hold your fire! Hold your fire!" at the other defenders, so Breckinridge didn't have to worry about getting his head accidentally shot off through one of the loopholes.

He couldn't reach the third arrow in time to keep it from striking the wall, but he arrived a heartbeat later and yanked it loose. The fire hadn't had time to catch. He tossed the arrow down, stomped it out, and wondered if he needed to stay outside the wall to catch the next one.

It didn't seem that there was going to be a next one. Inside, Absalom Garwood shouted, "They're leaving! They're on the run!"

Breckinridge leaned over, put his hands on his knees, and caught his breath while he lifted his head and peered toward the river. Sure enough, half a dozen warriors had piled into canoes and were paddling away, heading back upstream. The defenders fired after them to hurry them on their way. Breck saw a few splashes as rifle balls plunked into the Yellowstone, but the shots didn't appear to do any damage. The Blackfeet soon disappeared around a bend.

"Breck, should we open the gates?" Morgan called.

"Hold on a spell," Breckinridge replied. "Let's make sure they ain't tryin' some sort of trick."

He didn't believe that was the case. He didn't know how large the war party had been to start with, but with the four men he and Morgan had killed yesterday and all the warriors who had been shot down today, their numbers had to be seriously depleted.

Nobody was more stubborn about seeking revenge than Indians, but they were practical rascals, too. When the price of vengeance was too high, they would cut their losses and leave. Breckinridge had a hunch that was what had just happened here.

"At least let us open one of the gates enough for you to slip inside," Morgan said. "We don't want any of them sneaking up to take a potshot at you."

Morgan had a point, Breckinridge thought. He said, "All right, I'm comin' in."

Morgan, Garwood, and Desdemona were waiting for him just inside when he slipped through a narrow gap between the gates. The men who had opened them quickly shoved them closed again.

"You could have been killed out there!" Desdemona said.

"We all could've been killed if they'd managed to burn that wall down," Breckinridge said. "Although from what I could tell, it would've been a pretty fair fight. We might have run 'em off anyway, but more fellas would've been killed."

"Did we lose anyone?" Garwood asked.

"Edward was killed," Desdemona told him. "He was down at the river fetching water. Mr. Wallace and I were with him when an arrow struck him." She glanced at Breckinridge. "I wouldn't have made it back here if it hadn't been for Mr. Wallace."

"Good Lord," Garwood muttered. "I didn't know that the situation had been so desperate." He put an arm around Desdemona's shoulders and hugged her, then said, "Why don't you go on inside and reassure your sisters that everything is all right? I imagine they're quite worried."

Desdemona nodded and headed for the building.

Garwood turned to Breckinridge and went on, "My deepest thanks, Mr. Wallace, not only for helping to save all of us, but especially for what you did for my daughter."

Breckinridge shook his head. "We were both runnin' hell-for-leather, sir, and fightin' Blackfeet along the way. I reckon she saved me just as much as I saved her."

"You're too modest. Just know that you have my sincere appreciation." Garwood looked around at the others. "All of you men do."

"I wish I'd been able to do somethin' for Blue Feather . . . Edward, you called him. But them Blackfeet were able to sneak up without me knowin' they were around. Nobody's better at that than them. I've had run-ins with 'em before."

"How will we know that it's safe, that they'll leave us alone?"

"You won't," Breckinridge said. "Now that they know the tradin' post is here, there'll always be a chance they'll come raidin' back this way. You'd do well to keep the gates closed and men posted on guard all the time."

Garwood frowned. "That sounds very dangerous."

"Yep," Breckinridge agreed. "It sort of goes with the territory."

Chapter 7

At midday, everyone from the trading post gathered in a meadow surrounded by trees several hundred yards from the stockade. A couple of the Mandan men who had come upriver with Absalom Garwood had spent the morning building a scaffold where the body of Edward Blue Feather, as Breckinridge figured he ought to be called, would be laid. Several members of Breck's party had dragged off the bodies of the slain warriors. Eight Blackfeet had been killed in the fight.

The trappers were all armed and alert as Blue Feather's body, dressed in his finest buckskins, was brought from the trading post and placed carefully on the scaffold with his head pointing toward the north-west and his feet to the southeast. Breckinridge didn't know much about the Mandans, but it was easy to see this was their sacred ritual when someone died.

One of the other men, who spoke English as well as Blue Feather had, spoke after the body was in place. "It is the custom of our people for the family of the one who has gone on to gather here at his resting place and mourn his passing for four sunrises and sunsets. Blue Feather had no family. All of them were taken by the great sickness that almost wiped out our people many moons ago. So those of us who were his friends will mourn for him instead."

"And we will say prayers for his immortal soul, as is the way of our people," Absalom Garwood said. "May he rest in peace."

With that ceremony taken care of, there was nothing to do except return to the trading post. Two of the Indians stayed behind, resting on their knees next to the scaffold that held Blue Feather's body. Breckinridge figured they would take turns mourning, and he respected that, but here outside the stockade wall, with the possibility of murderous Blackfeet still lurking in the area, they weren't exactly safe.

He drew Charlie Moss aside and said quietly, "I think the boys should take turns standin' guard out here. They can post themselves over yonder under that tree, so they won't intrude on the grievin', but that's close enough to keep an eye on things and make sure nobody sneaks up on these poor folks."

Moss nodded. "That's a good idea, Breck. I'll take the first watch myself and tell Richmond to come spell me after a while."

Breckinridge clapped a hand on his shoulder and said, "Thanks. I'll take a turn myself, whenever I need to."

With that taken care of, he paused for a moment to look up at Edward Blue Feather's body on the scaffold. He had known the man for only a few minutes, had only the one brief conversation with him, but he felt the loss anyway. Blue Feather had left a tragic past behind him and come west with the hope of finding something better, only to wind up in a cursed valley, meeting a brutal, unexpected death.

Maybe most men carried the seeds of their own damnation within them, Breckinridge thought. He would have liked to believe that wasn't the case, but since setting out on his own, he had seen evidence of it again and again. The only thing a fella could do was keep battling to change that inexorable fate. He would be doomed to failure, more than likely, but the struggle itself was worth something.

He pushed those gloomy thoughts away and turned to follow the others back to the trading post. Morgan was waiting for him and fell in alongside him.

"I heard what you told Charlie about standing guard," Morgan said. "Do you plan on us staying here for the next four days, until they get through mourning that man? I thought we'd start looking for Carnahan again."

"Carnahan's been on the loose for a good while already. A few more days ain't gonna make any difference. We'll find him, no matter how long it takes."

Morgan nodded. "All right. Honestly, I won't mind spending some time here. After everything that's happened, I don't have quite the stamina that I used to. And I'm certainly not going to complain about the company." He smiled. "Eugenia is quite lovely and intelligent, and Ophelia has a considerable amount of, ah, earthy charm."

"What about Desdemona?" Breckinridge asked.

"She's a bit on the prickly side, I'd say, and I'm not fond of the way she dresses like a man. But she's not without appeal." Morgan looked over at Breckinridge.

"I'd say she only has eyes for you, though, and takes little interest in me."

"What in blazes are you talkin' about? She hasn't done much more than argue and snap at me."

"And that doesn't mean a blasted thing and you know it," Morgan said.

Breckinridge shook his head. "I'm not lookin' to get mixed up with any gal for a while. My luck in that area ain't been too good in the past, you may recall."

"Maybe not, but you don't strike me as the sort who gives up easily. You never have."

He had just been thinking that there was some honor merely in the struggle to achieve something worthwhile from life, Breckinridge reminded himself. Could be that applied to courting the ladies as well. But not yet. He had more important things to take care of first.

Like settling the score with Jud Carnahan.

A couple of days passed without any trouble, leading Breckinridge to believe that the surviving Blackfeet probably had left this part of the country, heading back north to their usual hunting and raiding grounds. He didn't think they should let down their guard, however. Just because one danger had passed didn't mean another couldn't show up at any time.

Of course, some problems were homegrown. Ophelia couldn't seem to stop herself from flirting with the men, which led to a number of arguments and a few shoving matches and fistfights, although these happened outdoors and didn't involve the whole group, as the first brawl had. Ophelia clearly enjoyed the attention, although both of her sisters just shook their heads and looked on with disdain.

Absalom Garwood seemed to have mixed emotions about the whole thing. Once Breckinridge, Morgan, and the other men moved on, things would settle down around the trading post, but for the time being, they were spending some of that money he had paid them for the furs, as well as their presence making it safer if any hostile Indians came along.

Three days after the battle with the Blackfeet, Breckinridge and Morgan were sitting in the trading post with Garwood when George Donnelly hurried into the building and announced, "Canoes on the river."

Garwood sat up straight. "Indians?"

Donnelly shook his head and said, "They're still a ways off, but they look like white men."

Breckinridge, Morgan, and Garwood got to their feet and started toward the door. Eugenia, who was sitting at a nearby table entering figures in a ledger, and Ophelia, who was behind the bar, raised their heads and looked like they were about to join the men.

Garwood lifted a hand and waved his daughters back, even though they hadn't actually moved from their places yet.

"You girls stay here," he told them. "At least until we find out what's going on."

"But George said they were white men," Ophelia protested. "Surely they don't mean any trouble."

Breckinridge said, "I've seen white men cause a whole *heap* more trouble than Indians, Miss Ophelia. There's more of us than there is of them, I reckon, so it stands to reason there'd be more varmints amongst us, too."

The three of them went outside with Donnelly. Breckinridge went to one of the loopholes in the stockade wall and peered through it toward the river. He saw the canoes approaching the bank. It was a large party, six canoes that Breck could see, with at least two men in each one. Some of the canoes held three men.

He straightened from the loophole and asked Donnelly, "Who's out at Blue Feather's grave?"

The scaffold on which the body lay wasn't really a grave, but that was the way Breckinridge thought of it.

"Richmond and a couple of the Mandan women."

"Go get 'em," Breckinridge said. Without really thinking about it, he had assumed command of the men, even though he was the youngest of the bunch. Maybe that was because of his size, or because he had more actual experience on the frontier despite his youth, but whatever the reason, no one had raised any objections to him giving the orders.

Donnelly hurried over to the gates. John Rocklin had already removed the bar and now opened one of them enough for Donnelly to slip out. He trotted quickly toward the site where Blue Feather had been laid to rest.

Garwood said, "Since they're white men, should we go down to the river to meet them?"

Breckinridge shook his head. "Let them come to you. It'll give you a chance to look 'em over good." He pointed to the wall. "You probably ought to build yourself a watchtower there. Be a lot handier for keepin' an eye on what's goin' on around here."

"An excellent idea," Garwood agreed. "I'll start the

men working on it right away, as soon as we see what we're dealing with here."

Rocklin had left the gate open so Donnelly could get back in with Richmond and the two Mandan women. Breckinridge, Morgan, and Garwood looked through the gap between the gates and watched as the newcomers grounded their canoes on the riverbank. Some wore buckskins, others the sort of rough work clothes common in St. Louis and farther east. Plenty of rifles were visible, but that was common, too, and none of the men appeared threatening. Breck could hear some of them laughing and talking, although he couldn't make out any of the words. When all the canoes were ashore, the men began walking toward the trading post.

Breckinridge and his two companions stepped aside so Donnelly, Richmond, and the Mandans could hurry back into the compound. Rocklin started to close the gate, but Breck motioned for him to stop.

"Leave it open so we can get a better look at those fellas," he said. "Just be ready to close it in a hurry if we need to." He looked at the others who were gathered around. "The rest of you boys spread out and take positions at the loopholes. When I give you the word, put your rifles through them."

Everyone seemed to understand the orders. They did as Breckinridge told them, and the tense air behind the stockade wall was evidence that they were all ready for trouble.

The newcomers were all close enough now to confirm Breckinridge's initial impression of them. Then he tensed as he unexpectedly recognized one of them.

"That's Cabe there with 'em," he said.

"By God, you're right," Morgan said. "I didn't think we'd see him again, after he left the way he did."

"Looks like he found some new friends."

Breckinridge was right. Cabe was smiling and talking with the other men as they approached. Then he looked at the gates and lifted a hand in greeting.

"Howdy, boys," he called. "I'm back."

George Donnelly, who had clashed with Cabe to start that brawl, said from his position at a nearby loophole, "I ain't so sure that's a good thing."

"Let's wait and see what happens," Breckinridge said. It wasn't that common for him to be the one counseling patience and restraint, but in this situation it seemed the wisest course of action.

Of course, being prepared for trouble was wise, too, so he added, "Rifles up, boys."

The men thrust their flintlocks through the loopholes, and the sight of all those rifle muzzles suddenly staring at them brought the newcomers to an abrupt halt. One of them called, "Hey, what are you doing?"

"Bein' careful," Breckinridge replied through the gap between the gates. He held his rifle ready, too, and he made sure the men outside the wall could see it. "Who are you fellas, and what are you doin' here?"

The man who had spoken before took a step forward, placing him in front of the others, and glared at Breckinridge.

"This is a piss-poor way of doin' business," he said. "If you own this trading post, mister, you shouldn't be pointing guns at your customers."

"He don't own it," Cabe said. "A fella name of Garwood does. I see him in there, though, standin' with Wallace."

Garwood spoke up, saying, "We're not looking for any trouble, men. We were attacked by a band of Blackfoot the other day, and it's got us a little skittish, I suppose."

"Well, you can look at us and tell we aren't Blackfoot, or any other kind of savage," the group's leader said. "My name is Henry Joslyn. We're headed west to do some trapping. We ran into Cabe here, and he told us about this place. We could do with restocking some of our supplies, and this is probably going to be where we bring our pelts to sell them later on. That is, if being threatened isn't the common practice around here."

Breckinridge looked over at Absalom Garwood, who displayed both suspicion and business interest on his face. Business won out, and he said, "They seem to be telling the truth and don't mean us any harm."

Breckinridge hesitated, thinking for a long moment before he finally nodded to Rocklin and took hold of the other gate himself.

"Let 'em in," he said.

Chapter 8

There were eighteen men in the party of new-comers, including Cabe. Henry Joslyn continued acting as if he were their leader. He was a tall, thick-bodied man with a mostly bald head, which he revealed as he took off his wide-brimmed black hat and set it on a table inside the trading post's main room. A fringe of dark hair surrounded his ears and wrapped around his face to form a close-cropped beard.

"I'd like to buy you a drink, Mr. Garwood," he said as he gestured toward the table.

"No, thanks," Garwood replied. "I'm not much of a drinking man. I'd be happy to have a cup of coffee with you, though."

Joslyn smiled and nodded, then looked at Breckinridge and Morgan. "You young men are welcome to join us. You're in charge of this other party, I take it?"

"We are," Morgan said. He held out his hand. "I'm Morgan Baxter. This is Breckinridge Wallace."

"Cabe mentioned both of you," Joslyn said as he shook hands with both of them. "I hope you're not upset that we seem to have stolen him away from you."

"That's his choice," Breckinridge said. "One good thing about the frontier, a fella's free to come and go as he pleases, at least most of the time."

Ophelia brought cups and a pot of coffee over to the table where the four men sat. Breckinridge saw Joslyn eyeing her appreciatively, but he wasn't too blatant or insulting about it. When she had returned to the bar, Joslyn picked up his cup and offered a toast.

"To a successful season of trapping."

The men drank, then Morgan asked, "Is this your first trip west, Mr. Joslyn?"

"As a matter of fact, it is. Do I look like that much of a neophyte?"

"Out here you'd be more likely to be called a greenhorn," Morgan said with a smile. "But no, you look like you have a pretty good idea how to take care of yourself. All your men do."

That was true. The newcomers seemed friendly enough, but they had an air of hardness about them. They looked like they had known trouble in the past . . . and vanquished it.

They were all clustered together at the bar, drinking and talking to Ophelia but not associating with any of Breckinridge's bunch. Charlie Moss, Ben Pentecost, and George Donnelly sat together at one of the tables. John Rocklin was outside on guard duty, and Richmond had gone back to watching over the two Mandan women keeping their vigil at Blue Feather's resting place.

Joslyn took another sip of his coffee and then said, "Tell me more about that attack you mentioned. I was under the impression that this region was relatively peaceful where the Indians are concerned."

"A place can be peaceful most of the time," Breckinridge said, "but when the Blackfeet come around, it ain't."

He sat back and let Morgan and Garwood fill in the details of the battle. It made him a little uncomfortable when they talked about how he had saved them all by putting out the fire on the wall and then keeping the other flaming arrows from doing any damage.

"That's remarkable," Joslyn said. "And you didn't lose any men?"

"Only one of the Mandan Indians I brought out here with me," Garwood said. "He was killed as soon as the attack began."

"How many of those redskins do you have working for you?"

"Five men and four women, now that poor Edward is gone. They've proven to be quite loyal and hardworking."

Joslyn nodded. "And you've got a fine establishment here." He raised his cup again. "Here's hoping we'll be doing a great deal of profitable business together over the years to come."

"I'll certainly drink to that," Garwood agreed.

Joslyn looked at Breckinridge and Morgan and said, "You've come to try your hand at trapping, too?"

"We've been out here before," Breckinridge said. He wasn't necessarily trying to be rude, but his voice was rather curt.

"We just sold a large load of pelts to Mr. Garwood," Morgan added.

Joslyn's bushy eyebrows rose. "This early in the season?"

"Some of 'em were left over from last fall," Breckinridge said. He didn't offer any other explanation.

"Well, that gives you a jump on the rest of us, I suppose, but that's all right. Nothing wrong with a little friendly competition, eh?"

"You'll have a chance to catch up," Morgan said. "We're not going to be doing any trapping for a while."

"No?" Joslyn looked puzzled. "Why else would anyone be out here in this wilderness?"

Morgan leaned forward in his chair. "We're looking for someone. A man named Carnahan. You wouldn't have happened to run into him, would you?"

"Carnahan . . ." Joslyn repeated slowly. He shook his head. "If I've ever run into the man, we weren't introduced. I don't recall anyone by that name. What does he look like?"

"Sort of a short fella," Breckinridge said, "but he's not little. He's almost as wide as he is tall, and it's all muscle. Has a long, bushy black beard and wears a coonskin cap with the coon's head still on it."

Joslyn laughed. "He sounds like quite a distinctive character. I still don't remember ever encountering him. Why are you looking for him?"

Morgan opened his mouth to answer, but before he could, Breckinridge said, "We've got some business to take care of with him. Nothing that important."

That last part was a lie—nothing was more important to Breckinridge right now than settling the score with Jud Carnahan—but he was starting to feel like it probably wasn't a good idea to go spreading their intentions all over the place. The frontier was sparsely populated, but gossip still got around surprisingly well.

Joslyn didn't press for more of an answer than that, and in fact he changed the subject by saying, "I'm surprised to see three such lovely young women out here in the middle of nowhere, Mr. Garwood, although Cabe did mention to us that your daughters work here at the trading post."

"I wouldn't know how to get along without them," Garwood said proudly. "Desdemona's turned out to be a mighty fine hunter. Keeps us in fresh meat. Ophelia takes care of the bar, and Eugenia keeps track of all the figures much better than I could ever hope to."

"Some strapping young frontiersmen are liable to come along and woo them away from you," Joslyn said with a chuckle. He nodded toward Breckinridge and Morgan. "Perhaps these two."

"The last thing in the world I'm lookin' for is a wife," Breckinridge said. He noticed that Morgan just cleared his throat and didn't say anything.

That made Breckinridge wonder just what Morgan would do in the long run, after they found Jud Carnahan and evened accounts with him. The previous year, Morgan had professed a desire to remain partners with Breck and lead a trapper's life, but that was before the injury that had cost him part of his right leg. Although Morgan got around fairly well on his peg, Breck knew it pained him quite often, and he would never have the strength he once had, nor the stamina, as Morgan himself had admitted.

Morgan Baxter came from a wealthy, privileged background, and he'd been downright arrogant when Breckinridge first met him. The danger and hardships they had encountered had left him little choice except to get over that attitude and grow up, and Morgan had adjusted to life on the frontier better than Breck had ever expected.

But was it a good idea for him to remain out here permanently? Breckinridge wasn't sure about that.

Morgan would have an easier life if he went back East where the rest of his family and his father's businesses were. They were Morgan's businesses now, Breck supposed, since he'd inherited them when his father died.

It was something to think about. Breckinridge knew he would miss Morgan if his friend returned home, but it was more important that Morgan do whatever was best for him.

Joslyn and his companions stayed at the trading post that day instead of pushing on. Breckinridge could tell the men were glad for the chance to rest a bit before journeying deeper into the mountains.

The two bunches still kept to themselves rather than mingling, but there was no trouble between them. No clashes over the attentions of the Garwood daughters. That wouldn't have surprised Breckinridge if it had happened, but thankfully it didn't.

The Mandan mourners returned to the trading post at sundown. One more day of grieving for Blue Feather would complete their ritual. The body would remain exposed to the elements until it was nothing but bones, and then those bones would be gathered and buried.

Except for the skull, one of the other men had explained to Breckinridge. The skull would be kept by the Mandans as an honored relic. That seemed a mite gruesome to Breck, but other folks had a right to their own customs, he supposed.

Members of Breckinridge's party were still standing guard all day, and there were two men on sentry duty at night. After supper, as dusk was settling over the landscape, Henry Joslyn came to Breck and suggested, "Why don't you let some of my men take over tonight? We're accustomed to standing watch as well, and that would give your men a full night's rest for a change."

"There's no need for that. We're used to what we've been doin'."

"It was just meant as a friendly gesture," Joslyn said.

Breckinridge heard the stiffness in the other man's voice and said, "Why don't we split it up? One of your men could stand guard with a fella from our bunch."

That put a smile on Joslyn's bearded face. "An excellent idea. I'll stand the first watch myself."

"And I'll join you," Breckinridge said.

Joslyn seemed satisfied with that arrangement. Slowly but surely, everyone else turned in. The light from a candle that showed through the trading post's windows winked out. The men had spread their bedrolls outside, so it wasn't long until the sounds of snoring filled the night air around the compound.

Breckinridge and Joslyn met at the gates. "How do you handle this?" Joslyn asked. He had a flintlock rifle cradled in his left arm, and the butts of two pistols stuck up from behind his belt.

"One man stays here by the gates while the other walks around inside the wall and keeps an eye out for anybody tryin' to climb over from outside or cause any other mischief. They trade places every now and then, when they feel like it."

"Whatever you prefer is fine with me."

"I'll walk around," Breckinridge said. "Always feels good to stretch my legs."

Joslyn nodded his agreement. The moon was low in the sky and wasn't providing much light yet, but millions of stars glittered overhead and provided enough illumination for Breckinridge to see where he was going as he set off on his first circuit of the compound.

When he was near the barn, he heard something moving around inside. That made him frown. The barn was empty at the moment. Garwood had built it so that any trappers who came this way on horseback would have a place to stable their mounts, and he had mentioned that in the next year or so he planned to have some cattle brought up from St. Louis so he would have milk and calves to build a small herd. That bit of domestication seemed completely out of place to Breckinridge, out here on the frontier. But it agreed with what Morgan had said about Absalom Garwood harboring a dream of there being a town here someday, with him its leading, most influential, and no doubt wealthiest citizen.

But for the time being, the barn didn't have any animals in it, and Breckinridge couldn't think of any reason for any of the men to have ventured out here. Might be an animal inside there, he thought. A big cat could have climbed over the wall in search of prey. If that was what had happened, the men sleeping on the other side of the main building might be in danger. He needed to check it out.

Holding the rifle ready, he moved to the double doors on the front of the barn. They weren't fastened, and in fact one of them stood open a foot or so. Breckinridge nudged it open even more with his foot and then stopped to listen. He didn't hear anything else and wondered if he had imagined the sound a few moments earlier.

That wasn't likely, he decided. He wasn't given to flights of fancy. He sniffed, but didn't smell anything out of the ordinary. So it wasn't a skunk, or if it was, the polecat hadn't sprayed recently.

Breckinridge wasn't foolish enough to step into pitch-darkness where a mountain lion or even a bear might be waiting. He backed off, keeping the rifle leveled at the open door, and waited.

A couple of minutes later, a raccoon waddled out of the barn, paused, and rose up on its haunches to look around. Breckinridge chuckled and shook his head. Maybe he was getting a mite too skittish, if he could be spooked by a furry little bandit like that.

"Best run along, mister," he said softly, "before somebody else sees you and decides to make a cap out of you."

The sound of his voice made the raccoon drop to all fours again and scamper away into the shadows at the side of the barn.

Breckinridge had just started to turn away himself when something crashed against the back of his head with incredible force and dropped him to his knees. He tried to hang on to consciousness and fight his way back to his feet, and as he lifted his head, he saw a shadowy figure moving around in front of him. He peered up at the face of the very Devil himself.

If the Devil was short, wide, had a bushy black beard, and called himself Jud Carnahan.

Chapter 9

Carnahan swung the rifle he held and smashed the stock against Breckinridge's head. The blow stretched Breck out flat on the ground and left him stunned, powerless to move.

But even this second brutal, treacherous blow failed to knock him out completely. He could still hear and had a vague sense of what was going on around him. He was even thinking well enough to realize that Carnahan must have been in the barn, too, and when the wandering raccoon had convinced Breckinridge everything was all right, Carnahan had seized the opportunity to step out and strike at his old enemy.

Breckinridge willed his muscles to move. He knew that if he just lay here, he was doomed. Carnahan would kill him. He was a mite surprised the man hadn't cut his throat already, or just hit him again and again until his skull was a shattered, gory mess.

Maybe Carnahan wanted to stretch things out, to make him really suffer before he died.

What Carnahan didn't know was that Breckinridge couldn't suffer much more than he already had these past months, living with all the physical and emotional damage the man's evil had inflicted on Breck and those he cared about.

Actually, the delay was explained a moment later when he heard a quiet voice say, "There you are. I thought I heard something back here. Is Wallace dead?"

"No, I heard you coming and wanted to make sure you weren't one of his friends." That was Jud Carnahan's familiar rumble. Breckinridge was unlikely to ever forget it. "Now I'll go ahead and kill him."

"Since he's just knocked out, wouldn't it be better to tie him up? We might be able to make use of him. Baxter and the others will be more likely to cooperate if Wallace's life is at stake."

Carnahan's voice held a low edge of menace as he said, "Who's the boss here, Joslyn, you or me?"

"You're giving the orders, Jud, as always," Henry Joslyn replied quickly. "I was just offering a suggestion."

"You don't know how dangerous this big, dumb galoot is, or how hard to kill. I'm not passing up this chance—"

"Hold it, both of you! Don't move or I'll shoot!"

The command rang out clearly in a voice new to this conversation. Breckinridge recognized it as well. If his vocal cords hadn't been as paralyzed as the rest of him, he might have let out a groan.

Desdemona Garwood was no match for Carnahan, or even for a lying polecat like Joslyn. From the sound of it, she had the drop on them, but Breckinridge didn't expect that to last.

"Who the hell is that?" Carnahan asked, apparently unconcerned.

"One of Garwood's daughters," Joslyn replied. "The one who seems to want to be a man."

"I don't want to be a man," Desdemona snapped, "but I can shoot like one if I have to. Both of you, step away from him. Joslyn, my father trusted you. I ought to shoot you right now."

Joslyn chuckled. "You won't pull that trigger."

"How do you know?"

"Because there's only one of you, you have only one shot, and even if you kill me, my friend here will deal with you. And, trust me, you'll wish that he'd killed you right away . . . but he won't."

"Damn right I won't," Carnahan growled.

Breckinridge didn't know what Desdemona was doing out here, but her presence made him clench his jaw in frustration. If she hadn't come wandering outside, she would still be in the trading post, safe.

But safe for how long? Joslyn, and no doubt all the other men who had shown up today, were working for Carnahan. Joslyn had put on a good act. It sickened Breckinridge to know that he'd been fooled, but so had Morgan and everybody else.

And now they would all pay the price for falling for that deception.

Unless Breckinridge could do something to stop it.

Again, his iron will exerted itself. This time, the muscles in his arms and legs quivered slightly. His nerves tingled. The fog in his head was receding. Once again, his strength and his hardy constitution were allowing him to throw off the effects of an injury. If Desdemona could keep Carnahan and Joslyn talking for just a few more minutes, he would be able to move again—he knew it.

In fact, he was able to lift his head now, so he could see what was going on. His vision was blurry at first, but it cleared as he spotted two large shapes standing near him. Carnahan and Joslyn, he thought.

And slowly, subtly, they were moving apart from each other, spreading out so that Desdemona couldn't cover both of them with her rifle at the same time. Breckinridge searched for her, saw her slim, straight figure poised about twenty feet away. She started to back off as she swung the rifle from Carnahan to Joslyn and back again. She had realized what they were doing.

Yell for help, girl, Breckinridge urged her silently. Or go ahead and shoot one of them—preferably Carnahan—and then turn and run, try to make it back into the trading post . . .

"Now!" Carnahan barked.

He and Joslyn lunged toward Desdemona. Joslyn was closer. He was able to get a hand on the barrel of Desdemona's rifle and wrench it upward. She pulled the trigger anyway, but instead of a booming report that would alert everyone inside the trading post that something was wrong, the charge generated only a slight spark when the hammer fell. Of all the times for a misfire!

But the attack on her cleared the last of the cobwebs from Breckinridge's brain and sent new strength flowing to his muscles. He made it to his feet, and as Carnahan grabbed Desdemona and clapped a hand over her mouth to keep her from yelling, Breck tackled them both.

He hadn't gone very far, but he had built up enough momentum so that the collision spilled all three of them to the ground. That knocked Desdemona loose from Carnahan's grip. She rolled away fast while Breckinridge and Carnahan wrestled desperately for the upper hand in their struggle.

Carnahan was as strong as ever, while Breckinridge was still weakened and somewhat disoriented from the blows to the head. He knew that if he didn't summon up all the strength he had, Carnahan would kill him. That would mean all his friends would die, too, and sooner or later, so would Absalom Garwood, his daughters, and the Mandan Indians who worked at the trading post. With that grim knowledge driving him, Breck got his left hand on Carnahan's throat under the bristling beard and hammered his right fist into the man's body.

Unfortunately, it was like punching a barrel. Carnahan didn't even seem to feel the blows. He lashed out at Breckinridge. Breck ducked his head so that Carnahan's fists just scraped the sides of it. He tried to dig his knee into Carnahan's groin, but the man twisted aside.

Breckinridge heard a pistol roar somewhere close by, but he couldn't take his attention off Carnahan to see who had fired the shot. He didn't know if Desdemona was alive or dead. But at least the men in the trading post would have heard the shot. They would know something was wrong, and Morgan and the others would have a fighting chance, although they were outnumbered.

Carnahan landed a punch to Breckinridge's chin that clicked his teeth together. Breck tightened his grip on Carnahan's throat. Carnahan bucked up from the ground and tried to throw Breck off. They rolled again, and this time when they came to a stop, Carnahan was on top.

He didn't stay there long. A heavy thud sounded, and Carnahan pitched to the side. Breckinridge looked up and saw Desdemona standing there, holding her rifle by the barrel. The weapon's stock was broken. Breck knew she had swung it like a club and brained Carnahan. Carnahan was stunned, but there was no telling for how long.

Breckinridge scrambled to his feet. Desdemona dropped the rifle and grabbed his hand. "Are you all right?" she gasped.

Breckinridge didn't take the time to answer her. He spotted a dark, bulky shape on the ground not far away. That would be Henry Joslyn.

"You killed Joslyn?"

"I shot him with my pistol," Desdemona said, "but I don't know whether he's dead."

Breckinridge reached for the tomahawk stuck behind his belt. Checking on Joslyn could wait for a minute. He wanted to smash Jud Carnahan's skull to bits while he had the chance. Every minute Carnahan remained among the living, he remained a threat to everything Breck cared about.

But before he could pull the tomahawk free, let alone strike with it, a rolling roar of gun-thunder came from inside the trading post. Joslyn's men— well, Carnahan's men, actually—must have heard the shot outside and decided that was the signal to launch their attack on Breckinridge's party.

Desdemona let go of Breckinridge's hand and turned to run toward the building. Breck's long legs allowed him to catch her in one swift stride. He looped his left arm around her waist and swung her off her feet.

"Hold on!" he said. "You can't go in there with all that lead flyin' around!"

"My pa! My sisters!"

"Those varmints won't hurt 'em," Breckinridge said. Of course, he didn't know that. He didn't think Carnahan's bunch would deliberately wipe out the Garwoods right away, but with all that shooting going on, there was no telling what might happen. "Get outside the gate and hide somewhere until this is all over."

"No!" She kicked and struggled in his grip. "I won't desert my family!"

That was an honorable attitude, but not a very smart one right now. And she was keeping him from killing Jud Carnahan—

That thought made Breckinridge glance over his shoulder. Carnahan was no longer lying nearby. Breck caught his breath and looked around. He didn't see Carnahan anywhere. The man must have gone back into the barn or fled somewhere else. As much as it pained him to realize that, Breck didn't have time to look for him. Not with Desdemona's life in danger, and her stubbornness to contend with, to boot.

Still holding her with her feet off the ground, Breckinridge circled the corral and loped toward the gate.

As he did, the door of the trading post flew open and dark shapes spilled out of it. Pistols roared, and the muzzle flashes revealed the faces of Morgan, Charlie Moss, and the other members of Breckinridge's group. They fled toward the gate as well, backing across the compound and keeping up a sporadic fire at the doorway to prevent the enemy from following them.

Breckinridge hurried to join them. The safest place right now was *outside* the stockade wall, regardless of how that was contrary to the conventional wisdom on the frontier. Breck didn't see Asbalom Garwood, Ophelia, or Eugenia among them. He hoped those three weren't already dead, cut down by the unexpected fusillade inside the building.

"Breck!" Morgan called.

Breckinridge shoved Desdemona into his friend's arms. "Hang on to her!" he ordered, then he turned to the gates. The bar sitting in the brackets could be lifted by one man, but usually two handled the job of removing the thick, heavy beam.

In the heat of the moment, Breckinridge grabbed the bar, lifted it, and threw it aside like it was a twig. He put a hand against each gate and shoved, as if he were Samson pushing down the pillars of the temple, back in Bible times.

"Go!" he told the others. "Get outside and take cover in the trees along the river!"

"Damn you!" Desdemona screamed at him as Morgan carried her out of the compound. He didn't know if she would ever forgive him for taking her away from her father and sisters, but right now he was saving her life, and that was all he could be sure of doing.

Muzzle flames spurted from the doorway, and rifle and pistol balls hummed around Breckinridge's head and thudded into the logs of the wall. His friends sprinted past him through the opening. One of them stumbled suddenly—in the bad light Breck couldn't tell who it was—and he figured the man had been hit. Breck pulled both pistols from behind his belt, eared back the hammers, and fired toward the trading post.

The pistols were double-shotted and packed a heavy charge of powder. Breck didn't know if he hit anything, but the volley made the men inside the building hold their fire for a second. That gave Breck time to duck through the gap between the gates and take off toward the river.

His jaw was clenched tight in anger and frustration. His brain was working well enough now that he could see how the whole thing laid out. Carnahan and his men had run into Cabe and found out from him that Breckinridge and the rest of the party were at Absalom Garwood's trading post. Knowing that Breck and Morgan would recognize him instantly, Carnahan had sent the others on ahead of him to pretend to be friendly and be in position to launch a treacherous attack when the time came. Then Carnahan had slipped into the compound. From there, maybe everything hadn't played out exactly as Carnahan had planned it, but close enough. Breck and his friends had been driven out, and Carnahan held the trading post.

The only real question was whether or not he had hostages, too. Garwood, Ophelia, and Eugenia might well still be alive.

But how long would they stay that way in the hands of a man like Jud Carnahan?

Chapter 10

"You . . . you scoundrel!" Desdemona raged at Breckinridge as he joined the others in the trees along the river. Breck had a feeling she wanted to use stronger language than that, but despite dressing like a man, she couldn't bring herself to do it. "You *left* them there!"

"Standin' around and gettin' myself filled full o' lead wouldn't have done your pa and your sisters any good," Breckinridge said. "As it is, we're all still alive, so we've got a chance to defeat Carnahan and rescue 'em." He looked around. "We *are* all still alive, ain't we?"

"Pentecost is wounded," Morgan answered. "I think he'll live, but he won't be any good to us in a fight."

Breckinridge nodded as he counted in his head. "There are six of us, then."

"Seven," Desdemona corrected him. "I can shoot a rifle just fine, and I have my own weapon with me, as well as powder and shot."

"We're not in great shape when it comes to arms, Breck," Charlie Moss said. "When all hell broke loose in there, not all of us were able to grab our rifles.

We've got six pistols and two rifles among us. Three rifles, countin' yours."

"Ammunition?"

"Enough to last us for a while, but we'll probably run out sooner rather than later."

Morgan said, "At this range, pistols aren't going to be very accurate."

"I know," Breckinridge said. "That's why we need two men with rifles aimed at that tradin' post all the time. If Carnahan and any of his men try to get out, knock 'em down. Charlie, you and Donnelly take that job right now. Richmond, Rocklin, you boys move along the river for a quarter mile or so, then circle around and get behind the place. I recollect there are some rocks and brush back there that you can use for cover. Get close enough you're in pistol range, so if anybody tries to climb over the fence, you can kill 'em, or at least make 'em think twice about it."

"We'll be on our own back there," Rocklin pointed out.

"You will," Breckinridge admitted, "but with the stockade between you and them, they can't launch a full-scale attack against you. And climbin' over ain't that easy, as I know from experience. You'll have time to blow a hole in anybody who tries."

"I hope you're right," Rocklin said gloomily. "Come on, Richmond."

The two men trotted off into the night, sticking to the thick shadows under the trees. Every so often, a rifle shot came from one of the loopholes in the stockade wall, but none of the balls came close to Breckinridge and the others. Just to be on the safe side, they kept some of the rough-barked trunks between them and the trading post as they held an informal council of war.

"What happened in there?" Breckinridge wanted to know.

"Everything seemed all right," Morgan said. "Joslyn's men seemed friendly enough, although they were still keeping to themselves. Miss Desdemona decided to go outside and check on you and Joslyn, Breck, even though her father didn't want her to."

Desdemona blew out a curt breath. "My father knows I have a mind of my own and it's a waste of time to argue with me."

"I'll just bet he does," Breckinridge said under his breath.

"What?" she asked sharply.

"Never mind. Go on, Morgan."

"Well, a few minutes after that, we heard a shot from outside. Our bunch started for the door to go see what had happened, and I guess we all expected Joslyn's men to do the same. But Charlie noticed just in time that they were turning their guns on us. We all dived for cover. If we hadn't done that, they might have wiped us out in one volley. Or at least most of us, anyway."

"Good thing you were quick to jump," Breckinridge said. "I reckon then you fought your way out?"

"Yeah. The place got full of powder smoke in a hurry, so we were able to make a dash for the door. There was nowhere else to go. They had us outnumbered so badly, if we'd stayed inside they would have killed us all."

"What about Cabe? Did he fight on their side?"

"I think he was as surprised as the rest of us. He

tried to get back on our side of the room, but they shot him down." Morgan's voice caught a little as he added, "He never had a chance."

"He wasn't a traitor, then. Just an ornery varmint who got fooled like the rest of us."

"I suppose so. What happened outside, Breck? Why would Joslyn's men try to kill us?"

"They ain't Joslyn's men," Breckinridge said. "They're workin' for Jud Carnahan."

That grim announcement brought a moment of silence from the other men. Then Charlie Moss, from his post behind a tree where he was aiming his rifle at the trading post, said, "You mean the varmint we set out to find?"

"That's right," Breckinridge said.

"So Carnahan came to us," Morgan said. "When Cabe ran into that bunch, why didn't he recognize Carnahan? We told everybody what he looked like."

"Could be Carnahan stayed out of sight so the others could find out who Cabe was," Breckinridge said. "He's pretty smart, you remember. Then, when he found out we were here at the tradin' post, he hatched the scheme with Joslyn to take us by surprise and wipe us out. It didn't quite work the way he'd planned, though. Joslyn may be dead—"

"He's dead, all right," Desdemona put in. "Now I've had a chance to think about it, he couldn't be anything else. I shot him right in the face with my pistol."

"Well, we can sure hope he is," Breckinridge said. "That'd be one less polecat we have to worry about."

"But there are still plenty of others," Morgan said. Desdemona turned to him and asked in a voice taut with worry, "Did you see what happened to my father and sisters?"

"I'm afraid I didn't," Morgan said. He sounded truly sorry. "There was so much confusion, so much powder smoke in the air . . . But I'm sure they all took cover when the shooting started. They should be fine."

"If you consider being the hostages of a madman fine," she said.

"Well, there's that," Morgan admitted. "But we're not going to leave them in there, are we, Breck?"

Breckinridge didn't answer that question directly. Instead he said, "There were sixteen men in that bunch, countin' Cabe after he threw in with 'em. But he's dead now, and so is Joslyn, more'n likely."

"He's dead," Desdemona insisted.

Breckinridge ignored her. "But Carnahan is with 'em now, so that leaves their number at eighteen. A little better than two-to-one odds against us, plus there's that stockade and the walls of the tradin' post itself between us and most of them. There's no way we can attack 'em head-on and do anything other than get ourselves killed."

"So what are we going to do?" Desdemona demanded.

"For now, try to wait 'em out and see if we can come up with some way to turn the tables on them."

After a few seconds of silence, Morgan said, "You mean we're going to lay siege to the place?"

"Reckon you could call it that."

"You *do* realize they have much greater supplies of food and ammunition than we do, don't you?"

Breckinridge glanced over his shoulder toward the Yellowstone River. "Miss Desdemona, how are they fixed in there for water?"

"Water!" she exclaimed. "You're right. There's only one barrel, and it's probably not full. One of the Mandans fetches water every morning. You remember, that's what Edward was doing when the Blackfeet killed him."

"I ain't likely to forget," Breckinridge said. "So your pa don't keep much of a supply inside the tradin' post?"

"With the river so handy, he never saw any real reason to do so." Desdemona paused. "It probably would have been wise, wouldn't it? This is another example of his inexperience at living on the frontier, isn't it?"

"Yeah," Breckinridge said, "but this time it might come in handy for us. The water they have won't last 'em more than a day or two, and then we'll have the upper hand. Maybe by then we'll have figured out how to take advantage of it."

It was long after midnight, according to the stars, when shots suddenly rang out from the other side of the compound. Breckinridge left the others where they were and circled around to check on Rocklin and Richmond. As he approached the area where he had told them to position themselves, he called out softly.

"I'm here," Rocklin replied from a nearby clump of rocks. "Richmond's over yonder behind that big stump."

"Both of you all right?" Breckinridge asked.

"Yeah. A couple of fellas tried to come over the wall, just like you said they might. I'm pretty sure we hit one of them pretty solid, and the other dropped back down inside in a big hurry. Might have winged him, too, but I can't say about that. The other one fell outside, though, and hasn't moved since. I've got a hunch he's done for."

"That dark place right by the base of the wall is him?"

"Yeah."

Breckinridge drew a bead with his rifle and fired. "He might've been tryin' to fool you."

Rocklin grunted and said, "You're a cold-blooded varmint, aren't you, Wallace?"

"I didn't use to be," Breckinridge replied honestly. "People keep tryin' to kill me and folks I care about, though. After a while, a man gets so he don't want to put up with that no more."

That forthright statement brought a chuckle from Richmond. "I don't reckon anybody could argue with that," he said.

"Keep your eyes open," Breckinridge told the men. He backed off into the night and then returned, the long way around, to the place along the river where the others were.

"Are those men all right back there?" Desdemona asked.

"They are. A couple of Carnahan's men tried to sneak out, probably figurin' they'd sneak up on us, but Rocklin and Richmond discouraged 'em. One of them got discouraged permanent-like."

Breckinridge didn't add that he had made sure of that with his rifle shot.

"Why is Carnahan doing all this? Does he hate you that much?"

"He's that scared of me," Breckinridge said. "He knows I've got a mighty big score to settle with him, and the only thing that'll do it is him dyin'. At my hands if I can manage it, but one way or another, I intend to see him dead."

Desdemona looked at him for a long moment, then shook her head. "I don't think I'd want you for an enemy, Breckinridge Wallace."

"Aw, you don't never have to worry about that. Pretty little thing like you, you could never do anything that'd make an enemy out of me."

She didn't say anything at first, then after a second laughed quietly.

"I might be offended by that," she said, "if I didn't know you meant well."

"Why, of course I did. I never would've—"

"Never mind. What do we do now?"

"Wait," Breckinridge said grimly.

Nothing else happened that night. The trading post remained dark and quiet. As dawn approached, Breckinridge took George Donnelly with him, and they circled out of sight of the compound to come in from the back and relieve Rocklin and Richmond, who were sent back to the river for water and rest.

"Desdemona's gonna go across the river and do some huntin', so we all ought to have some fresh meat fore the day's over," he told them.

"How about some coffee?" Richmond asked.

Breckinridge grinned wryly and shook his head. "Can't help you there. We'll just have to do without."

"One more good reason to kill all of 'em," Richmond grumbled. He and Rocklin slipped away and cat-footed off into the lingering darkness before the approaching sun dispelled it.

As the eastern sky lightened, Donnelly commented

from behind the rocks where he had taken cover, "Even though I tangled with Cabe and he stomped off and abandoned us, I was sorry to hear they killed him."

"Yeah, me, too," Breckinridge agreed. "He wasn't a bad sort, overall. Chances are, he would've cooled off and come back sooner or later, if he hadn't run into Carnahan's bunch. Too bad he didn't know that was the sort of snake pit he'd stepped into."

"I overheard some of the Injuns talkin' among themselves. Some of it was that gibberish they spout in their own language, but some of it was English. And I could've sworn I heard 'em say something about this valley bein' cursed. Something about it being called Damnation Valley. You know anything about that, Wallace?"

"I heard the same thing from one of them." *Just moments before the Blackfeet killed him,* Breckinridge added to himself. "And I'm startin' to think that maybe there's good reason for it."

Chapter 11

Inside the trading post

Absalom Garwood sat on the floor behind the bar with Ophelia beside him on the right and Eugenia on the left. One of Carnahan's men leaned on the bar, ordered to keep an eye on them but using that as an excuse to leer blatantly at the two young women. Anger burned inside Garwood, but right now there was nothing he could do.

Nothing except pray that Desdemona was unharmed, too, and that sooner or later all four of them would be together again.

The nine Mandan Indians who worked for Garwood had been herded into the barn earlier and were prisoners there now, watched over by two guards.

Also earlier, Carnahan had sent two men to climb the wall in the back of the compound so they could circle around and take Wallace and the others by surprise. That move had backfired, because one of them came in later, clutching a bloody arm, and informed Carnahan that the other man had been shot and apparently killed.

Garwood should have taken some satisfaction from that news, but as long as his daughters were in deadly danger—not to mention himself—he couldn't really think about anything else.

Carnahan had cursed bitterly while the wounded man was having his arm taken care of. The burly, bearded Carnahan came over to the bar, glared at Garwood and his daughters, and said, "You may think Wallace has outwitted me and it's only a matter of time until he rescues you, but I promise you, that's not the case. How much did he tell you about me?"

"Enough to know that he has good reason to hate you," Garwood had replied. "And even though I don't know the young man well, I could tell he's not the sort to give up."

"You'd better hope you're wrong about that, mister, if you want to survive. If you want your *girls* to survive."

Garwood thought a shrewd look appeared on the man's face then, although it was difficult to tell with that bushy beard.

"I'll make a deal with you," Carnahan went on. "Convince Wallace to surrender, along with his friend Baxter, and I'll let you and your daughters go. Hell, I'll let all the others go. I just want those two."

"Let me think about it," Garwood had hedged.

"Fine. Just don't think about it for too long. I'm already having a hard enough time keeping my men from having some sport with these two." Carnahan nodded toward Ophelia and Eugenia. "They'll have to content themselves with those redskin squaws out in the barn for the time being, but it won't be long before they're tired of waiting for a turn with your daughters. You just mull *that* over, Garwood."

The trading post owner had thought about Carnahan's threat. He could barely think of anything else, in fact.

But at the same time, Garwood knew how likely it was that Carnahan was lying. Carnahan would do or say anything to get what he most desired: Breckinridge Wallace's death.

And once Carnahan had that, he would have no reason to keep any of them alive. Ophelia, Eugenia, and some of the Mandan women might survive longer, so that the men could have their cruel sport with them, but in the end they would die, too. Garwood was sure of it.

Because of that, he would never cooperate with Carnahan. He might pretend to, but all the while, he would be looking for a way out of this mess.

Some of the men made pallets from blankets taken from Garwood's trade stock, stretched out on the floor, and soon began snoring. They took turns sleeping, however, and as long as some of them were awake, Garwood, Ophelia, and Eugenia had no chance to try to sneak out.

Besides, more guards were posted outside, at the loopholes along the wall, so getting out of the building wouldn't have done the three of them a bit of good. They were trapped, and so far Garwood saw no way out.

Fear could only fight off exhaustion for so long. Without even realizing when it happened, Absalom Garwood drifted off to sleep.

He came awake sometime later to the sound of heavy footsteps on the floor near him. He was trying to shake off the grogginess when Ophelia cried out beside him. That made his eyes fly open. He started to surge up from the rough floorboards when someone kicked him in the chest and knocked him back down. Garwood gasped for breath and looked around.

Carnahan stood in front of him, probably the one who had kicked him. One of the other men had dragged Ophelia to her feet and stood there holding her from behind, with one arm around her waist and the other nudging indecently against her bosom.

"Take it easy," Carnahan told Garwood. "Nobody's dying . . . yet. But you're coming with me."

"Eugenia—" Garwood began.

"That the little mouse's name? Don't worry, my men will watch her and make sure nothing happens to her." Carnahan followed that statement with a blatantly crude laugh. "Come on, Papa."

Garwood climbed awkwardly to his feet. He looked at Eugenia, who was peering up at him with big, terrified eyes in her pale face. She actually did look a little like a mouse, he realized.

"It'll be all right," he told her. He thought they all knew that was probably a lie.

The man holding Ophelia started toward the door with her. Carnahan gave Garwood a shove in that direction. As they all went outside, Garwood saw that the sun was up. The early-morning glare made him wince.

Carnahan kept prodding Garwood toward the gates. Ophelia struggled against her captor's grip, but she was no match for the man's strength. When they reached the gates, Garwood saw that the bar had been removed from its brackets. A man stood by each gate.

"Open 'em up," Carnahan said.

The men swung the gates back, not all the way but made enough of an opening that one person could step through it. Carnahan nodded to the man holding Ophelia. He forced her into the gap between the doors but didn't go any farther. None of the men in the trees along the river could shoot at him without hitting her.

Carnahan pulled a pistol and pointed it at Garwood's head. "Don't even think about trying anything funny," he warned. "The two best hostages I've got are those two girls. I don't have to keep *you* alive."

Garwood knew that. He swallowed hard and nodded. Carnahan still held the upper hand. He shoved the pistol back behind his belt, cupped his hands around his mouth, and shouted, "Wallace! Baxter! You hear me?"

A moment went by with no response.

"I know you can see that girl!" Carnahan went on. "You'd better talk to me if you don't want something bad to happen to her!"

Ophelia began to cry. The men in the trees probably couldn't hear her from where they were, but they might be able to see the sobs that shuddered through her.

"We hear you, Carnahan! What do you want?"

That was Morgan Baxter, Garwood thought. He would have expected Breckinridge Wallace to respond. What did that mean? Maybe Wallace had been killed in the fighting the night before?

"You know good and well what I want!" Carnahan bellowed. "You and Wallace give yourselves up, Baxter!

You do that and I'll let the girl and her sister go! I'll let all the hostages go!"

"We don't believe you! Let Ophelia go now, and maybe we'll talk some more! But you're going to have to release Eugenia, too, before you get what you want!"

Carnahan let out a bray of laughter. "What kind of idiot do you take me for? Those two girls are staying right here until I have you and Wallace where I want you. Where *is* Wallace? Why isn't he answering?"

So the same thought had occurred to Carnahan. If Wallace was dead, would that make any difference? From everything Garwood had heard, Carnahan ought to be carrying a bigger grudge against Breckinridge Wallace than Morgan Baxter. Baxter hadn't even been around when Wallace had destroyed Carnahan's previous gang of murderers and fur thieves.

"Breck's right here with me," Morgan called after a moment. "He just doesn't have any time to waste on you!"

That sounded blatantly false even to Garwood's ears. Carnahan didn't believe it, either, because he shouted, "You're not fooling me, Baxter! Is Wallace dead? Show me his body if he is!"

No response came from the trees. Carnahan waited a moment longer, then cursed and told the man holding Ophelia, "All right, get her back in here."

The man backed up, dragging the crying Ophelia with him. The man at the gates started to shove them closed, but Carnahan stopped them with a curt shake of his head.

"Leave them open like that and stay out of the way," he ordered.

As soon as Ophelia and the man holding her were

clear, Carnahan moved behind Garwood and prodded him forward with the pistol muzzle at the back of his head. Garwood, his heart hammering, had no choice but to obey.

"Stand there," Carnahan snapped as Garwood moved into the gap between the gates. "That's far enough. Raise your hands."

Garwood swallowed and lifted his hands to shoulder height.

"You see him?" Carnahan shouted. "This is the fella who owns the place. You ought to know him pretty well by now, Baxter!"

"We know him," Morgan replied. "I'm sorry, Mr. Garwood."

"Your apologies don't mean a thing to him right now," Carnahan said. "The only thing you can do to save his life is surrender, you and Wallace both, if he's still alive! If he's not, I'm gonna have to see his body before I spare any of these people!"

"You're not going to spare anybody! You're a killer and we all know it, Carnahan! But justice is coming for you!"

"Justice!" Carnahan jeered. "There's no such thing! Only two things truly exist in this world! Power and fear! I've got the power, Baxter, and you'd damned well better fear it! You'd damned well better know that I mean what I say! And there's only one way to make you believe it!"

Those words turned Absalom Garwood's insides to ice. He suddenly knew beyond a shadow of a doubt that his time had run out. All that was left for him to do was pray that some miracle would save the lives of his daughters—

That thought barely had time to form before Carnahan pulled the trigger.

Ophelia screamed as she heard the muffled boom and saw her father's head come apart from the close-range shot. Before Garwood's bloody corpse even hit the ground, Carnahan swiftly stepped back and to the side. Rifles blasted from the trees, but only a couple of balls whistled through the opening before the men pushed the doors closed again. The other shots thudded harmlessly against the thick barrier of logs.

Carnahan jerked a thumb toward the trading post and told the man holding Ophelia, "Get her inside." She didn't put up a fight this time as he hustled her toward the building. She was too stunned by witnessing her father's death.

The men at the loopholes returned the fire. It was unlikely that any of the shots would find their targets, but the volleys continued on both sides for several minutes.

Carnahan followed Ophelia and her captor inside, then told the man, "Put her with her sister."

Eugenia was still huddled against the wall behind the bar. The man gave Ophelia a hard shove in that direction, causing her to stumble. She fell to her knees beside her sister. Eugenia clutched desperately at her.

"Ophelia!" the younger girl cried. "Are you all right?"

Ophelia didn't answer. Her face was drained of color, and her blue eyes were wide with shock and horror.

"Ophelia!" Eugenia said again. "Where's Papa?"

"He's dead, girl," Carnahan answered instead of the stunned Ophelia. "I had to make those fools see that I mean what I say."

Eugenia stared up at him in a mixture of grief and horror. "You . . . you killed him?" she managed to say.

That was enough to make racking sobs come from Ophelia again. She sagged against Eugenia, who instinctively put her arms around her older sister.

Tears came to Eugenia's eyes, too, but she held tight to Ophelia and cast a glance up at Carnahan, who stood at the end of the bar with a cruel, self-satisfied smirk on his bearded face. Eugenia had never hated anyone as much in her life as she hated Jud Carnahan at that moment.

He was going to be sorry he had killed her father, she vowed. She had no idea how or when she would make good on that vow, but she swore to herself that sooner or later she would. She held Ophelia, patted her on the back, and attempted to comfort her by crooning soft words to her.

And all the while, she was trying to come up with a plan.

Chapter 12

From his position in the rocks behind the compound, Breckinridge heard the shouting and recognized the voices of Morgan and Carnahan, although he couldn't make out all the words. He understood enough to know that Carnahan was demanding he and Morgan surrender, as well as promising that he would let everyone else go free.

Breckinridge didn't believe that for a second. He knew Morgan didn't, either, and if they had any sense, neither would anybody else.

Think of the lowest, most treacherous thing a person could ever do—and that was what you could expect from Jud Carnahan. Or worse.

Even though Breckinridge knew that, he was still a little shocked to hear a sudden, single shot at the front of the compound, followed immediately by a volley of gunfire from the river. Carnahan had done *something* to set that off, and it had to be something bad.

From the clump of brush where he had hunkered down out of sight, Donnelly said, "Damn it, Wallace, don't we need to go see about that?"

"How are we gonna do that?" Breckinridge asked. "Climb over the fence back here? Carnahan's bound to have men watchin' all around the place, and we'd be easy targets tryin' to clamber over. I don't like it any more than you do, George, but for right now we got to sit tight and see what happens next."

Donnelly did some grumbling about that, but he didn't say much, and nothing directly to Breckinridge.

No matter how much the inaction ate away at Donnelly, though, it was worse for Breckinridge. Sitting and doing nothing while an evil man like Jud Carnahan threatened innocent folks scraped painfully against the grain for Breck. A glimmering of an idea began to form in his brain.

The shooting died away. Breckinridge and Donnelly continued to watch the compound. The morning dragged by and got warmer as the sun climbed higher in the sky. Beads of sweat began to pop out on Breck's forehead.

He heard a noise behind him and swung around quickly with his rifle ready, even though he didn't see how any of Carnahan's men could have gotten out and snuck up on them.

Morgan was crawling through the brush toward him. He held up a hand and motioned for Breckinridge to hold his fire. Breck lowered the rifle and waited for his friend to join him.

As Morgan moved into the rocks beside him, Breckinridge asked in a grim voice, "What happened?"

"Garwood is dead," Morgan replied, his tone equally bleak. "Carnahan shot him in the head."

Breckinridge's jaw clenched so hard it was painful. For a moment, he was too angry to speak. When he found his voice again, he rasped, "Why?"

"To make us take him seriously. I guess he figured he still had the two girls to use as hostages, so he didn't really need Garwood. He used him for . . . for an object lesson, instead."

"Good Lord," Breckinridge said. "Did Desdemona see it?"

"I'm afraid she did. Charlie had to grab her to keep her from charging the wall. It was all he could do to hang on to her." Morgan shook his head. "You wouldn't think somebody as small as that could put up such a fight."

"Badgers are small, too, but I wouldn't want to stick my head in a hole where one of 'em was. How's she doin' now?"

"She's still upset, of course. But she's settled down some. If she ever gets a chance to kill Carnahan, though, she may beat you to it, Breck."

"I don't care anymore who kills him," Breckinridge said. "He just needs to be dead."

"Nobody's going to argue with you about that. Question is, how are we going to do it?"

"We're gonna take a lesson from the Blackfeet," Breckinridge said. "They're ornery varmints, but nobody ever claimed they don't know how to fight. This didn't work for them, but we're gonna go at it a mite different. You take my place here, while I circle back around to the river."

"What are you going to do, Breck?"

"Make me a bow and some arrows." Despite the grim, desperate situation, Breckinridge smiled. "When I was a kid back home, runnin' around the Blue Ridge Mountains, I made more'n one bow. Got so I was pretty good at it."

Morgan frowned. "I don't understand. What good is a bow going to—" He stopped short. His eyebrows rose as he began to understand. "Flaming arrows!"

"Yep. We're a little closer than the Blackfeet were. If they'd been around on this side, we might not have been able to stop them from settin' the wall on fire. We're gonna give it a try. That ought to shake Carnahan up, if we can do it."

"He'll still outnumber us, and they'll be forted up inside that strong building."

"Then we'll have to make 'em come out."

Breckinridge didn't offer any more details. He left Morgan in the rocks and moved off through the brush, staying low so he wouldn't be spotted by anyone inside the compound.

Once he was out of sight, he stood up and loped around toward the river, then moved along the bank until he came to the spot opposite the trading post. The other men were crouched behind trees, aiming rifles and pistols at the wall.

Desdemona sat just below the bank's drop-off, on a log that had washed up there along with several others. Breckinridge angled toward her and dropped onto the log beside her.

Her face was pale and he could see streaks on the lightly freckled cheeks where tears had dried, but she wasn't crying now and seemed composed. Breckinridge said, "I'm mighty sorry about your pa, Desdemona."

"You ought to be," she replied. "I'm not saying that it's your fault Carnahan killed him. But if you hadn't been here, Carnahan wouldn't have attacked us."

"You don't know that. The fella's like a hydrophobia skunk. He'll lash out at anybody who gets in his way."

"But if he was headed on west, he would have stopped and then gone on his way. He wouldn't have any reason to cause trouble."

"Maybe . . . but I've got a hunch that when he saw you and your sisters, he would've wanted to take you along with him. Your pa wouldn't have stood for that. Things would have gone bad anyway."

She turned her head and gave him a cold stare. "I suppose we'll never know which of us is right, will we? And it doesn't matter. In the end, Carnahan is the one who pulled the trigger. He's to blame. And he's got to die for what he's done."

"Yes'm, he sure does. I'm workin' on it."

The possibility of action seemed to perk up Desdemona's interest. "What are you going to do?"

Breckinridge stood up from the log and took the tomahawk from his belt.

"First thing is to find me a good branch that I can make into a bow."

He had to look around for a while before he found a suitable branch on one of the trees. Once he had, he hewed it off the trunk, then trimmed the smaller branches and peeled the bark from it. After testing the branch for springiness and deciding it would work, he used his knife to notch both ends. Then he cut several pieces of fringe from his buckskin shirt, tied them together to make two longer pieces, and wove those pieces together so the makeshift bowstring would be stronger.

"There are better ways to do this," he told Desdemona, who was watching with interest, despite her grief. "Animal gut makes a stronger bowstring, and so do tendons. But that takes more time, and we ain't got that. Carnahan's like a wild animal—there ain't no tellin' what he might do, or when."

He strung the bow and tested it, putting enough pressure on the string to make sure it would hold. Then he began looking for smaller branches he could fashion into arrows.

"You're going to shoot flaming arrows at the wall the way the Blackfeet did," Desdemona guessed.

"Yep, but around in back, not here in front. The cover's closer in the back."

"My sisters are still in there," she said worriedly. "If you burn the whole place down, what's going to happen to them?"

Breckinridge shook his head. "Even if I set the wall on fire the way I'm plannin', it shouldn't burn down any of the buildin's except maybe the barn. There's a good-sized open space around the tradin' post itself. I don't think the flames will jump it. But then Carnahan and his bunch won't have the wall to hide behind no more."

"They'll still have the trading post," Desdemona pointed out. "It's very sturdy. My father built it for defense."

"I got an idea about that, too, but let's see if we can get that wall down first."

His boyhood spent roaming the Blue Ridge Mountains near his home had proven beneficial many times since he'd traveled west to the frontier, and now it did again. He was able to trim and shape several small branches into arrows. There were no birds in the trees at the moment—the gunfire had caused them all to flee—but he found a dead one on the ground and used feathers from it for fletching. There was no time to find flint and chip it into arrowheads, so he sharpened the tips of the arrows as much as he could. They wouldn't penetrate the logs, but Breckinridge planned to aim for the base and stick them into the ground there. He hoped that would be close enough for the flames to spread.

When he was satisfied with the arrows, he wrapped dry moss around the shafts just behind the tip. As he was finishing up, Desdemona said, "It's almost like you're an Indian yourself."

Breckinridge grinned. "I'll take that as a compliment. Most of 'em are fine folks, and they know better'n anybody else how to get along out here because they been doin' it all their lives. You got some who are pure poison, like the Blackfeet, and, shoot, probably a lot of them ain't all bad. Just the ones I've run into."

"I'm coming with you when you go back around to the other side."

"No, ma'am. You'll be safer here. The cover's better."

"You can't give me orders, Mr. Wallace." Her small chin rose defiantly. "Since my father's gone, I'm the oldest of the three sisters, which means I'm my own boss from now on."

"At least until you find a fella and get hitched."

She said, "Hmmph," as if getting married wouldn't change anything when it came to making up her own mind. Somehow, Breckinridge didn't doubt that.

Short of tying her up, he didn't really have any way

of stopping her, so he said, "Stay low and follow my lead."

"Fine."

He wasn't completely convinced she would do that, but he didn't have any choice but to hope so.

Breckinridge filled Charlie Moss in on the plan, then he and Desdemona trotted along the edge of the river, staying below the bank so they wouldn't be seen. Breck had to bend over in order to do that, but Desdemona was short enough she was able to stay upright. When they had gone far enough, they climbed out and began the wide circle that would bring them up behind the compound.

As they got closer, Breckinridge motioned for his companion to get down on her hands and knees.

"I know it ain't ladylike, but from here on, we got to crawl."

"Have I ever done anything that makes you think I'd worry about being ladylike, Wallace?"

Breckinridge knew this wasn't the right time for it, but he had to laugh at that question.

"No, I reckon not," he said. "But I learned a long time ago how changeable gals can be."

She just glared at him for a moment in response to that. But she got down on hands and knees and crawled through the brush behind him.

A few minutes later they came up to the rocks where Morgan was posted. He glanced over his shoulder when he heard them coming and looked surprised to see Desdemona with Breckinridge.

"Are we going to attack from this side if you can set the wall on fire?" he asked.

"No, they'll still have us outnumbered too much

for that," Breckinridge said. "But if any of 'em come out to fight the fire, we'll do our best to pick 'em off."

He gathered up dry twigs and leaves and mounded them behind one of the rocks. Then, taking out flint and steel, he began striking sparks. He had plenty of experience at starting fires, so it took only a few moments before small flames were flickering up.

Morgan was sprawled on his belly behind a rock. Desdemona had worked her way into a similar position a few yards away. Breckinridge looked at them and said, "You two ready?"

"Go ahead," Desdemona told him. "Rain down the fires of hell on them, Wallace."

"Might not be quite that much brimstone," Breckinridge said as he nocked the first arrow and held it in the flames to set the moss afire. Then he stood up, drew back the bow, and let fly.

Chapter 13

The arrow arched through the air. Breckinridge heard a man shout inside the compound and knew somebody had spotted the flaming missile, probably through one of the loopholes in the stockade wall. He had a pretty good idea what would happen next, so he ducked back down behind the rock.

As he did so, a rifle blasted. Breckinridge heard the ball hum past, well over his head.

"Breck, it fell just short!" Morgan called.

Breckinridge bit back a curse. It wasn't surprising that his first attempt was a little off—it usually took a couple of tries to get the range, after all—but a fella could hope, couldn't he?

He nocked another arrow and set it alight. Instead of firing immediately, he squirmed along the ground for several yards, so when he reared up he wasn't in exactly the same place as he'd been before. By now, more of Carnahan's men probably had hurried to the rear of the compound and would be watching through the loopholes, eager to get a shot at him.

More shots rang out. Rifle balls whined off the rocks.

"Stay down!" Breckinridge told Morgan and Desdemona. When the shots stopped for a moment, he came up on one knee, bent back a little so he could draw the bow, and loosed a second burning shaft toward the compound.

Once again he had to dive to the ground as shots whistled around him. While he was lying there on his belly, Morgan whooped and said, "This one landed perfectly! It dug into the ground right at the base of the wall and it's still burning good. Looks like it's going to catch—*Hell!*"

"Morgan, are you all right?" Breckinridge asked anxiously.

The answer came back right away, thankfully.

"Yeah, I'm fine. Just had a rifle ball skip along the ground a few inches in front of my nose. I'm back behind this rock now. Nothing to worry about."

"I can see the wall from where I am," Desdemona said. "It looks like the log next to where the arrow landed is starting to smolder. I wish I had a spyglass so I could see better . . . Yes! It's caught on fire now!"

Breckinridge crawled back to the fire. He had left the other arrow there, and in a matter of seconds he had it lit and was ready to send it speeding toward the compound. He heard quite a bit of shouting on the other side of that wall now. He thought Carnahan's men might try to throw some water over the top of the wall or even *through* it, hoping to get enough moisture through the tiny gaps in the wall to extinguish the flames. So far they didn't seem to be doing that, however, and the fire was getting bigger.

He reared up again, aimed at a different angle, and sent the third and final arrow toward a different section of the wall. This time the shots that came in response were even closer to him. He felt one of the balls flick the fringe on his left sleeve. He hit the dirt and listened to the shots whickering through the nearby brush.

Morgan laughed. "It's like you stirred up a nest of hornets and got them mad at you!"

"Yeah, them lead stingers can be pretty painful!" Breckinridge called back.

Then he felt bad for bantering with Morgan when Desdemona's father had been murdered so brutally just a short time earlier.

She didn't seem to be dwelling on that loss right at the moment. She had gotten caught up in what Breckinridge was trying to do. She said, "I can see through a little crack in the rocks, and that third arrow landed close enough that I think it's going to catch the wall on fire, too. That was good shooting, Wallace, especially with such a crude bow."

"I made a bunch of 'em when I was a kid. I spent more time wanderin' through the woods than anything else, teachin' myself how to survive."

She turned her head to look at him. "Did you know then that you were going to come out here and be a frontiersman?"

"I didn't have no idea," he replied honestly. "I might not have ever left that part of the country if it hadn't been for . . . well, things that happened. Things that made it better for me to light out for the tall and uncut."

He didn't want to explain all the bad judgment and

bad luck that had caused him to head west the first time. For one thing, a lot of his decisions had been plumb boneheaded, and he didn't want to revisit them. They didn't have any bearing on what was going on now.

A couple of thin columns of smoke wound into the sky. Carnahan's men weren't putting the fires out, or even trying to, from the looks of it. That puzzled Breckinridge, but he would take all the good fortune he could get.

When he risked a look again, the flames were leaping along the wall in both directions. By now the heat had probably forced Carnahan's men to pull back. Breckinridge readied his rifle. If part of the wall collapsed, he wanted to put a few shots into the compound. Even if he didn't hit any of the defenders, raking this rear area with rifle fire would make them retreat into the trading post itself.

Breckinridge wanted as many of them crowded in there as possible. The next part of his plan hinged on it.

Inside the trading post

The burning need for vengeance that Eugenia felt was a welcome distraction from the grief that threatened to overwhelm her. It was almost impossible for her mind to comprehend that her father was gone. Her mother had died while Eugenia was still fairly young, and her father had devoted himself to doing the best possible job of raising her and her sisters.

Some people might say that dragging them out here to the frontier from their home in Pennsylvania was hardly the way to go about that, and Eugenia supposed that to most, that would be correct. There were certainly a lot more dangers here, and now one of them had claimed Absalom Garwood's life.

But he had always harbored the dream of going west, ever since the first mountain men had started returning to the East some twenty years earlier with their tales of towering, snow-capped mountains and vast deserts and endless rolling prairies. Eugenia's father had wanted to see such things for himself. He'd planned to do so when all three of his daughters were safely and happily married.

When that hadn't happened by what most considered a reasonable time, Desdemona—herself inflicted with the same restless nature as her father—had started urging him to travel to the West anyway. It had taken some time to convince him not just to visit, but to move to the frontier permanently and start a business there. Absalom Garwood had owned a successful mercantile in their hometown for many years. Establishing a similar enterprise in the West would be perfect for him. And according to Desdemona's plan, she and Ophelia and Eugenia would go with him to help him. They wouldn't travel so far into the wilderness that they would be in great danger, she said.

Their father had resisted that for a long time, but once Desdemona won over the other two, the die was cast. Absalom Garwood wasn't able to resist his daughters for long. He had given in, sold his business, and made plans to found a trading post and establish what might well turn out to be a business empire in the bright new land west of civilization . . .

That was how they had come to Damnation Valley. They might not have picked this place to settle if they had known at the time what it was called, but maybe they would have. In every other way, it seemed to be perfect.

But horror could intrude into perfection. Eugenia knew that now, and she knew as well that their choices were to give in to that evil . . . or fight back against it.

She chose to fight.

She cradled the crying Ophelia against her and, inch by inch, scooted both of them along the wall. One of Carnahan's men was watching them, but he didn't seem to notice that Eugenia was several feet closer to a barrel sitting against the wall than she had been earlier. That was the barrel containing the water brought from the river. Every morning, one of the Mandans used buckets to bring water from the Yellowstone and replace what had been used the day before. It was generally kept about three-quarters full.

Eugenia worked her way over to the barrel and leaned her shoulder against it. Her head slumped forward. Her left arm was around Ophelia's shoulders. Ophelia seemed to have cried herself out at last. She slumped against Eugenia, and even though she was older and larger, she rested her head on Eugenia's shoulder like a weary child snuggling against her mother. Despair seemed etched into every line of their forms.

But at the same time, Eugenia's left hand had stolen behind the barrel, unseen by anyone. She searched for the plug—the bung—near the bottom of the barrel, which was there so the barrel could be drained and cleaned from time to time. That hadn't been done in the time since the trading post was established.

Under normal circumstances, that plug would be removed by whacking it with a bung starter. One of those mallets was on a shelf underneath the bar, but with Carnahan's men all around, Eugenia couldn't very well get it without drawing attention to herself, and she certainly couldn't put it to the use for which it was intended.

Her only option was to pull the plug out by hand. Her fingers closed on it and tested it to see how firmly it was planted. The plug didn't budge. She began pushing on it, working it from side to side. It had been hammered into place, and she didn't know if she could ever loosen it.

Draining the water would be a blow to Carnahan's plans, though, and right now it was the only thing Eugenia could think of that would cause trouble for him. There was plenty of food and ammunition in the trading post, so the men could hold out for a long siege as far as those things were concerned.

But this was the only water in the place, and if it was gone, Carnahan would have to send men to try to get more. Then Breckinridge Wallace, Morgan Baxter, and the others would kill them. That thought made her heart beat a little faster.

Any progress she made was maddeningly slow. She couldn't tell if she was actually doing any good or not. Her fingers ached from the effort. Ophelia's deep, regular breathing told Eugenia that her sister had gone to sleep, seeking refuge in slumber from the horrors that threatened to consume them both.

At first, Eugenia didn't realize something had changed. Then she rubbed her fingers together and realized they were wet. She wondered for a second if she had scraped them so raw while working at the plug that they had started bleeding. They weren't sticky, though. She held her breath as she felt a small but steady spurt of water against her hand.

The bung hadn't come out, but she had loosened it enough that the water was draining from the barrel. There were small gaps between the puncheons that formed the trading post's floor, so she hoped the water would trickle through them instead of forming a puddle around the bottom of the barrel, which might be noticed. The more water that drained out before anyone was aware of it, the better.

With that accomplished, Eugenia allowed herself to rest a little. She didn't go to sleep like Ophelia, though. She was too keyed up for that.

As she sat there, she felt her dress start to get wet. Some of the water had seeped over to where she was sitting. As far as she could tell, though, most of it was draining through the floor as she'd hoped.

She didn't go to sleep, but a stupor of sorts settled over her. She didn't know how much time had passed. It seemed like days, almost, but she knew it hadn't been that long. Several hours, though, punctuated by occasional bursts of gunfire outside. She prayed that Desdemona was safe with Breckinridge Wallace and the other men. Her oldest sister had taken to frontier life better than either she or Ophelia had. If any of the Garwood sisters was going to survive this ordeal, it would probably be Desdemona.

More gunfire roared outside, a veritable fusillade coming from the rear of the compound this time. Eugenia lifted her head and wondered if Breckinridge and the other men were attacking. Surely not, as badly as they were outnumbered.

Then one of the men rushed into the trading

post and shouted, "The fence is on fire in back! The varmints shot flamin' arrows at it, like red Injuns!"

Carnahan bellowed a curse and ordered his men, "Get buckets! There's got to be a water barrel in here somewhere! Find it! We need to put out that fire."

Men scurried around, grabbing buckets from a stack that had been for sale, and one of them came behind the bar and shoved the lid off the water barrel.

"This must be it!" he yelled. One of the other men tossed him a bucket, but he froze as he peered down into the barrel. "There ain't but a few inches of water left in here!"

"What?" Carnahan ran behind the bar and shouldered him aside. He looked into the barrel, too, and started spewing curses.

It was all Eugenia could do not to laugh.

Chapter 14

The upright logs that formed the stockade wall burned better than Breckinridge had expected, or even hoped for. It had been long enough since Absalom Garwood cut them down and built the wall that they'd had time to dry out.

And for some reason, Carnahan's men didn't appear to even be trying to put out the fire. They just let it burn as they retreated toward the trading post. Shots still blasted from behind the burning wall, but Breck, Morgan, and Desdemona returned them right through the flames. Breck saw at least one man fall as if badly wounded. He stayed down, too.

Morgan let out an exultant whoop. "It's going to burn all the way around!"

Breckinridge glanced over at him and would have agreed, but he also saw the look on Desdemona's face. She had already been through so much, and now she looked even sadder.

"Thinkin' about how your pa built that wall, and now it's burnin' up?" he asked her.

She nodded. "He and the Mandans worked really

hard at it. Now he's dead, Edward is dead, and there's no telling what's happened, or what's going to happen, to the other men. When we first came out here, I loved this place. I know what the Mandans said, but I never really believed the valley was cursed. Now . . . I'm not so sure."

"The frontier is a hard place, there's no gettin' around that. There's a million ways it can kill you. But it's clean and free, too, and dangerous or not, there's no other place I'd rather be. I didn't know your pa well enough to say for sure whether he felt that way, too, but I reckon there's a good chance he did."

Desdemona swallowed and nodded. "Yes, he did. Coming out here was something he wanted to do all his life, I suppose. Now I wish we had never encouraged him!"

Breckinridge couldn't blame her for feeling like that. Maybe she would look at things somewhat differently later on, once the pain of losing her father wasn't so sharp. That was something to consider for the future. Right now, the important thing was rescuing her sisters.

And making sure Jud Carnahan paid for all the monstrous evil he had done.

"The barn's caught on fire!" Morgan called, jolting both Breckinridge and Desdemona out of their thoughts. "Look at the roof!"

He was right. Embers from the burning wall had landed on the barn's roof and smoldered until they caught those logs on fire, too. Flames licked up, and Breckinridge knew they would spread quickly. There were no animals in the barn, as far as he knew, but some of Carnahan's men might be in there, in which case they would be forced to flee into the trading post, too.

That should have been a good thing, but for some reason, he was uneasy, as if he sensed somehow that more was going on here than he knew.

Inside the barn

The five men and four women from the Mandan tribe who had come west with Absalom Garwood sat together in one of the empty stalls with fear on their faces. They had heard all the shooting outside, and now they smelled the smoke from something burning. The two men Carnahan had given the job of guarding them looked worried, too. A lot was going on, and none of it seemed to be good.

One of the other white men came running into the barn. "The fence is burning back here!" he told the guards. "They shot flaming arrows at it and set it on fire!"

"Damn it!" one of the men said. "I knew that smoke smelled close. I could even hear the flames—"

"Look up there!" the third man yelled. "That's what you're hearing!"

Everyone in the barn looked up, white and Indian alike. Wisps of smoke curled down through the roof. In the gloom, tiny orange flickers of flame were visible. The roof was on fire, too.

"What are we gonna do?" one of Carnahan's men asked, obviously frightened. "We're supposed to watch these redskins, but the barn's liable to burn up. I'm not gonna be in here when it does!"

"We can't just let them go," said the man who had just run in to warn the guards. "Jud wouldn't like that." Callously, he added, "Might be better just to shoot 'em and be done with it."

All three white men turned to stare at the Mandans. The men looked increasingly desperate, and desperate men sometimes do unspeakable things. At least some of the captives realized this, and as Carnahan's men started to lift their rifles, three of the Mandan braves surged up from the floor of the stall and charged them, shouting their defiance.

The rifles thundered, but the shots were hasty and only one of them found its target. The Mandan who was hit clapped a hand over his chest where blood welled from the wound, but he managed to stay on his feet and barrel into the man who had shot him, driving the man off his feet.

The other two rounds missed and slammed into the barn's side wall. The Mandans tackled the guards and knocked them over backward. As they began to struggle, the other Indians leaped up and charged into the fray, even the women.

The white men didn't have much of a chance. The rifle was ripped out of one man's hand, and the butt crashed into his head again and again until it had been battered into a bloody mess that didn't even look human. One of the Mandans got his hand on a knife sheathed at his opponent's waist and ripped it free, then plunged it into the man's chest over and over. Only the third man was able to get his pistol out, and when it boomed as he triggered a wild shot, one of the women cried out and fell, with blood spurting from her neck where the ball had torn through it. Her killer died mere moments later as a Mandan wrenched the empty pistol away from him and hammered him into oblivion with it.

The man who had been shot in the chest was dead as well, but that left seven of the captives, who grabbed all the weapons they could from the white men and ran out of the burning barn. The structure's roof was fully ablaze now and would collapse soon. The fleeing Mandans dragged their slain companions out of the barn so their bodies wouldn't burn.

Then they raced toward the rear of the compound where the stockade wall was still burning in places and had collapsed in others. The Indians headed for one of the gaps. Some of Carnahan's men fired after them from the corners of the trading post, but so much smoke was in the air it was hard to achieve any accuracy. Rifle balls whistled past the Indians, but all the shots missed.

Then they were leaping over the debris, their moccasins smudged with ashes and embers, running for their lives toward the rocks and brush and trees some fifty yards away.

"Give 'em some coverin' fire!" Breckinridge called to Morgan and Desdemona as he aimed past the Mandan Indians who came running from the barn and through the fire-destroyed fence. He saw several of them carrying rifles, pistols, shot pouches, and powder horns. If the Mandans threw in with his group, that would go a long way toward evening the odds. He knew that some of Carnahan's men had been killed already. Carnahan couldn't have more than a dozen or so left, if that many.

The Indians angled to the left as they cleared the wall, giving Breckinridge, Morgan, and Desdemona more room to shoot past them. They reached the trees and took cover without any of them being hit, as far as Breck could tell.

"Keep those varmints in the tradin' post occupied," he told his companions. "I'm gonna go talk to those folks."

He backed away from the rocks and crawled through the brush until he could stand up and dart from tree to tree. It took him only a few minutes to reach the area where the Indians had taken refuge. The first one he saw was Rose. She impulsively stepped up to him and threw her arms around him in a hug.

"Oh, Mr. Breckinridge!" she cried. "Those evil men! They killed Andrew and Emily!"

Breckinridge knew those were the names Absalom Garwood had given two of the Mandans. He patted her a little awkwardly on the back and said, "I'm sure sorry, Rose. We'll settle the score for 'em, though, you can count on that."

"Settling the score will not bring them back."

Breckinridge shook his head and solemnly agreed, "No, it sure won't. I wish it would." He held Rose for a moment longer, letting her take comfort in his big, solid form, then stepped back and rested his hands on her shoulders. "Do you know if Miss Ophelia and Miss Eugenia are all right?"

"They were the last time I saw them. Those terrible men herded us out of the trading post and put us in the barn like animals! The young ladies were still unharmed when they did that. What about Miss Desdemona? She was not in the trading post."

"She's over yonder with Morgan." Breckinridge waved a hand in the direction of the rocks. "She's fine, other than bein' broken up about her pa dyin'.

But that ain't stoppin' her from fightin' side by side with us against Carnahan's bunch."

"We would fight with you, too," Rose declared, and the other Indians nodded their agreement.

"Figured you might," Breckinridge said with a smile. "A couple of you stay here, while the rest go back around to the river and find Charlie Moss and the other men." He pointed out the direction the Indians should go. "Stay low. You don't want those varmints in the tradin' post spottin' you."

All the Mandans spoke English, so they understood his directions. Two men volunteered to stay behind, while the other two men and the three women headed off through the trees to join the rest of Breckinridge's force. It wasn't much of an army, he reflected wryly as he led the two men with him back to the rocks where Desdemona and Morgan were still taking potshots at the trading post, but he had to make do with what was available. And so far, they had acquitted themselves fairly well.

By now a huge column of black smoke climbed into the sky from the burning barn. Every time another part of the building collapsed, sparks shot high above the destruction.

"I'm sure mighty sorry about havin' to burn down what your pa worked so hard to build," Breckinridge told Desdemona.

"Don't worry about that," she said. "Compared to everything else that's happened, that's nothing. I'd gladly see the whole place burned to the ground if it meant that Carnahan was dead."

"If my plan works, we won't have to go that far."

Morgan said, "Don't you think it's time you let the rest of us in on that plan, Breck?"

"There are no windows in the back of that tradin' post." Breckinridge asked Desdemona, "Do you recall if your pa put any rifle ports in the back wall when he was buildin' it?"

"No, I don't think so," she said. "He should have, I can see that now, but at the time he thought that with the barn and the stockade fence back there, the likelihood of anyone attacking us from that direction was pretty small." She shook her head. "He was much too inexperienced for this, wasn't he? We would have all gotten killed sooner or later."

"He'd have learned," Breckinridge said. "I don't have no doubts about that. He just didn't get the chance."

"Because the first ruthless killer who came along murdered him." Desdemona closed her eyes for a moment, then opened them and went on, "I'm sorry. I can't be thinking about that right now. To get back to your question, there are no loopholes or rifle ports back there, but there might be some chinks between the logs where somebody could look out."

"We'll keep 'em pinned down, then, and wait until nightfall so they can't see as good. Carnahan and his men are all inside, and with some good shootin' we can keep 'em there."

Morgan asked, "Are we going to sneak up on them from this side once it's dark and try to get into the building?"

Breckinridge shook his head. "Nope. That's too dangerous for Miss Ophelia and Miss Eugenia. Carnahan would be liable to kill 'em as soon as the fight started, just so we couldn't rescue 'em. And even if he didn't, you get a bunch of lead flyin' around in a sort of small space like that, and there ain't no tellin' who's gonna get in the way of it."

"Then what *are* we going to do?"

"Make them come out," Breckinridge said. "They got a fire goin' in the fireplace. I been seein' a little smoke comin' out of it all day. All I need to do is get on the roof, plug up the chimney, and let the smoke back up and drive 'em out."

"They could put out the fire," Desdemona said.

"Chances are, they won't notice what's goin' on until it's too late for that to help. And I can drop some moss down the chimney to make the fire smoke even worse before I stop up the openin'."

"It might work," Morgan said. "But they'll come out using those girls as hostages."

"That's why we'll have some men close by when that happens. You and these two Mandan fellas will be waitin' just behind the tradin' post. When Carnahan and the others start comin' out, it'll be your job to grab Miss Ophelia and Miss Eugenia and get them out of harm's way." Breckinridge shrugged. "It's still a mighty big risk. You're their sister, Miss Desdemona. What do you think?"

Without hesitation, she said, "I think if Carnahan is able to keep them in his hands, they're going to die sooner or later anyway, so we might as well give it a try. But there's going to be one change to your plan, Wallace."

"What's that?" Breckinridge asked warily.

"I'm going to be right there with Morgan and the other men to free my sisters."

That was what Breckinridge expected her to say, and he knew there was no point in arguing. Besides,

Desdemona had proven already that she was a good shot and cool under fire. He knew that she was probably praying she would get a shot at Jud Carnahan, too, and he certainly couldn't blame her for that.

"All right," he said. "Would it do any good to tell you to be careful?"

"Not one bit," she said.

Chapter 15

Breckinridge loped back around to the river to fill Charlie Moss in on the plan while Morgan, Desdemona, and the two Indians stayed where they were to keep an eye on the back of the trading post. If anyone tried to get out that way, a few well-placed shots would either kill them or drive them back inside.

Once Breckinridge had explained everything, Moss said, "If you'll give us a signal when they start comin' out of that building like rats, we'll close in from this side."

"You know what a bobcat sounds like?" Breckinridge asked.

Moss laughed. "I've heard one of the critters yowl many a time."

"Well, I can sound like a bobcat when I want to. That'll be the signal. When you hear it, come a-runnin'."

"But what if it's a real bobcat?" Richmond asked.

"There's been so much shootin' and yellin', any

real bobcat around these parts has lit a shuck a long time ago."

With the signal agreed upon, Breckinridge told them that he wouldn't put his plan into motion until after dark, so he would be less likely to be spotted from inside the trading post. Confident that he could count on Moss and the others, he headed along the river and then curved back toward the rocks where Morgan and Desdemona waited. He had filled a couple of water skins from the canoes and took them with him so the others could have a drink. They didn't have any food—Desdemona hadn't had a chance to do any hunting after all—so the water would have to be enough for now.

The afternoon dragged by, hot and interminable and broken up only by an occasional flurry of gunfire. The fire hadn't burned itself out completely, but it had died down a great deal now that the flames had largely consumed the stockade wall and the barn. From time to time a charred and smoldering chunk of wood let out a loud pop as a bubble of sap burst. That sounded like a gunshot and always made the people hidden in the rocks tense and get ready to return the fire, until Breckinridge reminded them what it really was.

Most of the barn had collapsed. Any time one of the remaining sections fell, it caused a lot of racket, sparks, and smoke. The fire hadn't reached the trading post itself, so it was still intact, but if Breckinridge's plan worked, it would reek of smoke inside before the night was over.

He couldn't help but wonder what was going on inside and how Ophelia and Eugenia were faring at the hands of their captors. He hoped they were all right.

Inside the trading post

As soon as Jud Carnahan saw that the water barrel was almost empty, he jerked around toward Eugenia and Ophelia with a savage snarl on his face.

"You did this!" he raged.

"We've been sitting right here with your men watching us all the time," Eugenia protested. Ophelia raised her head from her younger sister's shoulder, looking around and blinking in confusion. Eugenia went on, "And my sister's been asleep. She couldn't have done anything."

"Look around!" Carnahan yelled at his men. "See if there's any more water!"

There wasn't, other than one pitcher, and Eugenia knew it. It didn't take long for Carnahan's men to discover the same thing.

"Tip this barrel over and get what you can out of it," Carnahan ordered as he swept a hand toward the barrel next to Eugenia and Ophelia. Eugenia felt a shiver of fear go through her. If the men moved the barrel, they would see where the water had leaked out and would know she was responsible.

"Too late, boss," one of the other men said as he put his eye to a tiny crack between the logs of the rear wall. "Looks like the fence is burnin' all along the back, and the barn just caught on fire, too."

A flood of venomous curses came from Carnahan's mouth. He looked like he was about to lose control completely, but then one of the men said, "We'd better save what water's still in there, Jud. We'll need it for drinkin'."

Concerned muttering came from several other men. Water was going to be in short supply inside the trading post, and soon. Eugenia didn't expect much more to drain from the barrel, since from the sound of it the level was almost down to the bung, but that wouldn't leave much, either.

The men turned their attention back to shooting at their enemies who had taken cover along the river. Eugenia could tell from listening to their mostly profane comments that the fire was spreading to the stockade wall her father had worked so hard to build. That saddened her, but it was hardly the worst thing she had to worry about right now.

Ophelia whispered miserably, "What's going to happen to us? Are they going to kill us? Or . . . or worse?"

Eugenia's practical nature made her unsure there actually *was* anything worse than being killed, but it wouldn't do any good to say that to Ophelia, or to speculate on what these evil men might do.

Instead she said, "Mr. Wallace and Mr. Baxter are still out there. They seem very capable. And don't forget, Desdemona is, too. She's not going to let anything bad happen to us if there's anything in the world she can do to prevent it."

"She . . . she couldn't do anything to keep that man from sh-shooting Papa."

"I know," Eugenia said softly as she blinked to hold back tears of her own. "I know, but we can't give up hope."

"What's going on back there?" Carnahan demanded

in a harsh voice, addressing the man who had his eye
pressed to the crack in the back wall.

"Barn's burning more. The roof's on fire now.
Here come our men who were back there along the
wall. They're shooting at somebody on this side—"

The man's head jerked back. Eugenia happened to
be looking in his direction, and she saw the blood,
brain matter, and bone shards explode from the back
of his skull. He toppled backward and landed in a
limp sprawl on the floor. Blood swiftly pooled around
his head.

Carnahan roared a curse as he stared at the dead
man.

Eugenia's eyes were wide with amazement, too. She
knew what must have happened: One of the rifle balls
fired by the men outside the compound had hit that
crack in the wall at just the right angle to blast on
through it and into the man's eye. Then it had bored
through his brain and burst out the back of his head.
That was the only explanation.

Beside her, Ophelia made gagging sounds. She
had witnessed the man's shocking death, too, and
was sickened by it.

Eugenia couldn't bring herself to feel any sympathy
for him. As far as she was concerned, Jud Carnahan
and his allies deserved whatever fate awaited them.
The grislier and more painful, the better.

A moment later, one of the men inside swung open
the trading post door so several more men could
scramble in from outside. The door slammed closed
behind them. Carnahan glared at them and said,
"Where in blazes are the rest of you? I posted more
men than this back there!"

"Don't know what happened to 'em, Jud," one of

the men replied. "I heard some shootin' from the barn, I think. Maybe those redskins got loose."

That brought more vile exclamations from Carnahan. "Is there any end to the things that are gonna go wrong?" he demanded, but he didn't seem to expect an answer. He waved a hand wearily and went on, "Get back to the loopholes and keep shooting at them. Maybe we can whittle 'em down."

The gloomy atmosphere inside the trading post settled down to sporadic gunfire and a never-ending litany of curses. Eugenia and Ophelia huddled together behind the bar, reasonably safe from any rifle balls that happened to get inside—but not safe at all, considering the sort of cruel, ruthless men who held them prisoner.

Without meaning to, Eugenia dozed off. The strain had been too much for her, too, and her brain retreated into slumber. She had no idea how long she had been asleep when Ophelia nudged her awake.

"Eugenia," her sister whispered, "is it getting smoky in here?"

At that moment, a huge cloud of smoke billowed from the fireplace and filled at least half the room, causing Carnahan's men to curse and choke.

Breckinridge returned to the river in the late afternoon to scoop some mud from the edge and smear it on his face. He planned to approach the trading post as soon as it was sufficiently dark, before the moon rose. Despite that, anything he could do to make himself less visible was a good idea, he decided. His buckskins were fairly dark already and wouldn't show up much in the starlight.

Morgan looked like he wanted to make some comment when Breckinridge returned to the rocks, but he kept his mouth shut. He must have figured that after all the tragedy and violence today, now wasn't the time to poke fun at Breck's appearance.

While he was coming back through the woods, Breckinridge had gathered up an armful of dry moss. He took the makeshift bowstring he had used earlier off the bow and tied the moss into a bundle that he could sling around his neck. He would need both hands free while he was climbing onto the building.

Great care would be required, as well. If any of Carnahan's men realized he was up there, he could wind up trapped and an easy target for his enemies. They would have to come out of the trading post to shoot at him, but some of them might be willing to risk it for a chance to kill him.

Quietly, Desdemona said, "You asked me earlier if it would do any good for you to tell me to be careful. How about the other way around?"

Breckinridge chuckled. "People have been tellin' me for years how reckless and hotheaded I am. I don't think I'm that way at all. It's just that sometimes a fella's got to take a chance, and other times, a bunch of thinkin' clutters up his brain so much he can't do what needs to be done. But I ain't exactly foolhardy, Desdemona. You can count on that."

"Well, don't get your head shot off, Wallace. And don't go thinking that just because I say that, I've gotten sweet on you or anything like that."

"Never crossed my mind," Breckinridge said honestly. He admired Desdemona Garwood, and in another time and place—another life, really—he might have done more than admire her. Here and now, though, that was never going to happen.

As the sun went down and the sky began to darken, Breckinridge could tell that Morgan and Desdemona were getting more nervous. They knew the time was approaching to put his plan into action. The two Mandan Indians were as stolid as ever, much like Breck himself. He had never suffered from nerves before a battle, partly because of his confidence in himself and partly because of the fatalistic streak that ran through him. He would do the best he could, and destiny would have to take care of the rest.

When the stars were out and the shadows were thick, he slung the bundle of moss around his neck and checked both pistols thrust behind his belt. He couldn't take his rifle with him, but he had the pistols, his knife, and his tomahawk. When the smoke began to force his enemies out of the building, he intended to jump down among them and commence to spilling blood. Death dropping from the sky . . . He liked the sound of that.

"Be ready," he told Morgan and Desdemona. "When you hear the bobcat yowl, you'll know it's time to move."

"We'll be behind you, covering you once you get on the roof," Morgan promised. "Desdemona may not tell you to be careful, Breck, but I will."

Breckinridge clapped a hand on his friend's shoulder, squeezed for a second, and then cat-footed off into the darkness, toward the trading post.

His eyes were keen enough for him to see where he was going, but he didn't hurry. He picked his way over the charred debris that was left from the burned stockade wall. The fire had gone out except for an orange glowing ember here and there. He avoided those. Then, crouching low, he skirted the ruins of the barn and moved along the corral toward the trading post.

He had studied the building enough during the day that he'd been able to figure out the best place to climb onto the roof. Some of the logs Absalom Garwood had used still had bumps and protrusions on them where branches and limbs had been trimmed off. Breckinridge had traced a series of footholds and handholds that would take him up to the level of the roof's overhang. Once he reached it, he would have to grab hold and haul himself up by brute strength. Most men his size couldn't do that, but he believed he could.

Despite his young age, Breckinridge had years of experience at moving silently when he wanted to. He didn't get in any hurry as he approached the trading post. A few clouds floated in the night sky, which was a good thing because they created slowly moving shadows. Breck just blended in with them.

He reached the spot he wanted. The darkness was almost pitch-black here. He had to work by feel as he located his first handholds. Wedging his toe against a tiny knob, he pulled himself up.

He had to climb only a few feet before he was able to reach up and grasp the edge of the roof. When he was sure his grip with that hand was secure, he moved the other hand to the roof.

Then, after taking a deep breath, he held on and let his legs swing out so that he hung straight down. The muscles in his arms and shoulders bunched and bulged as he began lifting himself.

His head came above the roof level. A little more

and he was able to swing a leg up and hook his foot on the roof. Seconds later, he rolled quietly onto the roof and lay there with his arms and legs spread out to keep him stable.

After a moment, he started edging upward toward the peak. The chimney was at the end of the building to his left. He angled in that direction. His progress would have seemed maddeningly slow to anyone watching him, but speed wasn't the most important thing now. Stealth was.

Finally, he reached the roof peak next to the chimney. Grasping the rough stone on the outside of it, he pulled himself to his feet. His balance had always been excellent, so he had no trouble standing there as he slid the bundle of moss around in front of him and began pulling loose small bits of it. He dropped them down the chimney one by one, taking his time about it so that the men down below might not notice that the fire was growing bigger and brighter.

When he judged that it was ready, he set the moss aside and pulled his buckskin shirt up and over his head. He held it ready in one hand while he reached down and picked up the moss with the other.

Then he dropped what was left of it down the chimney onto the flames, half smothering them and causing a great deal of smoke to erupt. Even before the moss hit, Breckinridge had his shirt stuffed into the chimney's flue, blocking it.

Down below in the trading post, angry shouts rose. The door crashed open.

Grinning, Breckinridge tipped his head back and yowled like a bobcat.

Chapter 16

Breckinridge left his shirt where it was and ran lightly to the front edge of the roof. Men stumbled around, coughing, but some of them were already starting to figure out what had happened. One man yelled, "Up there!" and twisted around to point to the roof. He had a rifle in his hands, which he tried to lift and bring to bear.

Breckinridge didn't give the man a chance. He had already pulled both pistols from behind his belt. They were loaded and primed, and he thrust out the one in his left hand as he drew back the hammer. The flintlock snapped and sparked as the hammer fell. The charge in the pan ignited and then the main charge in the barrel thundered out. Flame gouted from the muzzle. The man on the ground went over backward as the ball slammed into his chest.

Breckinridge aimed the pistol in his right hand and fired it as well, downing another of Carnahan's men. He hadn't spotted Carnahan himself so far. The light was bad, and the smoke swirling out of the open door didn't help his vision.

But he had done all he could from the roof, and now it was time for close work. He jammed the pistols back behind his belt, yanked out the knife and tomahawk, and leaped off the building, aiming at one of the men on the ground.

Breckinridge's boots crashed into the man's chest and drove him to the ground. Breck felt bones snap and splinter under the impact and knew this man was out of the fight, if not dead. His momentum carried him forward, off his feet. He rolled and came up ready to fight, just as a man swung a rifle barrel at his head.

He ducked under the blow and drove in, backhanding his knife across the man's midsection. The razor-sharp blade went in easily and ripped from one side to the other, opening a gaping wound through which the man's guts spilled as he screamed. Breckinridge shouldered the dying man out of the way.

Guns blasted around him. Men bellowed curses. More screams of pain ripped through the darkness, and screams that were subtly different, too, cries of fear.

"Ophelia!" Breckinridge shouted. "Eugenia!" He hoped the young women would hear him and somehow make their way to him so he could protect them.

"Breck, look out!" That was Morgan. Breckinridge twisted and ducked just as a pistol went off nearby. He felt as much as heard the wind-rip of the ball as it passed by his ear. A rifle blasted, and the man who had just come within a whisker of shooting Breck dropped his pistol, doubled over, and collapsed.

Morgan hurried up and started reloading. "Breck, are you all right?"

"Yeah," Breckinridge replied. "Down!"

Morgan dropped to the ground as Breckinridge's arm flashed back and then forward. The knife he threw turned over once in midair, then buried itself hilt-deep in the chest of a man who was trying to draw a bead on Morgan. The man's rifle slipped from his fingers as he staggered forward. He pawed at the knife for a second before he collapsed.

"Where are the girls?" Breckinridge asked as he took hold of Morgan's arm and hauled his friend to his feet again.

Morgan coughed a little before replying. The smoke was stinging his eyes and nose and throat, too. He said, "I don't know. Desdemona was right with me, but then we got separated somehow, and now I don't see her!"

The pit of Breckinridge's stomach suddenly felt cold. In the shadows and confusion, he didn't see any of the Garwood sisters. Certainly, it was possible that they were here, very close by, in fact, but still, he couldn't locate them.

Two more shots boomed, and then an echoing silence fell over the area in front of the trading post, broken only by a groan from someone who sounded grievously injured, followed by a death rattle from elsewhere as another man breathed his last.

Then a scream, but it wasn't close. It came from somewhere in the distance, and Breckinridge could tell it originated in the throat of a woman.

One of his enemies—maybe more than one—was getting away, and the man had a hostage.

That cold ball in Breckinridge's gut expanded with the sudden hunch that the man fleeing was Jud Carnahan. Every time in the past, when things had gotten desperate enough, Carnahan had cut and run.

Breckinridge's head jerked from side to side as he

looked around. "Do you see *any* of the girls?" he asked Morgan.

"No, I don't," Morgan replied with a rising note of desperation in his voice.

"Charlie!" Breckinridge yelled.

"Right here," Charlie Moss replied as he came trotting up. He had a bloody scratch on his cheek, suffered in the fighting, but appeared to be unharmed otherwise.

"Charlie, have you seen any of the Garwood girls?"

"Not a one," Moss replied.

"You're comin' with me. I heard a scream from somewhere down the river a minute ago. We're gonna trail whoever it was."

Morgan began, "Breck, I can—"

"No, you can't," Breckinridge cut in. He spoke bluntly, knowing it might hurt his friend's feelings, but there was no time for sentiment, not with at least one of the young women still in danger. "You can't move fast enough. Stay here, light some torches, have a good look around. Those gals might be hidin' somewhere, afraid to come out until they know for sure it's safe."

Morgan still looked like he wanted to argue, but he nodded and said tightly, "All right, Breck. Good luck."

Breckinridge returned the nod, then he and Moss took off at a fast trot, heading for the river.

When they reached the Yellowstone, Breckinridge said, "There's a bunch of canoes here. Carnahan and whoever's with him could've grabbed some of 'em to head downriver."

"We could try to count 'em," Moss suggested.

Breckinridge shook his head. "No time for that. Help me shove off with one of 'em. We'll stay close to this side of the river, and maybe if they're on foot, we can still spot 'em." He glanced at the sky. "The moon'll be up soon, and the light will be better."

The two men took hold of one of the canoes, pushed it into the water, then climbed in and took up the paddles. Breckinridge was still bare from the waist up and didn't have his rifle, but he couldn't worry about that now. All that mattered was finding Desdemona, Ophelia, and Eugenia.

As his massive muscles dipped the paddle into the water, stroked, and sent the canoe gliding swiftly over the surface, he thought that maybe one or even two of the Garwood sisters were still back at the trading post, as he'd told Morgan. But Carnahan had dragged off at least one of them to use as a hostage—Breckinridge was sure of that. If some of Carnahan's men had gotten away with him, it was entirely possible all three of the girls were prisoners.

That knowledge put a sour, bitter taste under Breckinridge's tongue. All the fighting and destruction wouldn't have accomplished a thing if Carnahan had gotten away and the sisters were still in mortal danger. The trading post had been liberated—by destroying half of the compound—and Absalom Garwood was still dead. Carnahan had the devil's own luck, Breck thought.

The moon rose as the two men paddled downstream, helped along by the river's current. Breckinridge listened intently, hoping to hear voices or another outcry that would tell them they were on the right trail, but the only sound in the night was the splashing of paddles in the river.

Silver light from the moon rippled over the water as the two men continued their search. Then, as the canoe rounded a bend and entered a long, straight stretch of the river, Breckinridge spotted something several hundred yards ahead of them. The distance was too great to make out any details, but two and maybe three shapes were moving on the water. Breck knew his hunch had been right: Jud Carnahan and some of the other men had escaped, taking one or more of the Garwood sisters with them.

"Up there," he told Charlie Moss. "They're ahead of us."

"I see 'em, Breck. They've got a big lead on us, though. I don't know if we can catch up to them."

"We sure won't if we don't try." Breckinridge dug his paddle harder into the water.

"Never said we wouldn't try," Moss replied as he redoubled his efforts as well.

A chase like this all came down to stamina. Whoever could keep up the pace the longest and steadiest would win. Breckinridge had plenty of confidence in his own abilities, and Charlie Moss was a tough, seasoned veteran of the frontier. Both men would give it their all.

But hours passed as they pursued their quarry down the river without making a significant dent in the gap that separated them. Carnahan's men were strong and determined, too. Even Breckinridge's powerful muscles began to burn with fatigue as the sky lightened in the east. They had been paddling most of the night.

From time to time, they had to stop briefly to stretch and ease the stiffness and pain settling into their arms and shoulders. Those delays, brief though they were, ate at Breckinridge's nerves. The only thing that made them acceptable was that Carnahan and his men had to rest now and then, too, so their lead stayed generally the same.

"Once the sun comes up, I could try takin' some shots at them," Moss suggested. "My rifle will reach that far."

Breckinridge shook his head. "Too big a chance of hittin' one of the girls."

"We don't even know for sure they've got those girls with them."

"I heard one of 'em scream while Carnahan was gettin' away."

"Maybe she screamed because he was about to cut her throat. He could've killed her and left her layin' in the brush."

Breckinridge turned his head to frown over his shoulder at Moss, but deep down, he knew the man was right. This desperate pursuit might not save any of the Garwood sisters. It might be too late already for all three of them.

But he wasn't going to allow himself to think that just yet. The sun would be up soon, and maybe then he'd be able to tell who Carnahan was holding hostage and which canoe—or canoes—they were in.

A feeling as bitter as wormwood filled Desdemona Garwood. More than anything else, she hated being helpless. All her life, whenever trouble arose, she wanted to tackle it head-on, even when she was a little girl.

But when her mother fell ill and died, Desdemona hadn't been able to do a thing about it. When her father had been brutally murdered right before her eyes, she had to just stand there and watch in horror.

Being able to fight alongside Breckinridge Wallace, Morgan Baxter, and the others had helped dull that pain a little.

Then had come the moment when she'd rushed up to the trading post along with Morgan and the two Mandans, ready to deal pain and death to her enemies, and almost before she knew what was happening, a burly, bearlike form had emerged from the cloud of stinging smoke and wrapped a powerful arm around her waist to jerk her off her feet. She had tried to strike at her captor with the rifle she held, but before she could do any good, a fist had smashed against her head, stunning her and leaving her helpless for long moments.

Even when her senses came back to her, it still took her a while to figure out that she was draped over a brawny shoulder, being carried like a big bag of potatoes. Her hands and feet were tied, so she couldn't move other than to squirm a little.

She lifted her head, though, and screamed in a mixture of rage, frustration, and fear. The man carrying her jerked to a halt, slid her down from his shoulder, and slapped her face, forehand and then backhand, hard enough to send her spiraling back down into oblivion.

When she came to the next time, she was lying in the bottom of a canoe. A little water had gotten into the craft, so her buckskins were damp. At least her face wasn't lying in it, otherwise she might have drowned even though she was in the canoe.

She was trying to figure out whether she should pretend to still be unconscious, when some of the filthy water ran into her mouth and made her gag. It was an uncontrollable reflex, as was the way she pushed herself up as much as she could with the bonds still around her wrists and ankles.

"The little spitfire's awake," said the man in the back of the canoe. He was paddling hard as he gave her an ugly, gap-toothed grin. He looked vaguely familiar. Desdemona knew he was one of the men who had come to the trading post and pretended to be working for Henry Joslyn, when his real boss was Jud Carnahan.

"Better keep an eye on her," the man in the front of the canoe responded as he plied his paddle in the water. "Make sure she don't try anything."

"How can she try anything? She's trussed up like a pig on its way to market!"

That made both men laugh, despite what appeared to be a desperate situation, judging by how hard they were paddling. They acted like they were trying to get away from something—or somebody—and that thought made hope suddenly leap to life inside Desdemona.

Maybe Breckinridge Wallace was coming after them.

She raised herself high enough to look around them. Dawn light was breaking over the river. Two other canoes were on the water. Jud Carnahan was in the front of the one slightly in the lead. Ophelia was in that one as well, and she appeared to be tied up as tightly and uncomfortably as Desdemona was. Another man was in the back, helping Carnahan paddle.

Not surprisingly, Eugenia was in the middle of the third canoe, also with four of Carnahan's men. The fight back at the trading post must not have lasted long, Desdemona thought. Most of Carnahan's bunch had fled as quickly as they could, grabbing Desdemona and her sisters along the way.

She was pretty sure it was Jud Carnahan himself

who had captured her and knocked her out. Maybe the scream she'd been able to let loose when she regained her senses briefly had been enough to set Breckinridge Wallace on their trail. She craned her neck and tried to look back along the river.

Her spirits lifted as she spotted a canoe in the distance behind them. The man in front was bare-chested, with long, fiery red hair. There was no mistaking who he was.

Breckinridge Wallace.

"Yeah, there's a couple of 'em back there, gal," the gap-toothed man said, "but they ain't gonna help you. We still got 'em outnumbered three to one, *and* we got three hostages."

"You're wrong," Desdemona told him coldly. "Wallace will catch up to you, and then you'll be sorry you were ever born."

"I'd be even sorrier if Jud Carnahan was after me. I reckon he's the most dangerous fella I ever run across."

Desdemona hoped he was wrong about that.

The three canoes went around a sharp bend in the river. Desdemona couldn't see the pursuers anymore. She saw a large, rocky promontory on the right-hand side of the stream, though. Carnahan waved for the others to follow him and angled his canoe toward it.

"I'm tired of Wallace dogging my trail," Carnahan said as they grounded the canoes on the bank just above the promontory. He climbed out, lifted Ophelia, and slung her over his shoulder like a bag of grain, just like he had carried Desdemona after grabbing her the night before. Despite the fact that Ophelia was bigger and heavier than either of her sisters, Carnahan handled her with equal ease.

He went on, "Jenkins, come with me." A man from one of the other canoes stepped out onto the bank. "The rest of you keep on paddling downstream. Wallace will see you and think he's still after all of us. But Jenkins and I will be up in those rocks, ready to ambush him when he goes past." Carnahan let out an ugly laugh. "He won't stand a chance, and finally, I'll be done with Breckinridge Wallace!"

Chapter 17

Carnahan and the man called Jenkins hurried off to climb onto the boulder-littered knob that stuck out into the river. Carnahan was still carrying Ophelia. Desdemona wasn't sure why he took her sister with him, unless he wanted to keep one of the hostages close at hand in case his plan didn't work.

The other men pushed off into the river again and resumed paddling. Two of the canoes just had one man in them now, so their progress was slower. That would allow Breckinridge and whoever was with him to catch up faster, Desdemona thought, but it wouldn't do them any good. That just meant they would be in Carnahan's and Jenkins's gunsights that much sooner.

She writhed around in the canoe until she could look back and see the promontory. From where she was, she couldn't see Carnahan and Jenkins, or Ophelia, but she thought she spotted what looked like a pair of rifle barrels sticking up from the rocks. The two men were in position to carry out their ambush.

And there, around the river's bend, came the pursuing canoe. The sun was up now, splashing garish light over the scene, and Desdemona had no trouble seeing Breckinridge's red hair, which was brighter than her own.

Gap-Tooth pulled his paddle out of the water and lifted it to threaten her. "Get back down there, gal," he warned. "I'll brain you with this if you try anything."

"Carnahan wouldn't like that," she said. "And you're afraid of him, remember?"

"He'd like it even less if we let you cause trouble, so don't get cocky."

He went back to paddling, but he kept narrow, suspicious eyes on her.

Desdemona's brain raced. She had to do *something* to warn Breckinridge and his companion about the danger they were in. She was willing to bet that Carnahan and Jenkins were both good shots. From their position, they could take careful aim and kill their targets before either of the men knew what was happening.

Desdemona started to cry. She drew her legs up and curled around herself as sobs shook her shoulders.

Gap-Tooth laughed again. "That ain't gonna do you no good! A gal's tears don't mean a derned thing to me!"

The idiot didn't understand that she had to pull her legs up to get the leverage for what she was going to do next, and the tears kept him from realizing what she was doing. She rolled onto her back and straightened her bound legs, lashing out with a double kick as hard as she could.

Her heels crashed into his chest and knocked him backward. He wasn't expecting it, and as he flailed wildly with both arms, his balance deserted him and he toppled out of the canoe. That craft tipped far over because of that, and although Desdemona tried to catch herself, she failed.

She slipped out of the canoe and wound up in the river, too. For a second her head went under, filling her nose and mouth with water, but she kicked up hard and broke the surface, sputtering and coughing. She was able to gulp down enough air to let loose with a scream and then cried, "The rocks! The rocks!"

"Good Lord!" Breckinridge exclaimed when he saw the sudden flash of red hair. "That's Desdemona who just fell outta that canoe!"

"What's she yellin' about?" Charlie Moss wanted to know.

"Somethin' about rocks—"

Breckinridge broke off as he realized the biggest, most noticeable rocks on this stretch of the river were the boulders on the rugged promontory they were coming up on. He swung his gaze in that direction and saw the early-morning sunlight wink off metal.

His muscles bunched as he dug the paddle into the water and sent the canoe shooting off at an angle.

A split second later, rifles boomed and lead balls plunked into the river mere feet away from the canoe.

From the sound of the shots, Breckinridge believed there were two ambushers hidden in the rocks. If he and Moss could paddle swiftly to shore, they might be able to use the same rocks for cover and close in on the riflemen.

But before he could put that plan into action, he heard another scream and looked toward the spot where Desdemona had fallen out of the canoe. He didn't see her in the river, and that made him lean forward anxiously.

Suddenly, she popped up again, appearing to gasp for air as she thrashed around awkwardly in the water. Something was wrong, Breckinridge realized. Either she couldn't swim at all, or something was keeping her from doing it.

"Watch those rocks!" he called to Moss. "Let me do the paddlin'! If you see Carnahan or any of his bunch up there, ventilate 'em!"

He dug the paddle into the water and stroked harder than ever. The canoe shot forward. A rifle boomed again from the promontory, and a split second later, Moss's long-barreled flintlock thundered.

"Got one of the varmints!" Moss yelled in triumph.

From the corner of his eye, Breckinridge saw a man's body tumbling down loosely from the rocks. The limp form hit the water with a big splash and went under. From the way the man hadn't done anything to try to catch himself or stop his fall, Breck figured he was dead, or next thing to it.

No more shots came from the promontory as Breckinridge drove the canoe past it. Up ahead, not far now, were the three canoes he and Moss had been pursuing. Even closer was Desdemona, going under and then struggling back to the surface. Breck could tell now that her wrists were tied in front of her, and he knew there was a good chance her ankles were lashed together, too. That would make it difficult for her to paddle and kick and keep from sinking into the river.

The other canoes started to swing back around. The men in them were going to put up a fight. Breckinridge didn't see Carnahan among them, but he did spot a slender, dark-haired figure in one of the canoes. That was Eugenia, he thought, but he didn't see Ophelia.

A canoe with just one man in it surged toward him. The lone occupant dropped his paddle and snatched up a rifle. The range was still a little long for a pistol shot, but Breckinridge had to chance it. He yanked out one of his guns and fired just a hair ahead of the other man.

The rifle ball slammed into the canoe right at the waterline, tore through the wood, narrowly missed Breckinridge's leg, and blew a hole in the other side of the canoe. The craft immediately began to take on water.

Breckinridge's shot had found its target. The man came halfway up, pawing at his chest where the pistol ball had caught him, then he pitched forward, upsetting the canoe. It rolled over, dumping him into the water.

The canoe with two of Carnahan's men in it turned broadside so both of them could shoot at Breckinridge and Moss. Breck fired his other pistol and saw one of the men drop his rifle and clutch at a shattered shoulder. Moss's rifle blasted a second later and sent the other man falling backward into the river.

Eugenia was in that canoe by herself now. "Go after her!" Breckinridge told Moss.

He put his empty pistols down in the canoe and then went over the side in a long, clean dive.

Back home, Breckinridge had learned to swim in creeks and rivers and ponds at an early age. The Yellowstone had a fairly strong current but nothing that presented a real problem to Breck as he came up to the surface and began stroking strongly toward Desdemona.

The remaining member of Carnahan's bunch tried

to cut Breckinridge off by sending his canoe slicing through the water between Breck and Desdemona. He thrust a pistol at Breck and fired just as Breck took a deep breath and dived again. The ball plowed into the water and burrowed a path through it just in front of Breck's nose. The shadow of the canoe fell over his face as it glided above him.

Breckinridge kicked hard and came up with his shoulder against the canoe's bottom. He shoved hard on it and heard its occupant yell in alarm as one end of the canoe lifted from the water and turned over. That dumped the man into the river. He was still thrashing around when Breck loomed behind him, slid his arm around the man's neck, and clamped down on it. His struggles intensified at being caught like that, but he was no match for Breck's strength. He couldn't break free, and the next moment it didn't matter because Breck heaved hard and broke his neck. When Breck released him, his arms and legs dangled limply, and his head hung at an unnatural angle on his neck. Breck kicked away from the body and looked around.

He spotted Desdemona a few yards away. She had gone under again, and this time she wasn't fighting to get back to the surface. She floated limply, too, with her red hair streaming out around her head. Her face was calm in the blue-green underwater light as Breckinridge rushed toward her. Her eyes were closed.

He caught her in one arm and kicked for the surface. Water sprayed high in the air as they came up. Breckinridge wanted to check and see if her heart was still beating, but he figured it would be better if he got to shore first. There was nothing more he could do to help her as long as they were in the river.

He swam hard, cradling her in his left arm. A gravel bank along the edge of the stream loomed up in front of them. Breckinridge's feet touched the bottom. He clambered halfway out of the water and laid Desdemona down.

Her face was completely colorless, making the scattering of freckles stand out more than ever. Her head lolled loosely. Breckinridge leaned over her and rested a hand on her chest, searching for a heartbeat, as he called her name. She didn't seem to be breathing, and he couldn't find that elusive heartbeat . . .

Then she bucked up from the ground a little, gagged, turned her head to the side, and spewed water from her mouth. Shudders ran through her as she continued to cough up river water, but after a moment she was able to start dragging in raspy breaths of air. Her eyes opened and peered up at Breckinridge in blurry confusion as he knelt beside her in the shallows.

Suddenly, her gaze focused, and Breckinridge realized she was staring past him at something. He jerked his head around and saw a man lunging at him from the river, swinging a paddle. Breck had been so concerned with Desdemona that he hadn't even heard the man swimming toward him. The attacker's gaptoothed mouth was open as he bellowed an incoherent shout of rage.

Breckinridge tried to get out of the way of the blow but couldn't avoid the paddle completely. It clipped him on the head hard enough to send bright red explosions through his brain, but he didn't pass out, only sagged down for a second. He caught himself with one hand against the river bottom, and as the man tried to backhand him with the paddle, Breck thrust a foot out and swept the man's legs from under him. He went down with a splash but came right back up, this time with a knife in his right hand.

Breckinridge caught the man's wrist with his left hand, stopping the knife as it slashed toward him. He hammered a punch into the man's face with his right fist. The man's foot hooked around his ankle and pulled, and Breck's foot slid on the river bottom. Both of them fell over into the water, still struggling.

The man seemed to be an experienced fighter, and desperation and anger made him even stronger. The water made him slippery, too. Breckinridge grappled with him, held the knife away from his own body, and finally got both hands on the man's wrist. He heaved and twisted, turning the blade toward the man's body, and drove it in with a powerful shove. Bubbles burst from the man's mouth as he screamed. Breck shoved again, ripping cold steel through flesh and guts. Blood bloomed around them in the water like a crimson flower.

Breckinridge shoved the dying man away and came up out of the river again. By now, Desdemona had pushed herself up on one elbow. She was still pale and breathing hard, but she was definitely alive and Breck was thankful for that. He pulled his own knife from its sheath and began sawing at the rawhide bonds around her wrists, being careful so he didn't cut her with the keen blade.

"You . . . you saved me," she gasped. "My sisters . . . ?"

Breckinridge shook wet hair back out of his face. "Eugenia's all right, I reckon," he said. "She looked like it when I saw her in one of the canoes a few minutes ago."

The bonds around Desdemona's wrists fell away as

he finished cutting through them. Before starting to free her ankles, he looked over his shoulder. He'd heard someone paddling and wanted to make sure they weren't about to be attacked again.

They weren't. It was Charlie Moss coming toward him. Moss wasn't by himself, either. He had Eugenia in the canoe with him, still tied but evidently all right. Breckinridge knew Moss must have pulled up beside the canoe where Eugenia was and lifted her into his craft.

"What about Ophelia?" Desdemona asked.

Breckinridge didn't look at her. He concentrated on cutting the bonds around her ankles. But he said, "I don't know. Haven't seen her. It didn't look like she was in any of the canoes."

"She was! She was in the canoe with . . . Carnahan! But he . . . he took her with him . . . when he went up in those rocks with that other man to ambush you."

Breckinridge knew he hadn't seen Carnahan during the skirmish. Nor had Carnahan been the man who had fallen from the rocks when Charlie Moss shot him.

That meant Carnahan was still up there somewhere . . . and he had Ophelia with him.

Moss's canoe grated against the gravel bank. "Breck, are you all right?" he asked as he got out and pulled the craft higher with Eugenia still in it. She didn't weigh enough for that to present a problem.

"Yeah, I'm fine," Breckinridge replied. "Got a clout on the head from a paddle, but this old skull of mine is way too thick to dent that way."

"Desdemona!" Eugenia cried.

"I'm all right," Desdemona assured her sister. "I'm

soaking wet and I swallowed some water and I look like a drowned rat, but I'm fine." She paused. "Ophelia is gone, though."

"Gone!" Eugenia cried.

"She ain't dead," Breckinridge said hastily. "At least not that we know of." He added grimly, "Appears that Carnahan's got her." He came to his feet. "Gimme your rifle, Charlie. I'm gonna go have a look in those rocks where he was hidin', waitin' to ambush us. You stay here, cut Miss Eugenia loose, and watch over the gals."

"No one needs to watch over me," Desdemona said as she tried to get up. "I'm coming with you."

"No, you ain't," Breckinridge said as he took the loaded rifle Moss handed him. "You're too shaky. Anyway, Carnahan's already got one Garwood sister. I don't want to give him the chance to grab another one."

She looked like she wanted to argue, but instead she sighed and sank down weakly on the gravel, evidently aware that he was right.

Breckinridge headed back along the river toward the promontory. The rifle was ready in his hands.

Ten minutes of searching confirmed what he had been afraid he would find. There was no sign of Jud Carnahan among the boulders, other than a few smudged footprints. Ophelia wasn't there, either, and while that was disheartening, it was also good. Carnahan was such a ruthless animal, he might have cut Ophelia's throat and left her there so she wouldn't slow him down as he fled. Instead, it appeared that he had taken her with him.

Carnahan might have postponed the showdown by fleeing, but it was still coming. Breckinridge was a good tracker. Carnahan wasn't going to shake him. Wasn't going to escape the reckoning he had coming.

But first, Breckinridge had to go back down there to the river and tell Desdemona and Eugenia that their sister was still in the hands of that monster.

Chapter 18

They saw him coming and ran to meet him. Desdemona didn't look so shaken up now from her near-drowning, and Eugenia was free from her bonds. Their anxious expressions reflected the fear they felt because Ophelia wasn't with Breckinridge.

He came to a stop as they hurried up to him. Desdemona said, "Is . . . is she . . . ?"

Eugenia tried to talk at the same time, but all she got out in a choked voice was, "She can't be . . ."

"She ain't up there," Breckinridge said, getting that out of the way quickly. "And I didn't see any blood around, so chances are your sister's still fine."

"But she's gone," Desdemona said. The words were flat and hollow. "And so is Carnahan."

"Yeah, I reckon so."

Charlie Moss walked up and pointed to a corpse sprawled on its back on the gravel bank about twenty feet away.

"That varmint came floatin' up into the shallows, so I went ahead and pulled him in. That's the one I shot when he tried to ambush us from those rocks."

"You're sure about that?" Breckinridge asked.

"Yeah. It was only for a second, but I got a pretty good look at him over my rifle sights."

"That's him, all right," Desdemona said. "We all saw him and Carnahan leave the canoes and climb up onto that promontory."

"Then there's no question it's Carnahan who got away." Breckinridge wanted to add some bitter curses to that statement, but he swallowed them. That wouldn't do any good right now and wouldn't even make him feel any better. "Charlie, you get these gals back to the tradin' post. I need to get on Carnahan's trail."

Moss shook his head.

"How are you gonna do that?" he wanted to know. "I've got a little powder and shot I could give you, but not much. You don't have any food or other supplies. You don't even have a shirt!"

Breckinridge's teeth ground together as his jaw clenched. Tight-lipped, he said, "Carnahan's gettin' farther away with Ophelia while we're standin' here flappin' our gums—"

"Mr. Moss is right," Desdemona interrupted him. "You're not equipped to start a pursuit right now."

"That won't matter if I catch up to thcm in a hurry."

"But if you don't, then you'll have to return to the trading post anyway, and that will just delay you more."

Eugenia nodded and said, "Desdemona is right, Mr. Wallace. I'm as worried about Ophelia as anyone, but it makes more sense for you to prepare yourself. That ought to lead to a quicker rescue for her in the long run."

Breckinridge frowned as he mulled over what they

had said. He could see their point, but at the same time, any delay was going to gnaw at his guts. He didn't have any romantic interest in Ophelia, but he sympathized with her as a human being.

Mostly, though, he just wanted to kill Jud Carnahan as soon as possible.

Desdemona put a hand on Breckinridge's bare forearm. "Please, Mr. Wallace. You know we're right."

"Besides," Moss put in, "if we head back to the tradin' post, then me and some of the other boys can come with you when you go after Carnahan."

Breckinridge wasn't sure he wanted any help. He could move faster on his own.

On the other hand, Carnahan had a history of finding human polecats with the same sort of stripe down their backs that he had. He might run into some other fellas and throw in with them . . . especially if he had Ophelia with him to use as a bargaining chip.

That thought lifted Breckinridge's hopes that he would keep the blonde alive, rather than killing her if he decided she was slowing him down. That worry had nagged at him ever since he'd discovered that Carnahan and Ophelia were gone.

"Well, we can't afford to waste no more time jawin'," he said with an abrupt nod. "Let's get back to the tradin' post. Sooner we get outfitted and on their trail, the better."

"You're sure right about that," Charlie Moss said.

One of the canoes used by Carnahan and his men had drifted against a deadfall a hundred yards downstream. Moss retrieved the now-empty craft. To make their loads lighter and increase their speed, they rode two in each canoe—Breckinridge and Desdemona in one, Moss and Eugenia in the other.

Desdemona picked up a paddle. Breckinridge said, "You don't have to do that."

"We're going against the current now," she replied. "I know you're a big, strong brute, Wallace, but I'm going to help you paddle, anyway."

Breckinridge grunted. He had been called plenty of things in the past. "Brute" was hardly the worst of them.

"Fine. I'd be wastin' my time if I tried to argue with you, anyway."

She managed a small smile over her shoulder at him.

"I'm glad you're starting to understand."

Breckinridge just grunted and dug his paddle into the water, propelling the canoe upstream toward the trading post. Desdemona began plying her paddle as well, and soon they were working together in a regular rhythm.

Over in the other canoe, Eugenia lent a hand with the paddling, too, although she wasn't as good at it as Desdemona was. Physical agility and coordination just didn't come as naturally to her.

As always when he was working on something, Breckinridge concentrated on the task at hand, and while his hatred of Jud Carnahan and his worry about Ophelia Garwood persisted in the back of his mind, he was mostly lost in the glories of this late spring day in the wilderness. The sun was warm on his bare torso. The river was a deep blue, and the bubbling and chuckling of its passage over the rocky bed was like music to Breck's ears. The stream twisted through wooded hills and flowed past broad meadows where flowers were starting to bloom.

At the other end of the canoe, Desdemona worked her paddle as smoothly and steadily as Breckinridge did. The sun had dried her red hair. It curled around her shoulders, plucked now and then by the wind of their passage upriver. The still-damp buckskin shirt clung to her, and he admired the easy play of muscles in her arms and shoulders. He admired most things about her, Breck realized, even the sharp tongue that lashed him from time to time.

Then he pushed those thoughts away. This wasn't the time or place for them. Not with Ophelia a captive and Jud Carnahan still free to unleash his evil ways on the world.

It was well past the middle of the day when they reached the trading post. Morgan must have posted someone in the trees along the river to watch for them, because almost everyone was there on the shore to greet them: Morgan, Richmond, George Donnelly, John Rocklin, and the seven Mandan Indians who had survived the battle. Ben Pentecost was the only white man missing, and Breckinridge knew he had been wounded in the fighting. He hoped Pentecost was just resting and hadn't succumbed to his injuries.

"Thank God you're back," Morgan said fervently as Breckinridge and Charlie Moss pulled the canoes onto the bank. Then he realized not everyone had returned and went on, "Where's Ophelia?"

"Carnahan got away and took her with him,"

Breckinridge answered bluntly. "All the rest of his men are dead."

Morgan turned to Desdemona and Eugenia, who had climbed out of the canoes, and told them, "I'm so sorry. We'll do everything we can to get her back, I swear it. Breck, how certain are you that she's all right?"

"Pretty sure she was when Carnahan lit out with her. I'll tell you about it while I'm puttin' together an outfit. I'm gonna get on Carnahan's trail as quick as I can."

He began the explanation while they were walking to the trading post. All the fires were out now, with not even a wisp of smoke curling up from anywhere along the remains of the stockade or the rubble of the burned-down barn. Those things were a total loss, but they could be rebuilt. There were plenty of trees nearby to provide logs.

The trading post itself was intact and unharmed, as were the goods inside it. The business could continue, if the sisters wanted it to. Breckinridge figured they would head back East as soon as possible, though, especially if he was successful at rescuing Ophelia and bringing her back here fairly quickly.

"I'm headin' back downriver this afternoon," Breckinridge concluded. "I can paddle at night, and once the moon's up, it won't be hard to find that promontory where Carnahan ambushed us. I'll stop there, get a little sleep, and then take up the trail as soon as it's light enough in the morning."

"Carnahan will have almost a full day's lead on you," Morgan pointed out.

"Can't be helped. Anyway, I can make up a day.

He won't be able to move as fast as I will, since he's got a prisoner with him."

"I'm coming with you," Morgan and Desdemona said at the same time.

"No, you ain't," Breckinridge declared flatly. "Neither of you. And I ain't gonna argue about it. Takin' either of you along would be just throwin' away any advantage I've got."

He saw the hurt and anger in their eyes, and while he wished he hadn't had to cause them that pain, his words were absolutely true. He intended to move fast, and either of them would slow him down. They seemed to know that, but the knowledge only added to their frustration.

"Blast it, Breck—" Morgan began.

"No, he's right," Desdemona said. "I don't like it, but he's right. I've taken to life out here better than I ever dreamed I would, but even so, this task is beyond me."

Eugenia laid a hand on Morgan's arm and said, "It's not your fault that you were . . . injured."

"That I have to stump around on this peg leg, you mean," Morgan responded bitterly.

"Life deals out all sorts of bad luck to people. We have to deal with it the best we can. Desdemona and I, we . . . we've lost our father. We're truly orphans now."

"Where is he?" Desdemona asked. Her face and voice were grim. "He needs to be laid to rest properly."

"He is," Morgan said. "We buried him up on the hill where Edward's bones will be. I hated to do it while you girls weren't here, but . . ."

He spread his hands helplessly.

"You didn't have much choice," Desdemona said, nodding. "You didn't know when or even if we would be back."

"Were there at least . . . words spoken over him?" Eugenia asked.

"Absolutely. I spoke about him as best I could and led a prayer, and then two of the Mandan women sang a . . . a . . ."

"A death song for him," Desdemona said. "Honestly, that makes me feel a little better." She put her arm around her sister. "We'll go up there, pay our respects, and say our farewells."

"Wish I could, too," Breckinridge said, "but I got to get movin'."

He had pulled on a shirt, retrieved his own rifle, slung two powder horns and two shot pouches over his shoulder, and put together a bundle of supplies, including some jerky. He intended to live mostly off whatever game he could trap or shoot, but it never hurt to have some jerky along on a journey.

He had also said hello to Ben Pentecost, who was stretched out on the bed that had belonged to Absalom Garwood. Bandages were wrapped around his wounded leg and shoulder. With rest and proper nursing, he would recover from his injuries.

"Send Carnahan to hell for me, Breck," Pentecost had said at the conclusion of the brief visit.

"I got plenty of reasons to do that already," Breckinridge said, "but I'd sure be glad to add yours to the list, Ben."

Now, with everything taken care of, Breckinridge embraced Morgan roughly and clapped a hand on his back.

"Take care of yourself," he told his old friend, "and these gals, too."

"I suspect they'll do more taking care of me," Morgan said. He seemed to be struggling to find the words to add something, and after a moment he went on, "Breck, I . . . I can see something now. I can't just carry on as if I'm still whole."

"Blast it, you are in every way that counts."

Morgan shook his head. "No, not really. I'm not really cut out to be a trapper and a frontiersman and an adventurer anymore. But I can help run a trading post." He summoned up a smile. "Running a business is in my blood, after all. That is . . ." He turned his head to look at Desdemona and Eugenia. "That is, if these ladies would be interested in having my help. This trading post belongs to them now, after all."

"I think I'd like that," Eugenia said.

"It's a good idea," Desdemona added with a nod. "To tell you the truth, with everything that's happened I haven't even given the future any thought, but we'll need to talk about it. In a day or two, when things have settled down." She looked at Breckinridge. "And we can't make any final decisions until Breck has brought Ophelia back, of course."

Breckinridge couldn't help but notice that she'd just referred to him as Breck, not Wallace.

"No need for final decisions yet," Morgan said. "There'll be plenty of work around here to keep all of us busy for a good long time."

"You'll have the Mandans to help you," Breckinridge said. "And some of the other fellas might want to stay on for a spell, too."

"Not me," Charlie Moss announced from the trading post's doorway. "I'm going with you, Breck."

They turned to look and saw that he had an extra powder horn and shot pouch, too. Moss went on, "I won't slow you down, and you know it. Chasin' a devil like Carnahan, you're liable to need a hand sooner or later."

"I reckon that's true," Breckinridge agreed. "I'm obliged to you, Charlie."

Eugenia gave him a hug. In his embrace, up against his massive body, she seemed almost as tiny as a child. So did Desdemona when she put her arms around his waist and rested her head on his chest for a moment. Breckinridge wanted to raise his hand and stroke her hair, but he wasn't sure where that impulse came from, so he suppressed it and settled for an awkward pat on her back instead.

"So long," he murmured.

"Bring our sister back," she said.

"I will." Maybe he shouldn't be making a promise like that, he thought, but there was nothing else he could do.

"And yourself, too," Desdemona whispered. She tightened her arms around him again for a second, then let go and stepped back. Her green eyes peered up at him intently. He had to swallow and turn away.

"Let's go," he said to Charlie Moss.

A few minutes later, they were paddling down the Yellowstone toward the place where Jud Carnahan had disappeared, taking Ophelia with him.

Chapter 19

Ophelia Garwood didn't know if she was more tired, scared, or hungry. She and Carnahan had been on the move all day and deep into the night. Every time she tried to slow down, he grabbed her arm and jerked her along roughly. When she stumbled and almost fell, he cuffed her and knocked her to her knees, then yanked her back up and pushed her ahead. He stopped every now and then to let her rest, but it was on his schedule, not hers.

Her feet, shod in soft slippers, throbbed miserably. Every rock, every sharp plant she stepped on, just increased her agony. Her face and hands burned from being exposed to the sun all day. And yet he expected her to keep moving, growling threats at her whenever she slowed down more than was to his liking.

"I have reasons to keep you alive, girl," he told her, "but if you give me any trouble, maybe they aren't good *enough* reasons."

"I . . . I'm doing the best I can . . ."

"I'll be the judge of that."

Late in the day he had spotted a rabbit and killed

it by throwing his knife at it. Ophelia had thought that at least they would have something to eat, and she expected him to build a fire on which to cook the animal.

Instead he ripped the rabbit's hide off, hewed chunks of raw meat from its carcass, and tossed one of them to her.

"I can't eat this!" she had protested.

"Then give it back to me. If you expect me to cook it, don't waste your time. No fires. Not until we put more distance behind us."

More distance between him and Breckinridge Wallace, that was what he meant, she thought. He was afraid of Breck. The big frontiersman had bested him at every turn. Sooner or later, Breck would kill Carnahan . . . if Carnahan gave him the chance. Carnahan was determined not to let that happen.

Ophelia's stomach had been clenching painfully from hunger for quite a while. She tried to eat the raw rabbit haunch. The bloody meat was still warm. She managed to get it down, but her stomach spewed it right back up.

"Better get used to it," Carnahan had told her. "If you don't, you'll just go hungry."

Now it was dark. Carnahan took hold of her and forced her to the ground. Ophelia believed she knew what was coming. There was nothing she could do to stop him, no options except to lie there and hope that it would be over quickly.

Instead, he lashed her ankles together, using the same rawhide bonds he had taken off her earlier so she could walk. Her wrists were still tied.

"Now you won't get any ideas about running off," he told her as he straightened from the task. "And if you're thinking about trying to get hold of my knife or one of the guns, you can forget about that." He scattered dry, broken branches on the ground around her. "If you try to crawl very far, you'll make enough noise to wake me up."

He thought of everything. She would never get away from him. Despair welled up inside her as she realized her only real hope of escape . . . was if he decided to kill her.

Exhaustion claimed her, and she went to sleep with that bleak thought in her mind.

If anything, she was even more tired and hurt more when she woke up the next morning. But to her surprise, she smelled meat cooking and pushed herself up to see Carnahan hunkered next to a tiny fire.

"Don't expect me to take this much pity on you all the time," he said as he turned the piece of rabbit he had impaled on a sharp stick, roasting it over the small, leaping flames. After a minute, he stood up and handed it to her, still on the stick. She took it without hesitation, waited a moment for the meat to cool, and then carefully tore off a strip of it with her teeth.

The rabbit was only about half-cooked, but that was enough. She was able to eat it and keep it down while Carnahan kicked dirt over the fire to put it out. When she was done, she licked the last of the grease from her lips and said, "I could use some water."

"We'll come to a stream soon enough," he told her without looking at her. "You'll have to do without until then. Both of us will."

That was true. He had no canteen or water skin,

nor supplies of any kind other than powder and shot. And they were out here in the middle of a vast wilderness, Ophelia realized, a savage land that possessed myriad ways to kill any puny humans who ventured into it. She had been so afraid of Jud Carnahan that her fear had overwhelmed everything else, including a practical perspective on their situation.

She knew now that she had plenty of other things to fear, too.

Carnahan untied the bonds around her ankles so she could stand up. When she tried to, her legs were so unsteady that she almost fell down and had to lean against a small tree to hold herself up. She waited there for her muscles to settle down and support her.

Carnahan waved toward a nearby clump of brush and told her, "You can go in there to take care of any business you need to take care of. But I'll still be able to see your head, so don't try to run off."

"I won't run off," she said. As terrible as he was, the thought of being alone out here was even worse. Now that she had gotten some sleep and eaten something, she was beginning to think more clearly. A monster he might be, but Jud Carnahan was still a man, too. And for years, she had always been able to find some way to get a man to do whatever she wanted. She had been barely more than a child when she discovered this power she possessed.

It might take some time, and she might suffer considerably along the way, but sooner or later she would bend Carnahan to her will.

The sun hadn't been up long when they started moving again. They were headed south, Ophelia thought. She hadn't had a great deal of education, but she knew that the sun rose in the east and set in the west, and she could make a pretty good guess as to their direction based on its location.

What was south of where they had been on the Yellowstone? She had no idea, but she was sure she would find out eventually if they kept moving.

She had only *thought* she hurt the day before. This day was infinitely worse. Almost right away, it seemed, her slippers were torn and bloody, cut to ribbons by rocks and thorns and sharp branches. Of course, so were her feet. Clinging brush ripped her dress to shreds. The sun blistered her worse than ever. Every step, every breath, was painful. Beyond painful. She was suffering the torments of the damned.

Not surprisingly, Carnahan just made things worse by cursing her and forcing her along. They climbed ridges. They clambered over rocks and deadfalls. They trudged along dusty draws. Ophelia's thirst grew worse and worse, until it seemed like the inside of her mouth was coated with sand and her tongue was swollen to the point of choking her.

When they came to a small creek with trees growing along its banks, Ophelia forgot about all the pain and rushed forward, drawn by the sight of the water. She thought she could even smell it.

Behind her, Carnahan let out a harsh laugh.

"I thought you hurt too bad to go on, girl!" he called.

Ophelia ignored him. She reached the welcome shade underneath the trees and dropped to her knees on the bank. The creek was only a few feet wide, but it was flowing steadily. At that moment, Ophelia wouldn't have cared if it was stagnant. She would have plunged her arms into it and scooped up handfuls of scummy, brackish water to gulp down her parched throat.

Instead, the water was clear and cold and the most delicious thing she had ever tasted. She felt the urge to stick her whole head into the creek and drink and drink until she couldn't anymore. She suppressed that impulse for a moment, then decided it didn't matter. Leaning forward, she thrust her head into the stream and let its soothing coolness flow all around her.

She didn't come up until she had to breathe again. She lifted her head and gasped for air. The shoulders and front of her dress were soaked, and so was her blond hair. It hung in thick, wet curtains around her face and in her eyes.

Through it, she saw something on the other side of the creek. Several seconds went by before she realized that she was staring at an Indian mounted on a spotted pony.

Not just one Indian, either. There were two more mounted savages behind the one who had ridden up to the creek from the south. She didn't know anything about Indians, had no idea how to tell which tribe they belonged to by their clothes and decorations and the way they wore their hair. For all she knew, these could be more Blackfeet, like the ones who had killed poor Edward and attacked the trading post.

One thing was certain: they seemed almost as surprised to see her as she was to see them. The one in front stared at her with his dark eyes wide. He was young, maybe not any older than she was. He wore moccasins and buckskin leggings and no shirt. His long dark hair was pulled back and tied behind his neck so it hung down his back like a horse's tail. A necklace of what looked like animal claws of some kind was around his neck. He carried a bow in one hand and had a quiver of arrows slung over one shoulder.

The intensity of the gaze he directed at Ophelia made her glance down at herself. Her dress was ripped in numerous places so that her pale skin showed through it. The soaked cloth was plastered to her body like a second skin, and she was breathing so hard it made her breasts rise and fall quickly. He couldn't help but have his attention drawn to them. Ophelia saw the same look in his eyes that she had seen in the eyes of countless men, young and old, over the past seven or eight years.

The lust on his face disappeared and was replaced by a look of pain and shock as a gun boomed somewhere behind Ophelia. The young Indian rocked back on his pony. Blood spurted from the hole in his chest and splashed down on his belly. The spooked horse went one way and the Indian went the other as he toppled off the animal's back.

For a second the other two Indians who had come up behind him seemed frozen in place. Then they let out shrill cries of rage and kicked their mounts forward. They were armed with bows as well, and they swiftly drew arrows and nocked them.

Another gunshot roared. One of the Indians twisted under the impact of a pistol ball to the chest. He didn't fall off his pony, but he did drop his bow with the arrow unfired and clung to the pony's mane as his face contorted with agony.

The third man got his arrow away. The shaft whipped

through the air above Ophelia's head. She heard it thud against something and dreaded to look back because if the arrow had struck and killed Jud Carnahan, she would be at the mercy of the savage who had fired it.

She didn't know if that would improve her situation or make it even worse, but the uncertainty was too much for her to stand. She jerked her head around, which caused the wet hair to fly in front of her face. She pushed it back and saw Carnahan standing beside one of the trees with his rifle in his hands. His pistols lay on the ground at his feet where he had dropped them, and she knew he had used them to shoot the first two Indians.

Next to him, a foot away from his head, the arrow was stuck in the tree trunk. Its shaft still quivered from the impact.

Hooves pounded. Ophelia looked around again. The third Indian had whirled his horse and was trying to get away. Carnahan drew a bead on his back and pressed the trigger. The flintlock boomed. The Indian hadn't had time to get out of range, and Carnahan's aim was deadly. The man threw his arms out to the sides and pitched off the horse, landing in a limp heap.

The second man Carnahan had shot, the one who was still on his pony, groaned and fell, landing on the opposite bank. He writhed around, fumbling at his waist. Ophelia realized he was trying to draw a knife sheathed there.

The Indian hadn't managed to do that by the time Carnahan splashed across the shallow creek. Carnahan's own knife was in his hand. He leaned over and with one swift stroke slashed the Indian's throat, stepping back quickly so the blood that fountained high in the air didn't splatter him. With such a wide, deep wound, the Indian bled to death in a matter of seconds.

The first Indian, the young one who had looked so raptly at Ophelia, lay motionless nearby. He hadn't moved since Carnahan shot him. Carnahan stepped over to him and cut his throat anyway, just to make sure.

Then he turned to Ophelia and said, "Stay here while I go check on the other one."

He stalked off, leaving her there on the north bank of the creek.

Her hands were still tied, but her feet and legs were loose. She struggled to her feet. When she stepped into the creek, the water felt like ice, but it numbed the pain in her tortured feet. She would have stood there for a long time, relishing the relief, but she had her mind and her eye on something else.

The knife that Indian had been trying to get.

She stumbled out of the stream and over to the gory corpse. Blood had splashed all the way down past his waist and was on the bone handle of the knife. Ophelia didn't care. She glanced toward Carnahan and saw that his back was still toward her as he walked out to where the third Indian had fallen.

She bent down, pulled the knife from its sheath, and stuck it under her dress. She pressed her arm against it as best she could to hold it in place. She looked at the bows and arrows and was tempted for a second, but she realized there was no way she could use those weapons as long as her hands were tied. It was doubtful that she would have been able to shoot Carnahan with one of them even if she didn't have those bonds around her wrists. She'd never used a bow before.

But the knife . . . that was different. If she could just get close enough to him, she was strong enough to plant the whole blade in his body.

Still breathing hard, she watched him bend over the third Indian. Cutting his throat, too, she thought. Then Carnahan slowly approached the pony that stood a few yards away, eyeing him warily. Ophelia didn't think he would be able to catch the pony, but Carnahan surprised her. He seemed to have a knack for it and soon had the pony's reins in his hand. He led the animal back to the creek.

That was good, Ophelia realized. If he could catch one of the other ponies, they could ride. She didn't know how that would work out, but at least she wouldn't have to keep walking until her feet were nothing but bloody stumps, which seemed to be what he'd had in mind.

"By God, this is a stroke of good luck," he said as he came up to her. "Wallace will never catch up to us once we're mounted."

Ophelia hadn't thought about that. Carnahan was right. The chances of Breckinridge Wallace rescuing her had just dropped dramatically.

But at least she wouldn't have to walk anymore.

"You can throw that knife down now," Carnahan went on.

"Kn-knife?" Ophelia forced out.

"I know you've got it." Carnahan waved a hand toward the corpse she had taken the knife from. "His sheath's empty, for God's sake. Now throw it down, or I'll tear what's left of that dress off of you and find it."

Ophelia didn't doubt for a second that he would do exactly that. It might goad him into doing other things that he hadn't so far, too. She sighed, reached awkwardly into the dress, and slid the knife out. She tossed it onto the grassy bank between them.

"You might as well get it through your head right now, you're not going to put anything over on me, girl. But if you don't even try . . . if you don't give me any trouble . . . you'll live longer and life will be easier for you."

She looked down at the ground and muttered, "My name's Ophelia."

"What's that?" he asked sharply.

She jerked her head up and said defiantly, "My name is Ophelia, not 'girl.'"

He looked at her for a moment, then laughed.

"Is that so?" He stepped over to her and thrust the pony's reins into her hands. "Can you hang on to this horse, *Ophelia*, while I catch the other two? You'd better, unless you want to walk while I ride. We still have a lot of ground to cover, and it'll go faster on horseback."

She clutched the reins and nodded.

"That's good." He cocked his head a little to the side and studied her with a shrewd expression on his bearded face. "You know, having you around might just turn out to be a good thing after all."

She wasn't sure if she ought to be glad to hear him say that . . . or horrified.

Chapter 20

It was well after dark before Breckinridge and Charlie Moss reached the promontory where Carnahan and the other man had hidden to ambush them. Breck was confident he could find the place, even by moonlight, and that turned out to be true. The boulder-littered knob was easily visible in the silvery illumination.

They put in to shore, pulled the canoe well out of the water, and then climbed to the top of the ridge behind the promontory, taking their supplies with them.

"We'll make camp here and pick up the trail first thing in the morning," Breckinridge said. "Better get some sleep, Charlie. Tomorrow's liable to be a long day."

"I'm sure it will be, so you wake me up in a few hours and get some shut-eye yourself," Moss said.

"That's what I figured on doin'."

Moss spread the bedroll he'd carried on his back and stretched out. Within minutes, he was snoring. Breckinridge sat with his back propped against a rock and his rifle across his knees. Exhaustion sat heavily on him, but he was accustomed to staying awake when he needed to, no matter how tired he was. He didn't doze off as the stars wheeled through the ebony sky above him and the moon raced through the heavens.

When he woke up Moss and lay down himself, he went out like someone had walloped him on the head with a hammer.

Moss roused him from sleep when dawn was still a small, rosy arch on the eastern horizon. Moss built a fire and the two men made a fast, sparse breakfast of some fried salt pork. By then the sun wasn't up but the light was good enough for Breckinridge to start looking for tracks.

He found some leading south away from the river. Two different people had made them. One set of footprints was more sharply defined and deeper than the other. Jud Carnahan's boots had left those prints, Breckinridge thought. The other tracks, some of them mere smudges, were left by Ophelia Garwood, who had been wearing slippers when she was taken hostage.

That was more confirmation Ophelia was alive. Breckinridge welcomed that. He believed there was a good chance Carnahan would keep her alive, and he was going to hang on to that hope unless and until they found proof to the contrary.

Like Ophelia's body.

Breckinridge shoved that thought out of his head and gathered his gear. Charlie Moss did the same. The sun had just started to peek over the eastern horizon when the two men set out, heading south over mostly rolling prairie that was broken here and there by gullies, ridges, and hills. Mountain ranges bulked in the distance to the south and west. Breck wanted to catch up to their quarry before they reached any of those mountains, because the more rugged terrain would just make a rescue more difficult, but he would do whatever was necessary to save Ophelia and bring her back to her sisters.

They had water skins slung over their shoulders and from time to time drank sparingly from them. This country south of the river seemed to be pretty dry. Breckinridge was sure they would come to a creek or a smaller river sooner or later, though, and when they did they could refill the skins.

They stopped to rest now and then, as well, but both men were accustomed to the hard life on the frontier. The biggest challenge was following the trail left by Carnahan and Ophelia.

After a while that got easier, although Breckinridge didn't like the reason why. He began seeing small patches of dried blood and knew they came from Ophelia's feet. Her slippers had worn through on the rough ground, and her feet were bleeding with each step. That had to be miserably painful for her.

That mistreatment was one more mark against Jud Carnahan . . . not that he needed any to be deserving of whatever vengeance Breckinridge dealt out to him.

After a long, frustrating day, Breckinridge and Charlie Moss made camp again. Breck had hoped to catch up with Carnahan and Ophelia today, but he had also known how unlikely that was unless Carnahan stopped for some reason. Apparently, that hadn't happened. Breck had to be content with hoping that he and Moss had narrowed the lead Carnahan had on them.

There was a good chance this chase would last

several days, and each one that went by was another day when there was no telling what Carnahan might do to Ophelia.

That night, as they were sitting around for a few minutes after supper, Charlie Moss said, "You know, by the time we get back to that tradin' post, Morgan's liable to be sparking one or maybe both of those Garwood girls."

"Eugenia seemed to have taken quite a shine to him," Breckinridge agreed, "but I don't reckon Desdemona feels that way."

"You figure she's sweet on you?" Moss chuckled.

"I never said that," Breckinridge protested, although in truth he did believe he had seen a few signs of Desdemona developing some affection for him.

"Well, it might be true, but I'm quite a bit older than you, Breck, and I can tell you for a fact that no matter how a woman feels about a fella, if he ain't around she's gonna start lookin' around elsewhere. Women are the most practical creatures on God's green earth. If a fella ain't there, he can't do her no good. And when he can't do her no good, she'll just find somebody else."

Breckinridge frowned in the darkness. "You really think so?"

"Seen it happen over and over again. A friend of mine went back home after bein' out here trappin' for eight months and found his wife six months along in the family way. And his brother had been visitin', if you get my drift."

"What did he do?" Breckinridge asked, wondering if the "friend" Moss was talking about was actually him.

Moss shrugged and said, "Well, when the baby was born, it looked sort of like the fella, so he decided that was close enough and went right on. That was tolerable open-minded, if you ask me." Moss chuckled again.

"Maybe so," Breckinridge said. He'd had considerable experience with women, despite his young age, but when he stopped and thought about it, he realized that of the three gals who had meant the most to him, one of them had married somebody else, one was a prostitute, and one had turned her back on him. Either he'd had a run of remarkably bad luck, or else Moss might have something there.

But he'd had no claim at all on Desdemona Garwood, although he had come to admire her, and if she turned to Morgan that was none of his business.

He thought about what his old friend would do if both sisters were interested in him. If there was a way to turn such a situation to his advantage, Morgan Baxter would derned sure do it, Breckinridge thought with a smile.

They pushed on the next morning. The spots of blood that Breckinridge assumed were from Ophelia's feet had dried to a dark brown. Those grim markings made the trail easier to follow, but Breck's heart went out to the girl because of the misery she had to be suffering.

After a couple of hours, Breckinridge and Charlie Moss both stopped short at the same time. Moss said, "I reckon you're seein' the same thing I just spotted."

"Yeah," Breckinridge said. "And I don't like it."

Several hundred yards ahead of them, a line of trees marked the course of a stream. Above those trees, a pair of buzzards circled lazily in the sky. As

Breckinridge and Moss watched, the carrion birds dipped down and disappeared behind the trees.

"Could be worse," Moss said. "I've seen a dozen or more buzzards circlin' like that in one place."

"And it could be these two came late," Breckinridge said. He took a deep breath. "We'd better go see."

They strode forward, covering the ground between themselves and the creek fairly quickly. As they came closer, Breckinridge was able to peer through the screen of trees and see some dark figures moving around on the other side of the creek. Those were the two buzzards he and Moss had spotted a few minutes ago, he decided, plus some other winged scavengers.

There wouldn't be that many buzzards if there was only one body, he thought as he frowned. Maybe Carnahan and Ophelia had run into some hostile Indians and the savages had killed both of them. He hoped that wasn't the case. He didn't want anything that bad to have befallen Ophelia . . . and he didn't want to be cheated out of his vengeance on Jud Carnahan.

"I see two bodies," Moss said, "and I just saw another buzzard land out yonder a ways on the other side of the creek."

Breckinridge nodded. He had noticed the same thing, and it was puzzling. If the two bodies by the creek were Carnahan and Ophelia, who did the third corpse belong to? Assuming, of course, that was what the buzzard that had alighted out there was after.

The next few minutes cleared up the mystery. Breckinridge felt relief go through him as he realized the two dead people nearest the creek weren't the ones he and Moss were after. Buzzards had already been at the bodies and done so much damage that Breck figured they had died sometime the day before.

Both wore buckskin trousers, though, and enough flesh remained here and there on the bones for him to see the coppery hue of the skin. These two were Indians. The one lying out farther from the creek probably was, too.

As if reading Breckinridge's mind, Charlie Moss said, "I'll go have a look, while you see what you can tell around here."

That sounded like a good idea to Breckinridge. He began studying the ground around the bodies and along the creek bank.

What he noticed almost immediately was that horses had been here. Unshod horses, meaning they had belonged to the Indians. Breckinridge made a guess that the warriors were Cheyenne, but under the circumstances he couldn't be sure about that.

Moss came back and reported, "Another redskin, all right. Hard to tell, but I think he was shot in the back."

"Carnahan," Breckinridge said flatly.

"That'd be my guess."

Breckinridge half turned and gestured toward the stream.

"Carnahan and Ophelia came up to the creek from the north, and the three Indians rode up from the south. There are tracks of several ponies around."

"But no sign of the ponies themselves."

"Nope." Breckinridge had already figured out the implications of that. "Carnahan was able to catch them, so he and Ophelia are mounted now."

"You don't know that. The horses could've run off. Carnahan must've opened fire on those bucks without warning, otherwise it ain't likely he would have been able to kill all three of them. Look there."

Moss pointed to an arrow stuck in a tree trunk. Breckinridge had already noticed it and drawn the same conclusion.

"They put up a fight, but Carnahan killed two of them with his pistols," Moss went on, reconstructing the scene in his mind. "Then the third one tried to get away, but Carnahan knocked him off his pony with a rifle shot. That's the only way it makes sense."

Breckinridge nodded in agreement. He spotted a broken necklace of animal teeth lying on the ground near one of the mutilated bodies and picked it up. He slipped it inside his pack. It was possible they might run into friends or relatives of these men, and if they did, the necklace might help identify the corpses.

"We gonna bury 'em?" Moss asked.

"We don't have shovels," Breckinridge said, "and we don't know for sure how they'd want to be laid to rest. Besides, we need to get movin' again. If Carnahan and Ophelia are on horseback, we don't have any time to waste."

"If they're on horseback, we don't stand a chance in hell of catching them on foot. You know that, Breck."

Breckinridge glared. Logically, he knew his companion was right. No man afoot could catch a man on a horse. But he wasn't ready to give up and admit that Carnahan had gotten away from him . . . again.

Besides, a glimmering of an idea had just sprung to life in his brain. He said, "Listen, Charlie, if these three fellas were horse Injuns, it stands to reason that the rest of their bunch are horse Injuns, too. If we could find their village, maybe we could barter some ponies from 'em."

"You mean we ought to go *lookin'* for a whole village full of savages who want to lift our hair?"

"I think these three were Cheyenne, and the Cheyenne ain't like the Blackfeet. They ain't *always* hostile."

"They're unfriendly enough I ain't sure I want to go waltzin' right into one of their villages," Moss argued.

"It's our best chance of catchin' up to Carnahan and rescuin' Ophelia."

"Maybe, but you've got to think about this: we can't do that gal any good if we're bein' tortured to death by a bunch of redskins."

Something caught Breckinridge's attention. He looked past Moss and saw a column of dust rising to the south. When he looked closer, he was able to see several dark shapes at the base of that column.

"Looks like the decision's bein' taken out of our hands," he said. He nodded toward the dust in the distance. "If I ain't mistaken, there are some fellas probably from the same bunch as these headin' toward us at a gallop right now. They must've spotted those buzzards, too."

Curses burst out of Moss's mouth. He said, "We need to take cover somewhere they won't find us—"

"Where?" Breckinridge broke in. He waved a hand along the creek bank. "We could put up a fight from behind them trees, but they wouldn't keep the Injuns from findin' us. And if there's very many of 'em, sooner or later they'd get us. Our best chance is to try to make 'em understand that they don't have any reason to kill us."

Moss was a little pale under his permanent tan as he glanced toward the onrushing riders.

"You're puttin' an awful lot of faith in your ability to persuade 'em of that, Breck," he said. His hands tightened on his rifle. "But I reckon I'll follow your lead. Like you said, we ain't got much choice."

They stood there at the edge of the trees, waiting, as the men on horseback approached. Breckinridge could tell now that there were half a dozen of them, all riding hard. A couple of them drew out in front of the others, either mounted on faster ponies or determined to arrive first on the scene of this tragedy.

The buzzards that had been scavenging on the remains of the dead man farther out rose into the air as the hoofbeats approached swiftly. Awkward at first, as their kind always were, they became more graceful as they glided and soared away. The two riders in the lead drew rein and brought their mounts to skidding halts near the corpse.

They were definitely Indians—Breckinridge could see that now. One of them carried a lance. He looked down at the grisly sight on the ground for a long moment, then whirled his horse around, thrust the lance into the air above his head, and let out a shrill, piercing cry of rage.

He brought his horse to an abrupt halt facing the creek. Breckinridge knew the Indian had spotted him and Charlie Moss.

The warrior didn't wait around trying to figure out what to do next, either.

He lowered the lance and kicked his pony into a run straight toward the two white men, yipping furiously and obviously out for blood.

Chapter 21

Charlie Moss started to raise his rifle, but Breckinridge grabbed the flintlock's barrel and held it down.

"Shootin' that fella is the worst thing you can do right now, Charlie," he said.

"But he's gonna run one of us through with that lance!"

"I don't think so."

Breckinridge hoped he was right about that.

The Indian galloped toward them until he was about twenty feet away. Then he veered his horse to the side and flung the lance as hard as he could. He aimed it at Breckinridge, probably because Breck was the bigger target. Breck gave Moss a shove that pushed him out of the way, and he leaned in the other direction. The lance passed within inches of Breck's right arm and buried its point in the creek bank.

The Indian who had thrown it whirled his horse around and yelled. Breckinridge handed his rifle to Moss and strode forward in obvious challenge.

"I sure hope you know what you're doin'," Moss muttered behind him.

The Indian charged at Breckinridge again. His strident yips fell silent as he launched himself from the back of his speeding pony. He had a knife in his hand now as he flew through the air at Breck.

Setting his feet and bracing his powerful legs, Breckinridge caught the attacking warrior in midair, pivoted at the waist, and used the Indian's own momentum against him to fling him several yards. The Indian crashed to the ground and rolled over several times before he stopped himself and scrambled back to his feet. Somehow he had managed to hold on to the knife. He clutched it tightly as he bared his teeth in a grimace and ran at Breck.

"Use your knife!" Moss urged.

Breckinridge ignored him. The Indian feinted with the blade, but Breck didn't fall for it. As the knife darted in at his belly, he caught hold of the warrior's wrist and stopped it. His other hand came up in a fist and slammed into the man's face. The force of the blow drove the man off his feet. As the Indian went down, Breck twisted his wrist and the knife flew free. He let go and kicked the knife toward the creek.

The warrior shook his head for a second and then lunged at Breckinridge yet again. He was determined, Breck had to give him credit for that. Fast and slippery and strong, too. Despite Breck being quite a bit taller and heavier, the Indian got inside his grasping arms, tackled him around the thighs, and rammed a shoulder into his belly. Breck went over backward.

The Indian tried to thrust a knee into his groin. Breckinridge avoided it and got hold of the man's shoulders to heave him to the side. The Indian didn't go far, though. He twisted and aimed a kick at Breck's head. Breck jerked out of the way, but the man's heel still caught him a glancing blow just above the ear. It wasn't enough to knock him out or even stun him, but it did disorient him for a second.

The Indian must have seen that, because he jumped up and tried to leap on top again. Breckinridge met that by thrusting his foot into the man's belly and using his leg to lever him up and over. This time the man hit one of the tree trunks and bounced off, landing in a limp sprawl on the ground nearby. He was out of the fight for the time being.

The battle wasn't over, though. Two more of the Indians had raced up on their ponies, and as Breckinridge came to his feet, they dived off their mounts and tackled him at the same time. He couldn't stay upright under that much weight. He went down with both warriors on top of him.

But a moment later, one of the Indians flew one way, and the other man went the opposite direction. Breckinridge had tossed them away from him like dolls. He rolled onto his side and got a hand on the ground. As he shoved himself upright, one of the warriors recovered enough to lunge toward him again. Breck bent over, caught the man on his shoulder, and straightened, lifting his suddenly alarmed opponent into the air. A twist of his body turned Breck around and allowed him to heave the man he held into the other one, who was also trying to attack again. They crashed together and sprawled on the ground, then lay there moaning and moving feebly.

"Breck . . ." Charlie Moss said in a warning tone.

Breathing a little hard from all the exertion, Breckinridge looked around and saw that the other three

Indians had arrived. Instead of attacking as the first three warriors had, they sat on their horses several yards away. One man, the oldest of the bunch, by the looks of them, held a flintlock rifle with its barrel pointing in Breck's general direction. The other two had arrows nocked on their bowstrings.

Facing them, Breckinridge put a hand on his chest and said, "Friend. You understand the white man's tongue? Friend."

Charlie Moss said quietly, "Considerin' that you just beat three of 'em like they was drums, I ain't sure those other fellas are gonna believe you."

Breckinridge patted his chest again and insisted, "Friend."

The Indian with the rifle said, "Three of our young men are dead. How can the one who did this be a friend to the Cheyenne?"

His English was good. He'd probably learned it from one of the missionaries who had come west to convert the tribes they considered heathens, or else from fur trappers who had flocked to this region over the past couple of decades.

"We didn't do this, chief," Breckinridge said, guessing from the older man's bearing that he was a leader. "We just found these murdered warriors, like you did. But I know who killed them, and you're right, he's no friend to the Cheyenne. He's no friend to anybody."

The first man Breckinridge had tangled with, the one who had thrown the lance at him, had recovered some from his collision with the tree trunk and struggled to his feet. He spoke in fast, obviously angry, Cheyenne. Breck knew a few of the words, but not enough to make any sense of what the warrior said.

"You are here, and our young men are here, and

you must have killed them," the older man said. "This is what Elk That Stands Still believes."

"That's what he said, eh? Well, he's wrong. A varmint named Jud Carnahan killed your men. We've been trackin' him for the past couple of days. He has a friend of ours, a young woman, with him as a prisoner." Breckinridge waved a hand at the creek bank. "Study the tracks on both side of the creek. You'll see that I'm tellin' the truth. My friend and I just walked up here not long before you rode in. We saw the buzzards, too. Our tracks are fresh. The others were made yesterday. And you can tell by looking at these men, they didn't die today."

A long moment of silence dragged past. The older man with the rifle was the only one of the Indians who didn't look like he wanted to kill these white men without wasting any more time. And even he didn't seem convinced that wasn't a good idea. But finally he snapped what were clearly orders at the two men holding bows. They lowered the weapons, replaced the arrows in the quivers slung on their backs, and dismounted. They began examining the ground and the bodies, and Breckinridge knew they were checking the things he had pointed out.

"I sure never figured we'd still be breathin' this long," Moss said under his breath.

"Most folks will listen to reason if you give 'em a chance."

"And the ones who won't?"

"Well, them you got to *make* listen to reason, whether they want to or not. And if they still won't do it . . ."

Breckinridge's shrug was eloquent.

After a few minutes, one of the Indians on the

ground spoke to the chief still on horseback. The older man listened with a solemn expression on his face and nodded when the other Indian was finished. He looked at Breckinridge and Moss and told them, "The signs say you are telling the truth."

"I always try to," Breckinridge said.

"Who are you?"

"My name is Breckinridge Wallace. My friend here is Charlie Moss. Like I told you, we're lookin' for a man who attacked a tradin' post up on the Yellowstone, ran off with a girl, and tried a heap of times to kill us. I reckon your young men had the bad luck to run into him." Breckinridge reached inside his shirt and took out the claw necklace he had picked up earlier. "One of them was wearin' this, I think."

He nodded toward the body the necklace had been lying near.

He wouldn't have thought the chief's expression could get any more solemn, but it did. The man nodded slowly and said, "It is as I feared when they did not return to our village. That necklace belonged to my son, Rock Against the Sky."

"I'm sure sorry, Chief. The man we're after has brought a lot of grief to a lot of people. That's why we intend to kill him."

"The other two are my son's friends, Fast Water and Bent Tree. They were fine young warriors. My people will grieve for them all."

Breckinridge nodded. There was nothing else he and Moss could say.

The chief drew in a deep breath. His face was impassive now, but Breckinridge thought he could still see the pain lurking in the dark eyes.

"You will come with us to our village," the chief announced.

"We need to get back on the trail of the man we're after—"

"You will come to our village. We will give you horses. The evil man who did this stole the ponies belonging to my son and his friends."

"Yeah, I reckon he did."

"We will give you fast ponies, and some of my warriors will go with you."

Breckinridge wanted the horses but not the help. The scores he had to settle with Jud Carnahan were personal ones.

On the other hand, these Cheyenne felt the same way. Carnahan had brought grief to their tribe, and they wanted him to pay for it. They wanted to deliver justice to him themselves. Breckinridge couldn't blame them for feeling that way.

Besides, the Cheyenne knew this part of the country better than he did. He had never been in this particular area before. They might know some shortcuts that would cut down on Carnahan's lead even faster. Whether they would be fast enough to offset the delay of visiting the Indian village remained to be seen.

In the end, though, it came down to the fact that he and Moss were outnumbered, and despite the fact that the chief had accepted their story, the rest of the warriors still looked like lifting the two white men's scalps would be just fine and dandy with them. So Breckinridge just nodded and said, "It would be our honor to visit your people."

* * *

The chief's name was Wolf Tooth. He told two of his men to allow Breckinridge and Moss to ride double with them. The Cheyenne warriors didn't like that, but they obeyed their chief's orders. Breck rode with the lightest of the men, so the horse wouldn't break down under their combined weight.

The Indian village was about five miles southwest of where the three young men had been killed at the creek. The tracks left by the ponies Carnahan and Ophelia had ridden away from the site followed the same general route for a while, then angled off almost due south. Breckinridge had no idea where Carnahan was headed, and there was a good chance Carnahan didn't know, either. He was just putting distance between himself and any possible pursuit. He wouldn't worry about figuring out their ultimate destination until he felt like he was safe from Breck's vengeance.

He could never go far enough for that to be true.

"My son and the others left the village to hunt yesterday," Wolf Tooth explained as they rode. "But they did not take supplies to stay out overnight. When they did not come back by this morning, we rode out to search for them. Our medicine man, Bull Moose, said the signs were bad. I did not expect to find my son alive. But I hoped that I would."

"I wish you had, Chief," Breckinridge said.

Wolf Tooth stared straight ahead and his jaw was tight as he said, "They died as warriors. No man of the Cheyenne can ask for a better fate."

Breckinridge doubted that was what had happened. He suspected that some sort of treachery on Carnahan's part had been involved, at least to a certain extent. That was just the man's nature. But Breck didn't see where any purpose would be served by explaining that to Wolf Tooth, so he kept his mouth shut.

The Cheyenne left behind in the village must have been watching for the search party's return, because Breckinridge heard wailing before the riders ever reached the first of the lodges. Seeing the searchers come back without the young men they had gone out looking for led to only one inescapable conclusion. The mourning had already begun, even before the news had been delivered officially.

Warriors on foot crowded around the ponies. Most of them glared at Breckinridge and Charlie Moss. Breck looked over at Moss and saw that his companion looked nervous. Anybody with any sense would. He hoped that Moss would be able to keep a cool head while they were here.

The Indians reined in and dismounted in front of the largest lodge, which Breckinridge supposed belonged to Wolf Tooth. A handsome, middle-aged woman with gray streaks in her dark hair stepped up to the chief. She didn't say anything, but her expression made it clear that she was waiting to hear whatever he had to say. He spoke to her quietly, in the Cheyenne tongue, and although her face didn't change immediately, Breck saw pain flare in her eyes. He knew she had to be Wolf Tooth's wife and the mother of the young man called Rock Against the Sky. She turned away from the chief, some of the other women clustered around her, and the wailing resumed.

Wolf Tooth turned to Breckinridge and Moss and said, "You will be taken to a lodge and given food. You will rest there tonight and tomorrow. The bodies of our lost ones will be brought back and given to the spirits of the earth and the sky as is our custom, and then . . ." He had to stop and draw in a breath. "And then we will find the man who did this evil thing and deal with him as we would an animal that has gone mad."

"That's a pretty good description of Jud Carnahan," Breckinridge agreed.

Chapter 22

Charlie Moss stayed nervous as long as they remained in the Cheyenne village. The fatalistic streak that the past few years had instilled in Breckinridge took over and kept him from being too worried, at least about his own safety. He figured that whether he lived or died didn't really matter. The only thing that was important was living long enough to kill Carnahan and get Ophelia back safely to her sisters.

As long as Wolf Tooth was on his side, the Cheyenne were going to help him do that, so he didn't mind being here.

That night, the chief came to the lodge Breckinridge and Moss were sharing. They hadn't turned in yet. Wolf Tooth sat on the buffalo robes next to the fire with them and said, "The wise old men of our people believe I should have the two of you killed."

"I knew it," Moss said. "I knew we couldn't trust—"

Breckinridge stopped him with a lifted hand.

"But you told them you weren't going to do that," he said to Wolf Tooth, "because we have the same enemy and should be friends."

Wolf Tooth frowned and said, "I do not think the Cheyenne will ever be friends with the white man."

"Even when we desire the same vengeance?"

"We can seek that without being friends."

Breckinridge shrugged and said, "I reckon so. But it might be easier if we were."

"You will not be killed," Wolf Tooth declared. "You are safe in our village. You will be given horses, as I said before. More than that, I cannot offer you."

"You said you were going to ride with us after Carnahan."

Slowly, and with apparent reluctance, Wolf Tooth shook his head.

"This I cannot do. Some of our scouts saw a Pawnee war party east of here. They may be coming to raid our village and steal our horses and women. I cannot take our warriors and leave, much as I wish to avenge the death of my son and the other two young men. You have sworn to me that you will kill this man Carnahan."

"I have," Breckinridge agreed. "And I never meant anything more in my whole life."

"It is good," Wolf Tooth said, nodding. He reached into a pouch he wore at his waist and brought out something that Breckinridge recognized: the necklace of animal claws that the chief's son had worn.

Solemnly, Wolf Tooth extended the necklace to Breckinridge. Equally solemnly, Breck took it.

"Wear that, and the spirit of my son will travel with you. He will be there when you slay the evil Carnahan. While Carnahan still lives, you will tell him that he dies to avenge the death of Rock Against the Sky, as well as for all the hurts he caused to you and those you love. Then, my son's spirit will be free."

"I swear it," Breckinridge said. "You have my word on it."

Wolf Tooth nodded and got ready to stand up. Instead he paused and said, "I have not had dealings with many white men, but there have been enough that I have learned already their word is not to be trusted. For some reason, I believe that you are different, Breckinridge Wallace." The chief made a face. "Your name is long and uncomfortable on my tongue."

"Back where I come from, the Indians I knew sometimes called me Flamehair."

Wolf Tooth thought for a moment and then nodded.

"Flamehair," he said. "Yes. It suits you. Flamehair now carries the spirit of Rock Against the Sky with him, and together they will have vengeance on the evil one called Carnahan."

"You can count on it," Breckinridge said.

To tell the truth, he wasn't disappointed that Wolf Tooth and some of the Cheyenne warriors weren't going with them, Breckinridge reflected the next morning as he and Charlie Moss got ready to ride. Wolf Tooth was a chief, and as such, he would expect to be in charge. Breckinridge had never cared much for anybody giving him orders.

There was another thing to consider. He and Moss still got plenty of unfriendly looks from the inhabitants of this village. He didn't think the Cheyenne believed the two white men were responsible for the deaths of the three young hunters. It was more like they just didn't like Breckinridge and Moss on general principles. If Wolf Tooth and the other warriors had gone along, and something had happened to the chief, Breck had a hunch that the rest of them would decide it was better to kill him and Moss. Their bodies would feed the buzzards and the coyotes, and their bones would bleach in the sun.

One of those none-too-friendly fellas had come and gotten them this morning, after a couple of women brought food for breakfast. He motioned curtly for Breckinridge and Moss to follow him. When they stepped outside, he pointed to two ponies standing there with their reins dangling and said, "Horses."

"Yep, they are," Breckinridge said.

The Indian motioned again, first at the two white men, then at the ponies. The word *horses* might be all the English he spoke, Breckinridge realized. Breck nodded, tapped his chest, gestured toward Moss and then toward the horses to show that he understood. The Cheyenne grunted and stalked off.

"We are mighty lucky to be gettin' outta here with our hair still on our heads," Moss said.

"You ain't far wrong. Let's gather our gear."

"We're gonna have to go back to where we veered off Carnahan's trail to pick it up again, ain't we?"

Before Breckinridge could answer that question, Wolf Tooth walked up. He had a stick in his hand.

"I will show you where to ride," he said.

He hunkered down and began drawing in the dirt. Breckinridge and Moss knelt, too, and studied what Wolf Tooth was doing.

The chief spent several minutes sketching in landmarks, including the creek where the killings had taken place and the location of the Cheyenne village.

"This is the way the tracks left by Carnahan and the woman were going," he said as he drew that trail. "There are mountains here, in their way. But there is a pass here"—he touched the stick to the drawing—"where they can ride through. If they do not take that pass, they must travel many days to the east to go around the mountains."

"So you're sayin' we should head for that pass, too," Breckinridge said.

Wolf Tooth shook his head and moved the stick's tip.

"There is another pass—smaller, higher, harder to reach—here to the west. But it is closer to this village. If you take it, you will save a day's travel, perhaps more. And if you follow this route"—he traced an angled line in the dirt—"you will come to the trail left by Carnahan. No matter which way he goes, you will cross his trail sooner or later."

Breckinridge nodded. "Then that's what we'll do. We're sure obliged to you, Chief, for the horses, your hospitality, and this advice, too."

"You will owe me no debt," Wolf Tooth said, "as soon as the man Carnahan is dead and my son's spirit is free."

"That can't be too soon to suit me."

The Indian ponies were a little skittish, and Charlie Moss didn't have any experience riding with just a blanket instead of a saddle. He fell off a few times before he got used to it, and in spite of the grim nature of the quest they were on, Breckinridge had to work to keep from laughing. He had ridden bareback or with a blanket many times, so he didn't have any trouble.

Once Moss got the hang of it, they made better time as they rode toward the high pass Wolf Tooth had told them about. Breckinridge could see it in the distance, a small notch in the mountains that ran east and west. Those mountains were not tremendously tall, but they were rugged enough that it would be difficult to cross them without making use of a pass.

Once they entered the foothills around midday, the terrain got rougher and rockier, the vegetation more sparse. The ponies were big for Indian mounts. Breckinridge knew Wolf Tooth had picked them out because the white men were larger and heavier than the Cheyenne. Even so, the horses struggled at times on the slopes, and Breck and Moss had to dismount and lead them.

Being slowed down like that chafed at Breck, but there was nothing he could do about it. They had to keep their mounts in good shape. Being set afoot out here might not be fatal, but it would ruin any chance they had of catching up to Carnahan.

It was late in the day by the time they reached the pass. Down on flatter ground, the sun had been warm, the breezes pleasant. Up here, the wind that blew was a chilly one.

"We'll push on," Breckinridge said. "We can get part of the way down from here before it's late enough that we'll have to make camp."

"I sure hope that Injun was right about this savin' us some time," Moss said.

Breckinridge reached up and touched the claw necklace he had placed around his neck after Wolf Tooth gave it to him. The claws had been restrung carefully on a new strip of rawhide that replaced the broken one. Breck figured the boy's mother had done that.

Maybe someday he would come back to these parts, he thought, and find that band of Cheyenne again. It would be fitting to return the necklace to Wolf Tooth and his wife and let them know that their son had been avenged.

"He told us right," Breckinridge said. "He's got as much at stake in this as we do."

They were about halfway down the southern slope below the pass when they found a somewhat level spot that would serve as a good campsite. Breckinridge called a halt. Moss arranged a circle of rocks, stacking them high enough that he could build a small fire inside to cook their supper without the flames being seen from far away. Breck picketed the ponies where there were a few clumps of hardy grass growing from the rocky landscape.

With those chores done, they sat and ate and watched the last of the pink and orange glow from the sunset die in the western sky. To the east, darkness flowed steadily toward them, with the heavens shading from purple to blue to black. A few streaks of cloud showed up dramatically pink in the gathering dusk. The world was quiet.

To the south were more rolling hills and flatlands. As Breckinridge sat there, his keen eyes swept over the far distances, searching for any faint glow that might mark the location of a campfire.

If Carnahan was out there, though, he had made a cold camp. Breckinridge didn't see a thing.

His frustration over that futility grew during the next day, as he and Moss descended the rest of the way from the pass and followed a generally south-eastward course, detouring only when they had to in order to avoid one of the deep, rocky ravines that cut across this part of the country. Breckinridge wasn't sure how long it ought to take them to cut Carnahan's trail, but it didn't happen that day.

A similar lack of success the next day grated at him until he was snapping at Moss every time the other man said anything. Finally, Moss responded, "Blast it, I don't know where they went! I thought we'd find their tracks before now, too."

"Either Carnahan's coverin' 'em up really good, or else they didn't come this way after all," Breckinridge said with a frown. They had stopped the horses and were sitting and peering at the ground. No matter how hard Breck stared, it didn't make tracks appear.

"Where else could he have gone?"

Wearily, Breckinridge scrubbed a big hand over his face.

"I don't know. If they didn't come through the mountains, they had to go either east or west. West would've put them deeper in Cheyenne country, but I don't know if Carnahan knew that or not. East would take 'em . . . shoot, all the way back to St. Louis, if they went far enough."

"You think Carnahan would do that?" Moss asked with a frown. "He's got a kidnapped gal with him. All she'd have to do once they got back to civilization is yell her fool head off about what Carnahan did, and the law would be after him. Seems like he wouldn't want to risk that."

Deep in thought, Breckinridge scraped his right thumbnail along the line of his jaw, then tugged at that ear.

"He's got to head for a settlement somewhere. He can't just wander around out in the middle of the wilderness, alone with Ophelia, from now on. He could go back to St. Louis, but more folks know him there. Maybe he's figurin' on driftin' on down to New Orleans. And there are Spanish settlements a long ways south of here, down in Nuevo Mexico. Santa Fe, one of 'em is called, I think. Nobody would know him there."

"They still got to have law," Moss said. "The girl could still try to get help from them."

"You reckon after travelin' with Carnahan for weeks or maybe even months, Ophelia's gonna be brave enough to try to get the law on him? By then he'll have her so beat down she probably won't dare to try anything like that." Breckinridge sighed. "That is, if he don't just get tired of her and kill her somewhere along the way."

A grim silence hung between the two men for a few moments. Then Moss said, "So what are we gonna do? Give up?"

"Not hardly," Breckinridge said without hesitation. His eyes narrowed as he stared into the distance. "I'll never quit lookin' for Jud Carnahan until all the skin wears off my soul."

Chapter 23

Two months later

Spring had turned to summer. Heat lay hard on the land. At least, down on the flats it did. Up here in the mountains, the nights were still cool, anyway.

But Breckinridge and Charlie Moss were at the very edge of the mountains, so that when they looked eastward from the ledge on which they stood, they could see forever across the plains in that direction.

"You reckon they're out there somewhere?" Moss asked as he stood with the butt of his flintlock rifle on the ground, leaning tiredly on the weapon.

The past two months had caused a deep weariness to set in for both men. They sported long beards, and their faces were gaunt. They had long since run out of the supplies they'd taken with them from the Cheyenne village and had been living on wild game and whatever edible plants they could scrounge for quite some time.

More than just the physical, their appearance and attitude mirrored the frustration they felt. Breckinridge knew that given half a chance, Moss would give up on the chase.

Not Breckinridge, though. He was still as determined as ever to find Jud Carnahan and settle with him. He was just . . . tired, that's all.

Unable to find any trail left by Carnahan and Ophelia Garwood south of the mountains they had crossed after taking their leave of the Cheyenne, Breckinridge and Moss had had no choice but to double back and cross the mountains to the north, using the pass they had believed their quarry would take.

A day of casting back and forth had finally turned up the tracks of three unshod ponies, one of them carrying a lighter load than the other two. Carnahan and Ophelia had taken all three horses from the young Cheyenne braves Carnahan had killed. They were using one as a spare, Breckinridge figured. That would allow them to keep up a somewhat faster pace, although not as fast as if they'd had two extra horses so both riders could switch back and forth.

The tracks led east. Carnahan had decided to go around the mountains after all, instead of cutting through them by way of the pass. Eventually, they left the mountains behind but continued straight as an arrow across what some people were starting to call the Great American Desert.

It wasn't actually a desert, of course. In fact, there were plenty of stretches where grass grew. Thick, hardy stuff that came up to their horses' hocks. But trees were mighty few and far between, and when Breckinridge and Moss came across one, it was usually a stunted, gnarled thing. The few exceptions were cottonwoods that grew along the banks of the small creeks they came to.

No matter how hard they tried, the two men couldn't seem to gain any ground on Carnahan and Ophelia. Whenever it looked like they might, bad luck always intervened. Sometimes they lost the trail and had to search for half a day or more before finding it again. Twice they had to hunker down and wait out massive thunderstorms with lightning flashing all around. Out here on the flats, it was too dangerous to ride horseback while that was going on. They would be the tallest objects around and might attract those deadly bolts if they continued to ride. They even had to get the horses to lie down flat, where it was safer.

During one of those storms, Breckinridge had heard a sudden roaring sound unlike anything he had ever heard before. He lifted his head enough to look and saw a huge column of what appeared to be black, spinning air reaching down from the clouds to the ground. It was a cyclone, he realized. He had heard of them but never seen one with his own eyes. The thing was dark because of all the dirt and debris it had sucked up from the ground. Looking at it, Breck felt an instinctive fear. He would match his strength and fighting ability against almost anything, but he knew that against a storm like that, he would be utterly powerless.

The cyclone danced across the prairie about half a mile away and gradually went out of sight. Breckinridge and Moss stayed right where they were, though, because of the lightning and the possibility that another of those madly whirling monsters might come along. They didn't move along until the storm was miles to the south.

The rain had washed out the tracks they'd been following, of course, so once again Breckinridge and

Moss had to search for a long time, splitting up and riding back and forth seemingly endlessly, before they found the now-familiar hoofprints again. And as Breck well knew, all that time spent searching was more time Carnahan and Ophelia were using to get ahead of them.

The only glimmer of hope the two men had in those early days was that the tracks of two horses carrying riders proved Ophelia was still alive.

Gradually the trail began to curve to the south. Breckinridge had expected Carnahan to turn in that direction as soon as they cleared the mountains, but it hadn't happened. Eventually the tracks had led due south, and after a few days of riding that way, Breck and Charlie Moss spotted something looming up from the prairie ahead of them. The land was so flat they could see it for miles before they reached it.

The thing was a fort, a huge structure made of logs with tall, thick walls, with guard towers rising on two of the corners and a sturdy, two-story guardhouse inside the wall next to the gate.

Charlie Moss had let out a whistle of admiration and said, "If Absalom Garwood had built something like that, nobody would have ever gotten in to bother him."

"I reckon that's what he had in mind," Breckinridge had replied as they halted their horses and studied the impressive structure. "See those flags?"

He pointed to a flagpole flying two flags, one the Stars and Stripes, the other also red, white, and blue, but with the colors divided vertically rather than horizontally. Pennant-shaped, rather than rectangular like the American flag, it had writing of some sort in the white field in the middle.

"That's the American Fur Company flag, ain't it?" Moss asked. "I've seen it before."

"Yeah. I think I've heard of this place. Fort John, I think they call it."

Moss had swept a hand toward a long line of ruts that led across the prairie in a roughly east–west direction, passing near the fort, and said, "Then that must be what they've started callin' the Oregon Trail."

Breckinridge nodded. He had heard a lot of talk about the trail that had been blazed through these parts so immigrant wagons could follow it all the way from Missouri to the Pacific Northwest.

He wasn't sure how he felt about that. He could understand why folks wanted to spread out and see some new country. He had been like that himself, before he ever came west. But while he could sympathize with the people joining up with those wagon trains to go to the Oregon country, they weren't hunters and trappers and explorers, like him. They were *farmers,* from what he had heard. And storekeepers. The sort of folks who didn't just look around and leave a place like they found it. They *changed* things.

Breckinridge didn't much want the frontier changed. Sure, it had brought him a lot of suffering and loss, but those were the risks a fella ran when he set out for someplace new. Whatever he found was bound to be a mixture of good and bad, because that's the way life was everywhere.

One thing was for sure, though. There was nothing Breckinridge or anybody else could do to stop that tide once it started flowing westward. The Indians thought it was bad having a few fur trappers roaming around the mountains. Things were fixing to get a lot worse for them, and he wasn't sure they could survive it.

Breck and Moss had ridden on in to Fort John. There were no wagon trains there at the moment, but a dozen or so trappers were there, having come in to sell their furs. Breckinridge didn't know any of them, but Charlie Moss recognized a couple of them and introduced them to Breck as Harmon Russell and Jim Faherty. While they were having a drink with the men in the tavern attached to the fort's store, Breck took advantage of the opportunity to ask them about Carnahan and Ophelia.

"Carnahan," Russell had repeated, stroking his chin. "Name's vaguely familiar, but I don't think I know the man. What's he look like?"

"You couldn't miss him if you ever saw him," Breckinridge said. He described Carnahan's tree-stump shape and the long, bushy beard, then added, "He's traveling with a young woman. Blond hair, mighty easy on the eyes."

That had brought grins from both of the trappers.

"Now, her I'd remember for sure," Faherty said. "I can tell plain, Wallace, we ain't seen 'em."

A man sitting at a nearby table spoke up. He was a thin, cadaverous-looking fellow in a black swallowtail coat. His head was bald, but he had a black, pointed beard.

"I saw those two," he said. "They were here about ten days ago, I'd say."

"That was before Jim and me got here," Russell put in.

"Was the woman all right?" Breckinridge asked quickly.

"She mean something to you, friend?" the man in the swallowtail coat drawled.

"She ain't my sister or my wife, if that's what you

mean," Breckinridge said, "but I wouldn't want to see anything bad happen to her."

"I suppose that depends on your definition of *bad*." The man shrugged. Breckinridge suppressed the impulse to get mad at him for his nonchalant attitude and waited for him to go on. "She didn't appear to have been physically harmed. She limped a little, as if one of her feet was sore, but other than that she seemed fine."

Breckinridge remembered all the bloody footprints he had seen when they were first trailing Carnahan and Ophelia. They had been riding long enough that the damage should have healed by now, but maybe it had been bad enough that it left Ophelia with foot trouble permanent-like.

"As for her state of mind, I can't speak to that," the stranger went on. "She seemed pretty cowed. Kept her head down, never said anything. And when the man with her let it be known that gents could spend some time with her, for a price, she never objected or acted like it bothered her."

When he heard that, Breckinridge had to grip the edge of the table and hold on hard to keep from standing up and bellowing in anger. The news that Carnahan was whoring Ophelia out didn't come as any real surprise, but it enraged him anyway. Moss looked upset, too.

"I reckon we had to expect it," the older man muttered, "but dang, that's low of Carnahan."

"He's done worse, I reckon," Breckinridge said curtly. To the stranger, he said, "Do you know where they went when they left here?"

"I believe they headed east," the man said. "That's

all I can tell you . . . except that they were some richer than when they started out."

Breckinridge knew what he meant by that comment, and it almost made him mad again. But he just grunted his thanks, stood up, left his drink on the table, and stalked out of the tavern. With some obvious reluctance, Charlie Moss followed him.

Breckinridge was headed for the horses when Moss caught up to him.

"We ought to stay here a day or two," Moss said. "We've been pushin' those Injun ponies for a long time, and pushin' ourselves, too."

"Maybe we can trade these horses for some fresher ones."

"Maybe. But we can't trade away how worn out we are."

Breckinridge swung around sharply and said, "Blast it, Charlie, you heard what Carnahan's doin'. That poor girl—"

"It's already done, Breck. I don't mean to sound callous about it, but anything that could be taken away from her has done been took."

"It's got to be hell for her."

"I expect it is. That's more marks on the wall against Carnahan. But as far ahead of us as they already are, a couple of days ain't gonna make a difference. The time when speed counted was at the beginnin' of this chase, and like it or not . . . Carnahan gave us the slip. Now we got to be slow and steady and determined. He'll think that he's got away clean, and he'll stop tryin' as hard. Sooner or later he'll stop somewhere, relax, and that's when we'll come up and get him."

Moss's words made sense. Breckinridge had to

admit that, even though doing so put a bitter taste in his mouth.

"All right. I still have the money Garwood paid us for those furs. We'll see if we can trade these ponies, maybe put some cash with 'em, and get a packhorse and some supplies, too. And we'll rest up tomorrow and start out first thing the next mornin'. How's that sound to you?"

"Like good ideas," Moss said.

Good ideas they might have been, and having better horses and some supplies made the traveling easier, but Jud Carnahan continued to elude them as the weeks passed. The man had followed the Oregon Trail back toward Missouri, and for a while Breckinridge was convinced Carnahan intended to go all the way to St. Louis.

But then he and Ophelia dropped south again. Breckinridge and Moss might not have known that if they hadn't stopped at a small trading post being operated out of a couple of wagons. The men who owned them had decided to set up shop about halfway between Independence, Missouri, where the immigrant trains actually started, and Fort John. Carnahan and Ophelia had been through there, stopped over for a night, and then headed south, away from the settlers' route. Breck suspected the two traders had had their way with Ophelia, but he didn't ask them about that. Best not to dwell on it until he could do something about it, he told himself.

The weather had been good, no more thunderstorms, and one day they came upon familiar tracks, old but still visible.

"Is that them?" Moss asked in amazement.

"I believe it is," Breckinridge said.

"But they're headed west again! What in blazes is Carnahan doin'? Does he plan on wanderin' back and forth from one end of the blamed frontier to the other?"

"He's still afraid that we're behind him," Breckinridge said, nodding slowly. "He's smart enough to know that I ain't the sort to give up easy. So yeah, he's gonna wander around like a drunk Indian on a blind mule. Figures that'll throw us off the scent. He's come pretty close to doin' just that a few times."

"Yeah." Moss rubbed fingertips on his beard-stubbled chin. Both men had shaved while they were at Fort John, and their beards hadn't come back out full yet. "Luck's been with us, though. What if it turns on us one of these days, Breck?"

"We'll keep goin' anyway until it turns back in our favor."

That was what they had done—kept going. Across the plains and into the mountains again. The sun went down and rose again. Whenever they encountered anyone, white or red, they asked about the bushy-bearded man and the blond woman. Every so often, then ran into somebody who had seen Carnahan and Ophelia. The last man they had met on the trail, a half-crazy old-timer who claimed to be a preacher out to bring the Holy Gospel to the savages, as he put it, had pointed them out of the mountains.

"The bearded brother asked me if I knew where Bent's Fort was," the would-be sky pilot told them. "I said I'd been there recently my own self and pointed out the path to him and the woman. That's my job, pointing out the paths folks should take that will bring them to the Lord."

"The last thing Carnahan wants is to find the

Lord," Moss said. "More likely he'd want to march into hell and take over from the Devil."

"He's gonna get his chance to do that, one of these days," Breckinridge said. "What's Bent's Fort? Seems I've heard tell of it, but I don't remember."

"Some fellas built it as a trading post, down on the Arkansas River," the old-timer said. "It's right on the Santa Fe Trail."

Breckinridge and Moss looked at each other. Moss said, "You speculated a long time ago, Breck, that he might head down into Mex country."

"I didn't think he'd meander around all over creation gettin' there," Breckinridge said. "But it sure sounds like that's where he's headed at last."

The preacher said, "Do you intend violence toward this man, brothers?"

"We da—darned sure do," Moss said.

"Violence only begets more violence, you know."

Breckinridge said, "It's the only way to help that gal. And he's got it comin', no doubt about it."

"Well, then, I'll pray that you stay safe."

They parted ways with the old-timer, and now they were ready to ride back down out of the mountains and find Bent's Fort.

"You think he'll still be there?" Moss asked as they nudged their horses into motion and started down from the ridge.

"Only one way to find out," Breckinridge said.

Chapter 24

Bent's Fort was laid out much like Fort John, a large, rectangular compound with guard towers at the corners. Instead of logs, though, the walls of this post were made of adobe, fifteen feet high, four feet thick, and impregnable to anything short of a prolonged cannon bombardment.

The buildings inside backed up to those massive walls and faced inward on a central plaza with a well in the middle of it. At the rear of the compound was a large corral, also surrounded by adobe walls.

The fort sat by itself in the middle of the prairie with the Arkansas River following its winding course a short distance to the south. During wet weather, the ground around the outside tended to get boggy except in certain areas, which made it even more difficult to attack.

Now, at the height of summer, the river was fairly low and the hard-packed dirt around the fort had tipis set up on it where friendly Indians had come to trade and scrounge. As Breckinridge and Charlie Moss rode slowly toward the fort, Breck looked at the ruts left by the wagons traveling on the Santa Fe Trail and knew those wagon trains probably stopped here quite often. After the long trek across the middle of the country, this outpost of civilization would be a welcome sight.

The gates were on the north wall of the compound, so Breckinridge and Moss approached from that direction. At the moment, the gates were open, and several buckskin-clad men lounged around the entrance, smoking pipes and talking. Some of them held rifles, and more of the long-barreled flintlocks were leaning against the wall nearby. The ground in front of the fort was flat and open and the men at the gates could see trouble coming for a long way. Breck knew they were watching him and Moss, but the two of them evidently didn't represent a threat, because the loungers continued to lounge.

They did, however, become a little more alert as Breckinridge and Moss reined to a stop in front of the gates. One of the men, a burly fellow with two white streaks extending down from the corners of his mouth through his black beard, said, "Howdy, boys. Welcome to Bent's Fort. You come to trade?"

"Nope," Breckinridge said. "Lookin' for somebody. Fella name of Jud Carnahan. Sawed-off gent, about as wide as he is tall. Got a beard comes down to the middle of his chest, or at least he did the last time we saw him."

"Friend of yours, is he?"

"Not exactly." Breckinridge wasn't sure how much to say. Carnahan could act friendly when he wanted to, so there was no telling who might be sympathetic to him and want to mislead any enemies on his trail. "We've got business with him, though. Is he here?"

"Hell, I don't know," the man replied. He looked

around at the others, who shrugged. "Ain't been here all that long myself, so I ain't sure who's around. Talk to St. Vrain. He could tell you, I reckon."

"Who's that?" Breckinridge asked. "We're not from around these parts."

"Ceran St. Vrain. Him and William Bent built this place. Their company owns it. Bent's off down in Santa Fe right now, but I seen St. Vrain just a little while ago, goin' into the blacksmith shop."

"Much obliged to you."

Breckinridge and Moss nudged their horses forward. None of the men tried to stop them as they rode through the open gates and the tunnel-like entrance to the fort.

Inside, it was like being in a miniature town. Various establishments lined the walls, including a store, a saloon, a gunsmith, and the blacksmith shop, which Breckinridge located by following the sound of a hammer ringing against an anvil. Breck and Moss dismounted and led their horses across the plaza, past the well and the hitch rails where other mounts were tied.

A sturdy-looking man who had a fringe of brown beard running down his jaw and under his chin but was otherwise clean-shaven stood just inside the blacksmith shop's entrance. He had been talking to the brawny smith in his thick leather apron, but the man turned to nod to Breckinridge and Moss as they strode up.

"Gentlemen," he said. "Welcome to Bent's Fort. You're new here, are you not?"

"Just rode in," Breckinridge confirmed. "I'm Breckinridge Wallace. This here is Charlie Moss."

"Ceran St. Vrain," the man introduced himself. "A pleasure to meet you. Did you bring furs to trade?"

St. Vrain could see for himself that there were no pelts on the packhorse tied to Moss's saddle, but asking the question like that gave newcomers the opportunity to provide as much or as little information as they wanted. People on the frontier quickly learned that it wasn't polite to be too curious about strangers.

"No, we're trappers, sure enough, but right now we're on other business. Lookin' for a fella named Jud Carnahan."

A frown of what appeared to be disapproval immediately creased St. Vrain's high forehead.

"A friend of yours?" he asked, as had the man at the gate.

Given St. Vrain's reaction, Breckinridge felt comfortable this time in saying, "Not hardly."

"Good, because he seemed like a thoroughly unsavory man."

Charlie Moss said, "I'd describe him as more of a no-good son of a—"

"Is he here?" Breckinridge broke in impatiently.

St. Vrain shook his head and said, "No. He was, two weeks ago, I would say. Like so many who come here, he was bound for Santa Fe. To that end, he attached himself to a train of freight wagons headed for the same destination. There's more safety traveling in numbers, you know."

"Those freighters agreed to let him go along, just like that?"

St. Vrain shrugged.

"Carnahan was one more gun, in case of trouble. The Indians in this region are, by and large, peaceable to white men and Mexicans. My partner, William Bent, is married to a woman of the Southern Cheyenne and is well respected in that tribe and among the Arapaho as well. But between here and Santa Fe, the Navajo are intermittently hostile and have been known to attack wagon trains. Carnahan appeared to be a competent fighter."

"He's that, all right," Breckinridge said grudgingly. "I have to give him that much."

"And there was the added inducement of Carnahan's . . . companion."

Something about the way St. Vrain said that made a chill go through Breckinridge, even though it didn't really surprise him.

"You're talkin' about the gal travelin' with him."

St. Vrain inclined his head and said, "An attractive young blond woman. Carnahan made it known among the freighters that they could enjoy her company during the journey, in return for the added safety of traveling with them."

"There ought to be a special place in hell for varmints like him," Charlie Moss said.

"I'm in business, gentlemen, which means I don't debate morality. I must admit, though, I felt some sympathy for the young woman."

"But not enough to put a stop to what Carnahan's doin'," Moss snapped.

Breckinridge raised a hand to keep Moss from saying anything else. It was a rare day when Breckinridge Wallace was the voice of reason, but Breck knew it wouldn't do any good to get in an argument with a powerful man like St. Vrain.

"Did she seem to be all right? Other than what Carnahan was makin' her do, I mean."

St. Vrain shrugged again and said, "She appeared to be healthy enough. Of course, in that line of work, it's unlikely she'll stay that way for a very long time. But she did not seem to be . . . mistreated physically."

Breckinridge nodded, glad to hear that Ophelia was bearing up under the hardships she'd been made to suffer. He thought about Desdemona and Eugenia, up there at the Garwood trading post, and was glad as well that they didn't know what their sister was going through. Sooner or later, they were bound to find out about it, but at least they were being spared that worry for the time being. They were probably doing plenty of worrying just about whether or not Ophelia was still alive. Breck wished there were some way he could get word to them that she was.

"Two weeks ago they were here, you said?"

"Approximately. I couldn't tell you the exact day they left." St. Vrain laughed. "Well, actually, I suppose I could, since there are records of my dealings with those freighters. I consigned some goods to their wagons. Bent and I have a store in Santa Fe, too, you know, and our own wagons deliver merchandise there. But sometimes I need to get goods there while our wagons are not available, as in this case. Would you like for me to check in my office and see what I can find out?"

"That's not necessary. We'll be headin' on to Santa Fe first thing in the mornin' anyway, so it don't really matter when Carnahan left. I reckon it's all right that we stay here tonight, let our horses rest a mite, and pick up a few supplies?"

St. Vrain smiled and said, "That is why this fort exists, my friend."

Moss said, "I don't reckon we'll have any trouble findin' the way to Santa Fe?"

St. Vrain waved a hand in the general direction of

the broad, rutted path that ran past the fort and didn't say a word. He didn't have to.

Spending the night at Bent's Fort gave Breckinridge and Charlie Moss the chance to have a meal they hadn't cooked themselves over a lonely campfire, and wash it down with some beer, as well. The buildings that lined the fort's walls sort of ran into each other and had doors between, so a fella could walk from the store into the saloon and on into an eating place without ever going out into the plaza. Breck and Moss were at a table sawing chunks off steaks when a man came up to them and said, "Did I hear tell that you gents are looking for Judson Carnahan?"

"Judson?" Breckinridge repeated. "I never heard him called anything but Jud. But yeah, we've been tryin' to find him for a while."

"Mind if I sit?" the stranger asked as he gestured at the empty chair beside the table. He was tall, thin, and lantern-jawed, dressed in a threadbare dark suit.

"Help yourself. You know Carnahan?"

The man settled himself at the table and cast a thirsty gaze toward the mugs of beer sitting in front of Breckinridge and Moss. He licked his lips and then said, "Indeed I do. We grew up together in the same town, back in Ohio."

"Ohio, eh?" Moss said. "I figured he was born and raised in hell."

Breckinridge motioned one of the serving girls over and told her to bring a beer for the newcomer. He figured the man might talk more if his tongue had the proper lubrication. Although, he and Moss already knew Carnahan was headed for Santa Fe.

Breck wasn't sure what else they needed to know. But there was no telling when some bit of knowledge might come in handy.

"Our town wasn't hell, but Judson's father might as well have been the Devil. He terrorized his wife and children and anybody else who crossed him. Judson was the oldest, and he became the old man's willing accomplice. Probably because he knew that if he didn't go along, he'd be just another target for his father's wrath."

The man stopped and picked up the mug the girl put in front of him. He took a long swallow, said, "Ah," and licked his lips again.

"So Carnahan was raised to be bad," Breckinridge said.

"Actually, I believe he was born that way. But having his father for an example certainly didn't help matters. When Judson was fifteen, his twelve-year-old brother tried to stand up for himself." The man paused. "Judson beat him to death. Then he left town and none of us ever saw him again. Everyone agreed it was only a matter of time until he killed someone. It's a shame to say so, but I think most people in town were grateful that it was a member of his own family and not someone else. Although the boy didn't deserve it, of course."

"And you just happened to run into him out here?" Breckinridge asked.

"That's right. I clerk for Mr. Bent and Mr. St. Vrain. Everyone who comes through this part of the country stops here sooner or later. I see old friends from back home now and then."

"Like Carnahan."

The man shook his head and said, "Good Lord, no.

Judson Carnahan was never my friend. I'm not sure he ever *had* any friends. Just victims."

"He ain't changed much," Moss said.

"No, I don't suppose he has. You men clearly know him. I was going to warn you that if you knew him only by name and hadn't made his acquaintance, you needed to be careful."

"We know him," Breckinridge agreed. "Did you talk to him while he was here?"

The man responded with a vehement shake of his head.

"I kept my distance. As I said, we weren't friends back home, and I didn't particularly want to remind him of those days. I, ah, felt sorry for the young woman with him, but there was nothing I could do for her, you understand."

He was right about that, Breckinridge thought. This man was no match for Carnahan and would have just gotten himself hurt, if not killed, if he'd tried to interfere, and that wouldn't have done Ophelia a bit of good.

Finding out a little about Carnahan's background was interesting, but it didn't really change anything. No matter what sort of stock a man was bred from, or how he was raised, it was still up to him to choose between good and evil. Nothing in Jud Carnahan's past could ever excuse the things he had done.

"If you don't mind my asking," their newfound acquaintance went on, "just what is it you intend to do when you find Judson?"

"We're gonna get that girl away from him," Moss said. "And then we're gonna kill him."

The man gave a dubious shake of his head and downed the rest of his beer.

"I'd wish you luck, but I'm not sure that will be enough," he said. "Not against a man like that. If I were you . . . I think I'd turn around and go back where I came from. It's too late to save that girl from whatever Carnahan has turned her into, and I'm not sure even two men such as yourselves can kill him."

"Anybody can be killed," Moss protested.

The man stood up, gave them a pitying look, and walked back toward the saloon part of the establishment.

Moss grunted and then said, "You reckon he's right, Breck? Is what we're doing just a waste of our time that's gonna get us killed?"

"I ain't sure," Breckinridge said, "but we've come too blasted far to turn back now."

Chapter 25

Bunks were available for sleeping in a big room that ran along one of the walls, and Breckinridge and Moss took advantage of that. This was their first night spent indoors since leaving the trading post on the Yellowstone all those weeks ago. They were up early the next morning, had a good breakfast including a pot of coffee, bought some supplies in the store, and then got their mounts and packhorse from the stable. The sun was almost up, and it was time to hit the trail.

"You reckon Carnahan plans on stayin' in Santa Fe," Moss asked as they rode away from Bent's Fort, "or will he move on again?"

"Hard to say, but my hunch is he might stay put for a while. By now he's bound to believe we ain't followin' him no more. By all rights, he should've given us the slip half a dozen times in the past two months. We've been lucky."

"And stubborn as all get-out," Moss said.

"That, too," Breckinridge agreed with a grin.

That morning, while they were buying supplies,

one of the clerks in the store had mentioned a wagon train that had left the fort several days earlier. Breckinridge asked about it, thinking it had been longer than that since the freight wagons had pulled out and Carnahan and Ophelia had gone with them.

"No, not the freight wagons," the clerk had explained. "This was a bunch of immigrants planning to take up farming down there in New Mexico. I'm afraid they're going to be disappointed. That land's not really suited for farming. But you can't tell that to folks who have their hearts set on it."

"The Mexican government lets American settlers come in?" Breckinridge asked. "That sort of thing led to a big fight somewheres else, didn't it?"

"Over in Texas, you mean." The clerk nodded. "Yeah, that was part of it. But the Mexes let some gringos in. That's what they call us, gringos. Means *foreigners*. You got to be careful down there, though. They've got their own way of doing things, and if you don't follow their rules, you're liable to wind up in a Mexican prison. That's pretty much the same as them dumping you in a deep, dark hole that you'll never climb out of."

As Breckinridge and Moss rode southwestward, paralleling the main trail but not following it precisely because they wanted to avoid the deep ruts, Breck thought about the wagon train ahead of them. The freight wagons, along with Carnahan and Ophelia, had been gone from Bent's Fort for long enough that the two men had no chance of catching up to them. That immigrant train was a different story, though. Those heavy wagons and the stolid oxen pulling them didn't move very fast. Breck expected to come up on them before they got to Santa Fe.

He and Moss didn't run into anyone for the first couple of days of the journey, which surprised Breckinridge a little since the Santa Fe Trail was supposed to be so heavily traveled. Around midmorning on the third day, after coming down through a steep pass in an offshoot of mountains from the main body of the Rockies, they were crossing a broad, open flat when Breck spotted something up ahead.

"What's that?" he asked, pointing to a number of low mounds to the left of the trail.

"I dunno," Moss said. "Looks like . . . Good Lord, Breck, those look like graves! Pretty recent ones, at that."

Breckinridge agreed. As they came closer, he was able to make out that small, crude wooden crosses had been erected at the head of each grave—because that was clearly what they were. Not only was the dirt mounded where it had been turned up and replaced, but rocks had been stacked on them, too, to form cairns.

The burial sites were about a hundred yards from the trail. Breckinridge and Moss detoured over to them and reined in to get a better look.

"No names on the markers," Moss commented. "Not even a date. It's like they're sayin' somebody's buried here, but whoever put these up didn't know who they were or when they died."

"That'd be my guess," Breckinridge agreed. He counted. "Fourteen graves. That's a heap of dyin'."

"Who do you reckon they were?"

Breckinridge had to shake his head as he said, "I don't have any idea. But we know what was ahead of us on the trail: those freight wagons, and that wagon train full of settlers."

Moss looked over at him. "You reckon somebody jumped those freight wagons and killed everybody? Are you sayin' Carnahan and the gal could be buried here?"

"It's possible," Breckinridge said, although he didn't want to believe it was true. He wanted Jud Carnahan dead, sure, but he wanted to be the one to kill him. And after everything Ophelia had gone through, she might have preferred death, but he still hated to think about her winding up in a lonely, unmarked grave out here in the middle of this wilderness.

On the other hand, once you were dead, it didn't really matter much to you where you wound up, he thought bleakly.

They scouted around, looking for any other clues that might tell them what had happened here, but there was nothing. Just those fourteen graves. Maybe if they kept going, they would find out the truth, Breckinridge thought . . . or maybe not. It might remain an unsolved mystery.

It certainly did for the rest of that day and most of the next. But late in the afternoon of the fourth day after leaving Bent's Fort, Breckinridge and Moss heard something that made both of them rein in, sit up in the saddles they had bought at Fort John when they traded for the horses, and listen intently.

"Blast it, that sounds like shootin'," Moss said after a moment.

Breckinridge nodded and said, "Yeah, and a bunch of it, too."

"Are we about to ride into the middle of a war we didn't know about? The United States declared war on the Mexes, maybe?"

"Could be, but that don't sound like quite enough

guns to be a battle between two armies. We need to find out what it is, though."

Breckinridge kneed his horse into motion again. Moss was right behind him. They rode hard, although not at a full gallop because the packhorse had to keep up. Ahead of them, the trail dropped down through a wide, gentle, natural cut in a ridge that stood up across the terrain like a stair step.

At the bottom of the slope, where the trail leveled out and ran through a field of boulders, about twenty wagons were stopped. A haze of powder smoke hung over the scene. As Breckinridge reined in, he saw more puffs of gray smoke from behind many of the boulders where hidden gunmen were shooting at the wagons. Return fire came from the wagons. The battle seemed to be a standoff.

"Somebody was waitin' to ambush that wagon train!" Moss exclaimed.

"Yeah, looks like they shot the lead oxen on the first wagon, and that brought the whole thing to a stop," Breckinridge said. "Those pilgrims are stuck there."

"Can you make out who's behind the rocks? Injuns?"

Breckinridge held a hand over his eyes to shade them from the sun and squinted.

"I see some coonskin caps and felt hats," he said after a moment. "Those are white men. Bandits, I reckon."

"I can't abide a thief," Moss said. "What are we gonna do?"

"Well, there's two of us and probably twenty or thirty of them. Those ain't very good odds." Breckinridge smiled as he lifted his rifle, swung a leg over his horse's back, and slid to the ground. "What say we try to whittle 'em down a mite?"

Moss dismounted, too, and they put rocks on their horses' reins to keep the animals from wandering off. Then, carrying their rifles, they trotted along the edge of the ridge until they could see behind the boulders where the ambushers were hidden.

"Try to pick off the ones farthest away from the trail first," Breckinridge said. "With all the shootin' goin' on, maybe they won't notice what we're doin' until it's too late."

"We'll be shootin' 'em from behind, in no warnin'," Moss pointed out.

"I reckon they gave up the right to expect anything like that when they started tryin' to kill those settlers and loot the wagon train. 'Cause you know that's what they're after."

"Couldn't be anything else," Moss agreed. Grimly, he added, "I spotted a few fellas lyin' next to the wagons, and they weren't movin'."

"Yeah, I saw the same thing," Breckinridge said as he rested his rifle barrel on a rock and drew a bead on one of the bandits. "See that fella in the green flannel shirt? He's my meat."

"I'll take the varmint to his right, in the tall hat."

They aimed carefully and then squeezed the triggers. The rifles' blasts blended in with the continuing roll of gunfire across the plains.

The ball from Breckinridge's flintlock crashed into the back of the man in the green flannel shirt and drove him forward against the rock behind which he had hidden. He bounced off, dropped his rifle, and collapsed in a limp heap. A few yards away, the man

Moss had targeted had slumped forward over his rock and was pawing at it, trying to hold himself off as blood welled from the wound in his back. He slid down until he was on the ground and unmoving, too.

Breckinridge watched the other men attacking the wagon train to see if any of them had noticed the two men who'd been shot down. None of them seemed to. They continued firing at the wagons as if nothing had happened.

After reloading, Breckinridge and Moss picked out two more targets. These men went down under the deadly accurate fire, as well.

The ambushers were hidden on both sides of the trail. Breckinridge counted ten men on the near side, including the four he and Moss had killed, or at least put out of the fight.

"We get many more of 'em, they're gonna start to notice," Breckinridge said. "Let's move over to the other side of the gap and see if we can ventilate a few of 'em over there."

They dashed across the trail and moved along the ridge, staying back from the edge so they wouldn't be spotted until they were ready to move up and start searching for fresh targets. They carried out the maneuver with the same success they had enjoyed on the first round of shots. Four of the ten men on this side fell on their rifles.

"A couple more," Breckinridge decided after mulling it over for a moment. "Then we'll have cut the odds in half from what they were."

"Sounds good to me. You reckon those pilgrims can fight off the rest of 'em?"

"I don't know, but I don't plan on stoppin' there. Just figure to kill some more at closer range."

The ridge was fairly steep and rugged, but Breckinridge knew he could make it down there to the boulders. If he could get among the bandits before they knew he was there, he could wreak some pretty bloody havoc with his pistols, knife, and tomahawk. Once the ambushers on this side of the trail were wiped out, maybe he could rally the immigrants and lead a charge against the handful of remaining bandits on the other side.

The plan might well have worked, except that just as Charlie Moss squeezed his rifle's trigger, the man he had drawn a bead on shifted to one side. Instead of striking him in the middle of the back, the ball shattered his shoulder, spun him around, and knocked him against the rock instead. The wound was bad enough to put the man out of the fight, but it hadn't killed him instantly, as the other shots had done.

So he was able to yell his head off and warn the other four men on the near side of the trail.

"Get down!" Breckinridge said as the bandits swung around and opened fire toward the ridge. It had taken the men only a second to figure out that's where Breck and Moss had to be.

They dived to the ground as rifle balls hummed around them. One of the shots kicked up dirt and rocks at the edge of the slope.

"Hunt some cover," Breckinridge said. "We got a fight on our hands now, not a turkey shoot."

They crawled over to some rocks that were a far cry from being boulders but were large enough to provide some cover, especially since the bandits were having to shoot up at an angle. Breckinridge and Moss had the better of that. For several minutes the rifle balls flew madly between the two groups without any hits on either side.

Then one of the ambushers got careless, and someone in the wagon train was alert enough to notice that the man had exposed himself to fire from that angle. The bandit's head seemed to explode as a shot struck it from behind. The gory corpse flopping forward distracted one of the other men, and Breckinridge drilled him through the chest.

That just left two men on this side of the trail, and they had had enough. Breckinridge saw them duck back into the boulders and start running toward a nearby gully. Breck would have bet they had horses waiting there.

"See if you can get one of 'em on the wing!" he called to Moss as he reloaded.

Moss's rifle boomed, but both ambushers kept running without breaking stride. They disappeared into the gully.

"Dadgummit!" Moss exclaimed. "I thought I had him!"

"At least they're not tryin' to kill any of those farmers anymore. And look over yonder." Breckinridge pointed across the trail to where a cloud of dust was boiling up and moving away from the stalled wagons. "The varmints on that side are takin' off for the tall and uncut, too. I reckon they saw the bodies of the ones we got before and decided they'd lost enough men for one day."

"Are we goin' down there to introduce ourselves to the folks in the wagons?"

"We sure are," Breckinridge said. "For one thing, I want to ask them about those graves back there."

They returned to the spot where they had left their horses, mounted up, and rode slowly down the trail where it descended from the ridge. Breckinridge didn't get in any hurry because he wanted the immigrants to get a good long look at him and Moss. After having been under attack, they would be on edge, and he wasn't going to give them any excuse to panic and start shooting again.

He didn't have to worry about that. Someone in charge must have figured out that Breckinridge and Moss were the men who had come along to help them. Several men on horseback moved out from the wagon train and rode back along the trail toward them.

When they were close, Breckinridge and Moss slowed and let the riders come to them. Everyone had their rifles across their saddles, but that was just being careful, something a fella had to do out here on the frontier if he wanted to survive for very long.

The man who seemed to be the leader held up a hand to halt his companions. He was a stocky, florid-faced man with white hair under his hat and a white brush of a mustache. He said to Breckinridge and Moss, "You're the boys who gave us a hand just now?"

"We are," Breckinridge said. "This is Charlie Moss. My name's Wallace. Front handle is Breckinridge."

"We're mighty obliged to you, and pleased to meet you, as well. I'm Otis Shaftel, captain of this wagon train. We're bound for Santa Fe, although I suppose you knew that, since this is the Santa Fe Trail." Shaftel nodded toward his companions. "Silas Barker, Jack Bechdolt, and Earl Repp, the men who are helping me run things. Do you know anything about those skunks who ambushed us?"

"Not a blamed thing," Breckinridge replied. "Other than they were white, as far as I could tell."

Shaftel grunted. "We expected we might have trouble with Indians on the way out here but haven't seen a single hostile, just those friendly ones camped at Bent's Fort. Didn't think about running into outlaws. But I suppose there's lawlessness anywhere you go, isn't there?"

"Pretty much," Breckinridge agreed.

"I don't doubt that those no-good thieves were the same ones responsible for the massacre back up the trail."

"Massacre?" Breckinridge repeated, even though he had a very good idea what Shaftel was talking about.

"Yes, a few days ago we came up on what looked like a group of teamsters. They'd all been slaughtered, and their wagons were gone."

Chapter 26

Breckinridge let that dramatic pronouncement hang in the air for a second, then he said, "The people who'd been killed . . . was there a woman among 'em?"

"A woman?" Shaftel repeated in surprise as his bushy white eyebrows drew down in a frown. "No, they were all men. Fourteen of them." He looked around at his companions. "Did any of you boys see hide nor hair of a woman?"

The others shook their heads. One of them said drily, "I think we would've noticed that, Otis."

Shaftel regarded Breckinridge and Moss with suspicion. "Why would you ask such a thing?"

"Because we've been trackin' a man and a woman for a long time now," Breckinridge replied. "The woman is young, blond, mighty easy on the eyes. At least, she was the last time we saw her. But I reckon what she looks like don't matter, since you said there weren't any females in the bunch you came across."

"Nary a one," Shaftel said. "What about the man you're looking for?"

"Short and wide, but not fat. All muscle. He generally sports a dark, bushy beard that comes down on his chest. His name is Jud Carnahan."

Shaftel shook his head.

"None of those fellows were in any shape to tell us their names. They'd been dead awhile, and the scavengers had been at them. But I don't recollect any of them matching that description."

The other men from the wagon train chimed in, agreeing with their captain. They *could* be lying, Breckinridge supposed, but he didn't see any reason for them to do so. They seemed to be decent fellows. They had taken the time to bury each of those murdered teamsters in individual graves, after all, instead of dumping them all in one big hole or even leaving them for the animals and the elements.

Shaftel went on, "These two you're looking for, were they traveling with those teamsters?"

"That's what we were told at Bent's Fort."

One of the men said, "I'll bet the bunch that ambushed us today is the same one that jumped those freight wagons."

"Seems likely," Shaftel said, nodding. "Although I suppose there could be more than one band of outlaws operating in this area. The Santa Fe Trail stays pretty busy, after all. Lots of wagons to provide tempting targets." The suspicion he had demonstrated earlier seemed to have eased. "You men saved us, I reckon, and you're mighty good fighters. How would you like to throw in with us the rest of the way to Santa Fe?"

Breckinridge thought it over. What had happened

to Carnahan and Ophelia was a mystery. It was possible the outlaws had taken them along as prisoners after wiping out the rest of the party. Or maybe Carnahan and Ophelia had split off from the group for some reason before the freight wagons were ambushed.

He considered backtracking to the site of the massacre and trying to follow the outlaws' trail, but with the welter of hoofprints on both sides of the trail, that might be difficult. How could you pick out the tracks of the bandits' horses from the millions of other hoofprints? Trying to find the place where Carnahan and Ophelia had split off from the wagons, if indeed they had, would be even more of a challenge.

No, if Carnahan and Ophelia were still alive, then Santa Fe remained their most likely destination, Breckinridge decided. And as Moss had pointed out, time was no longer the most important factor. Persistence was.

Moss would go along with whatever he said. So Breckinridge nodded and told Shaftel, "I reckon we wouldn't mind ridin' with you folks, if you'll have us."

"You'll be mighty welcome," the white-haired captain said. "Come on. I know folks are anxious to meet the two men who saved our bacon."

Otis Shaftel was right about that. The immigrants crowded around to greet Breckinridge and Charlie Moss. The men shook their hands and slapped them on the back. The older women smiled and invited them to take supper with their families when the wagon train made camp that evening. The younger women smiled and batted their eyelashes, especially at Breck.

When they got a chance for a word alone, Moss nudged Breckinridge with an elbow and grinned.

"Better be careful, Breck. I think at least half of the mamas in this train are already plannin' on marryin' one of their daughters off to you."

Breckinridge blew out a breath and shook his head.

"Last thing in the world I want is a wife. Almost had one a time or two, and the way things worked out, I learned I ain't exactly the marryin' kind."

"Well, we'll see. Sometimes things you ain't expectin' come along and smack you in the head."

They were tending to their horses when a nice-looking woman with brown hair came up to them. They hadn't been introduced to her earlier, as far as Breckinridge could recall, but she remedied that by saying, "Hello. I'm Georgina Shaftel."

She had a wedding ring on her finger, Breckinridge noticed. She was a lot younger than Otis Shaftel, but such matches weren't uncommon. He nodded politely and said, "You're Captain Shaftel's wife, ma'am?"

"No, I'm his daughter-in-law. I'm married to . . . I *was* married to . . . his son Patrick." A faint, sad smile touched her lips. "He passed away last year."

Moss tugged his hat off and said, "We're mighty sorry to hear that, ma'am."

"What can we do for you?" Breckinridge asked.

Georgina Shaftel's smile was warmer and not as sad as she went on, "I know you probably received a lot of dinner invitations earlier, but my father-in-law would really like for you to eat with us tonight. So would I."

"I reckon we'd be pleased to," Moss replied before Breckinridge could say anything. Not that it mattered. Breck would have agreed, too. It didn't make any difference to him.

"All right. You'll be able to find our wagon without any trouble."

Georgina moved off toward the front of the line of wagons. The immigrants were getting ready to roll again, since there was still plenty of daylight left to cover more ground. Two men had been killed in the ambush. Their bodies had been wrapped in blankets and placed in their wagons. They would be laid to rest beside the trail that evening, after the group made camp.

There were probably thousands of lost, lonely graves along this trail, Breckinridge reflected. The final resting places of folks who had tried for something better in their lives and failed, falling victim to sickness or violence.

Breckinridge and Moss rode at the front of the wagon train with Otis Shaftel. The company had two scouts, a couple of leathery older men named Kanigher and Dawson, who rode a mile or so ahead to make sure there was no trouble lurking along the trail. Earlier, Breck had overheard them talking to Shaftel. Both men were extremely chagrined that they had allowed the wagons to roll right into that ambush. The outlaws had been well hidden, though.

As far as Breckinridge was concerned, he would keep a wary eye on Kanigher and Dawson. He didn't believe that the scouts were working with the bandits, but the possibility couldn't be ruled out.

If there *was* something shady about the two men, they would be less likely to lead the wagon train into a trap, now that Breckinridge and Moss had thrown in with the immigrants. Breck was *always* on the lookout for trouble.

That evening, after the wagons pulled into a circle and the teams of oxen were unhitched and herded into the center, the two men who had been killed were buried on a little hill overlooking the trail from about a quarter of a mile away. It was a solemn occasion. A couple of men who had fiddles played a hymn, and the whole company sang. Shaftel said proper words over the bodies and led a prayer. The sun had just set, so a brilliant red and gold cathedral-like arch was still on display in the western sky. A breeze kicked up a little dust and swirled it around so that it sparkled in the fading light. A fella could have a worse send-off, Breckinridge thought.

The bandits who'd been killed in the fighting earlier in the day certainly hadn't received such respectful treatment. Their bodies had been dumped into a nearby ravine and left there.

With the burial over, the pilgrims returned to camp, where the women set about preparing supper. Breckinridge and Moss made sure their horses and the packhorse were all right, then strolled over to the big Conestoga wagon belonging to Otis Shaftel. Georgina had a pot of stew simmering over a cooking fire. A Dutch oven with biscuits in it sat at the edge of the flames.

Two youngsters, a boy about eight years old and a girl a couple of years younger, played nearby. Moss took off his hat, nodded toward them, and asked Georgina, "Your young 'uns, ma'am?"

"That's right," she replied with a smile. "Walter and Sadie. And you don't have to call me *ma'am*, Mr. Moss."

"All right, then, uh, Miz Shaftel."

"Perhaps by the time we reach Santa Fe, you'll be calling me Georgina and I can call you Charles."

Moss was starting to look uncomfortable. He twisted the hat in his hands and said, "Um, ain't nobody called me Charles since my ma did, and she mostly did when I was in some sort of trouble. But I reckon you can call me Charles anytime you want, ma'am—I mean, Miz Shaftel."

She turned away, but not before Breckinridge spied the smile on her lips. Moss had ribbed him about all the attention the girls had paid to him, but from the looks of Georgina Shaftel, Moss was the one who had a gal seriously setting her cap for him already.

The meal was a pleasant one. The kids settled down and weren't too rowdy, and the stew was good, especially with light, fluffy biscuits and washed down with strong black coffee. There wasn't a lot of evidence to go on yet, but Georgina seemed to be a fine cook.

Curious, Breckinridge asked Otis Shaftel, "Did you have to make arrangements with the Mexican government before you folks could move in down there around Santa Fe?"

"Yes, I was in charge of forming the company and signing contracts with the territorial governor," Shaftel said. "We had to put up a sizable bond, but it'll be returned to us once we've settled and been there awhile. Less, of course, a certain amount for the governor." He chuckled. "I made a couple of trips down there to arrange everything, and it didn't take me long to figure out how things work south of the border. The Mexicans are still a little touchy about what happened over in Texas. That whole revolution was less than ten years ago, you know."

Breckinridge nodded. "I've heard a lot about Texas. Never been there, though."

"From what I understand, it's a hellish place. I'm not sure why anyone would want to fight over it." Shaftel shrugged. "But there's hardly anyplace that somebody's not willing to fight over."

"Do you have to be Mexican citizens?" Moss asked.

"No, but we have to abide by Mexican laws. It's pretty much the same as if we were citizens, I suppose."

Breckinridge drank the last of the coffee in his cup and said, "I wouldn't think the country down there would be very good for farming." He waved his free hand to indicate the rocky, semiarid terrain around them. "These parts sure wouldn't be."

"It's different over in the valley of the Rio Grande. That's the big river that runs through this part of the country. Not saying it'll be easy, but I'm convinced that with hard work, we can make a go of it."

Georgina said, "Whatever you do in life, you have to work hard to be successful at it."

"That's sure true," Moss agreed. His hat was pushed back on his head, and as he looked across the fire at Georgina, Breckinridge could tell that he was well and truly smitten.

Like Moss himself had said, sometimes something unexpected came up and smacked you across the face. Breckinridge figured that was what was happening to his friend now.

Later, they spread their bedrolls under one of the wagons. Breckinridge said quietly, "I reckon we ought to take turns stayin' awake tonight, just in case what was left of those varmints come back to try again."

"Cap'n Shaftel has guards posted every night," Moss said.

"I know. But I don't know how good those fellas are at stayin' alert. You and me, though, we've got a lot of experience at watchin' out for trouble."

Moss grunted and said, "That's for sure." He paused, then asked, "What do you think about Miz Shaftel, Breck?"

"Nice lady. Good cook. Seems to be a good mama to them kids. Why you askin', Charlie?"

"Oh hell, no reason," Moss replied gruffly. "Can't a fella just talk a mite without needin' to have some special reason for it?"

"Sure he can," Breckinridge said, trying not to grin. "You want to take first watch?"

"Yeah. I don't feel much like sleepin' right now, anyway."

Breckinridge was still smiling to himself as he rolled up in his blankets and dozed off.

Chapter 27

A couple of days on the trail passed without incident. At this rate, the wagon train would arrive in Santa Fe in another five or six days, Shaftel told Breckinridge and Moss.

Much to the disappointment of some of the young women in the train, the two newcomers ate breakfast and supper every day at the Shaftel wagon. Breckinridge saw Moss and Georgina talking every chance they could find, and although he didn't try to eavesdrop, he overheard enough of the conversations to know that they had reached the stage where they were calling each other Georgina and Charles already.

That was fine. If something came of this, Breckinridge would be happy for his friend. He had never intended to partner up with Charlie Moss from now on. Fate had sort of thrown them together and put them on the trail of Jud Carnahan, and Breck had always figured that once they were done with that quest, they would go their separate ways.

Anyway, he already had a trail partner—Morgan Baxter—and he planned to return to the Garwood trading post so he could tell Desdemona and Eugenia what had happened to Ophelia. That is, if he couldn't bring Ophelia herself back to them.

From what he had heard about the misfortunes that had befallen her, she might not want to go back to her sisters. If that turned out to be the case, Breckinridge knew he couldn't force her to return to her old life.

He wondered about Morgan, too. Would so much time have passed by the time Breckinridge got back up there to the Yellowstone country . . . would Morgan have gotten so comfortable there at the trading post . . . that he wouldn't want to leave and resume his life as a fur trapper? Breck couldn't blame him for that, and to tell the truth, it was much more what Morgan was suited for. Breck found himself actually hoping things turned out that way.

Of course, if it did, that meant he would be on his own again. But after the events of the past few years, Breckinridge had begun to wonder if such solitude was just his destiny . . .

After not seeing any more sign of the bandits for several days, Shaftel and the rest of the immigrants began to relax again. Not Breckinridge, though. He remained alert and tried to make sure Moss did, too, at least when Moss wasn't busy daydreaming about the winsome Georgina. The two of them still took turns standing guard at night, sitting up under the wagon where they had pitched their bedrolls and listening intently for any warning of trouble.

When it was Breckinridge's shift, he moved out from under the wagon and sat with his back propped against a wagon wheel and his rifle lying across his lap. He looked out at the landscape northwest of the trail.

There was a half-moon, and of course millions of stars twinkled in the heavens. That was enough light for him to see a dark line bulking along the horizon. Those were mountains, he knew. The trail had been running along parallel with them for quite a few miles. He had looked at the map Otis Shaftel had brought along. The mountains would continue to encroach closer and closer to the trail on both sides until they got to Santa Fe, which was nestled in a high valley between the peaks. The mountains, according to Shaftel's map, were called the Sangre de Cristos. *Blood of Christ.* Breckinridge hoped that no more blood would be spilled before the wagon train reached its destination.

His eyes narrowed suddenly. He thought he had glimpsed something moving out there in the darkened landscape. Probably nothing more than a shifting shadow, maybe a cloud over the moon, he thought as he sat up straighter and picked up the rifle, but he wanted to be sure.

Before he could do anything, a scream ripped through the night.

Breckinridge was on his feet in an instant. The cry had come from the other side of the camp, almost directly across the circle from the wagon where Breck and Moss were spending the night. Breck ran to the front of the vehicle and hurdled the wagon tongue. Flames leaped up across the way, blindingly bright against the surrounding darkness. One of the wagons was on fire.

"Breck!" Moss shouted as he emerged from underneath the wagon. "What's goin' on?"

"Don't know. There's a wagon burnin'—"

People were yelling all around the camp. With that

much racket going on, Breckinridge almost didn't hear the gunshots at first. But he spotted a spurt of orange flame in the shadows outside the camp and recognized it as a muzzle flash, then a second later heard the reports of several rifles being fired. The wagon train was under attack again.

"Head for the cap'n's wagon," he told Moss, knowing that his friend would want to go protect Georgina and her children. "Tell everybody you see to hunt some cover and stay down!"

"You reckon it's that same bunch of bandits?"

"I'd bet on it!" Breckinridge said as he took off at a run toward the burning wagon.

He had to dodge around livestock to get there. The horses were gathered inside a rope corral in the middle of the circle, but the oxen roamed free at night, with no desire to stray. As Breckinridge approached the wagon, he saw that men had gathered around it and were using buckets filled from water barrels to try to put out the flames.

One of the men hurrying toward the wagon suddenly dropped the bucket he was carrying, clapped both hands to his chest, and stumbled on for a few steps before pitching to the ground. Breckinridge had seen enough men shot to know that was what had just happened.

The plan was clear in his mind. One of the outlaws had crept up to the circle of wagons and set one of them on fire while the others remained hidden out in the shadows, ready to use the firelight to aim by as the blaze drew the settlers out into the open. While the immigrants were busy trying to put out the fire, the bandits would cut down as many as they could before sweeping in to overwhelm the others. Then they could loot the wagons and deal with any prisoners at their leisure.

Breckinridge didn't intend to let that happen. One wagon was an acceptable price to pay to save the rest of the train.

"Let it burn!" he bellowed. "Everybody get down! Ambushers outside the circle!"

He saw another muzzle flash, whipped the flintlock to his shoulder, and fired where that flash had been. He couldn't be sure in all the commotion, but he thought he heard a pained shout.

Another man fell, struck by a shot fired from outside, but the settlers were starting to realize what was going on. Some of the men herded women and children toward the center of the circle where they would be safer, while others grabbed rifles and bellied down behind wagon wheels to return the attackers' fire.

Breckinridge figured he could do more good elsewhere. Instead of reloading his rifle, he hurried back across the circle, getting as far away from the garish light of the burning wagon as possible. He crawled under the wagon where his bedroll was spread, left the rifle and his pistols there, along with the powder horn and shot pouch, and crawled out on the other side, armed only with his knife and tomahawk.

He stayed as low as possible as he crawled over the rocks and through the scrubby brush. The bandits were clustered on the other side of the camp, so he circled in that direction. They expected the defenders to hunker down and try to fight them off, Breckinridge figured. They wouldn't be looking for any of the pilgrims to bring the fight to them.

But Breckinridge Wallace was no pilgrim.

The muzzle flashes from the outlaws' guns were as

good as beacons as Breckinridge closed in on them. He had worked his way around so he was behind the attackers. The first man he came to was kneeling behind a slab of rock. Soundlessly, Breck rose from his crawl and poised himself behind the outlaw, who was reloading his rifle. When the man was finished, he started to bring the weapon to his shoulder.

Breckinridge struck first, looping his left arm around the man's neck to jerk him backward as he drove the knife forward with his right hand. The razor-sharp blade went smoothly and easily into the man's back. He spasmed as the tip penetrated his heart and killed him. Breck lowered the body to the ground.

The boom of a nearby rifle told him where he needed to go next. Again he dropped to the ground and approached at a crawl, coming up behind a man who crouched behind a clump of brush. Breckinridge heard the hammer on the man's rifle fall, but instead of a shot, this time there was only the fizzle of a misfire. He lowered the weapon and said, "Lousy damn—"

He died with that curse on his lips and Breckinridge's knife in his heart.

Breckinridge pulled the blade free and dropped the corpse. He tried to remember if eleven or twelve outlaws had escaped from the failed ambush a few days earlier. He couldn't recall and decided it probably wouldn't matter. He had taken care of two and intended to send more of them across the divide tonight.

As he moved along the line of bandits, he realized there were two men kneeling side by side ahead of him. One was always loading while the other was drawing a bead and firing toward the wagons, so they were keeping up a nearly constant barrage of lead. Breckinridge thought about skirting around them, but his natural stubbornness cropped up. Two-to-one odds were nothing he hadn't faced many times before.

He was going to need his tomahawk this time, though. He pulled it from behind his belt and sheathed the knife.

As silent as death, he had just loomed up behind the men when the one who was loading his rifle fumbled the ball and dropped it. He cursed and reached down to pick it up, and as he did, he turned his body just enough to see the huge shape behind them from the corner of his eye. He let out a yell and tried to twist more, but the tomahawk swooped down and smashed his skull with a grisly crunch of bone that sounded like an egg breaking.

Breckinridge swept the 'hawk to his right in a backhanded blow aimed at the other man's head. The shout had given the man enough of a warning that he had time to fall backward on his butt. The tomahawk missed him by inches. With a desperate yell of his own, he yanked a pistol from behind his belt, thrust it at the shape blotting out the stars, and pulled the trigger.

Breckinridge felt the heat of the pistol ball against his cheek, but it missed him. The next instant, the tomahawk in his hand cleaved deep into the top of the outlaw's head, splitting it for several inches and splattering blood and brains. Breck wrenched the 'hawk free.

The shouts and the pistol shot had warned the others that an unexpected threat was among them. Someone charged at Breckinridge and fired another pistol. The flash lit up a bearded, demonic face for a fraction of a second. Breck heard the ball whistle past his ear. He pulled the knife again, this time with his left hand, and stepped up to meet the man's charge. The blade sank into the surprised bandit's belly. Breck ripped it to the side and felt the hot spill of blood and guts over his hand.

With the other hand, the one holding the tomahawk, he grabbed the front of the dying man's shirt and hauled him around, obeying an instinctive warning. Another gun went off. Breckinridge felt the man's body jerk under the ball's impact. He dropped the human shield and threw the tomahawk. It wasn't quite a blind throw, but almost. Despite that, the 'hawk found its target. Breck heard a man gurgle and gasp and collapse.

He had lost count of how many he had killed, and he didn't know how many were left. But from the corner of his eye, silhouetted against the still-burning wagon, he saw several men charging toward the camp. Rather than fleeing from the bloodthirsty devil that had descended upon them out of the night, they were making a last-ditch bid for victory. If they could get into the camp and grab a few hostages, they might still come out of this with their hides intact and some ill-gotten gains.

Breckinridge set off after them.

As he came nearer the wagons, he saw a knot of men locked in a desperate hand-to-hand struggle. He charged up to them, grabbed two men he didn't recognize from the wagon train by the backs of their necks, and slammed their heads together with terrific force. Both dropped like rocks.

Another man broke away and ran toward a wagon. Breckinridge realized it was the vehicle belonging to Otis Shaftel, and as he did, he saw eight-year-old Walter scramble out from under the wagon and try to run. The outlaw darted toward him, reaching for him.

"No!"

That cry came from Georgina. She emerged from under the wagon, too, and got in the outlaw's way. He leered and reached for her, evidently thinking that a woman would be an even better hostage than a kid.

He didn't get the chance to capture her. Charlie Moss, left arm hanging limp and blood staining that shoulder of his shirt, lunged into the open and fired the pistol in his hand. It was a risky shot. Georgina was almost in the line of fire, but not quite. And Moss's aim was true. The bandit's head jerked back, and as he twisted to the ground, Breckinridge saw the line of blood running down from the hole in his forehead.

Georgina grabbed hold of Walter and tugged him back to the wagon, where Moss met them and put his right arm—with the smoking pistol still in his hand—around them and drew them to him. Georgina said, "Charles!" and clung to him, sobbing.

Moss was wounded but not fatally, Breckinridge decided. He didn't know what had happened or why Walter had jumped out from under the wagon like that, but it didn't matter right now. Breck looked around for more outlaws to kill.

There didn't seem to be any. Moss's shot was the last one. Its echoes died away over the New Mexico plains.

Otis Shaftel hurried up to Breckinridge, carrying a rifle. "Is it over?" he asked in a strained voice.

"Seems to be," Breckinridge replied.

"My family—"

"Appear to be all right, thanks to Charlie." Breckinridge changed the subject by asking, "Do you know if any of those murderin' varmints are still alive?"

"I don't know," Shaftel said. He was clearly anxious to get to his daughter-in-law and grandchildren, but he paused long enough to ask, "Why?"

"Because I've got some questions," Breckinridge said, "and, by God, I intend to get some answers."

Chapter 28

Shaftel had to hug Georgina and the children, too. While the wagon train captain was doing that, Breckinridge spoke to Charlie Moss, who had sat down on the lowered tailgate of the Shaftel wagon.

"How bad are you hurt, Charlie?"

"I reckon I'll live," Moss said. "I got shot through the shoulder. Lost quite a bit of blood, and although it pains me to admit it, I reckon I passed out for a while. When I came to, I looked out from under the wagon and saw that varmint about to grab Georgina. I couldn't let that happen." He had placed the empty pistol on the tailgate beside him. As he paused in his answer, he reached up and rubbed a shaky hand over his face. "It makes me kinda sick now to think about what a big risk I took. If I'd missed, I might've hit Georgina."

"You didn't miss," Breckinridge said. "That's all that matters. Well, that and gettin' that shoulder patched up."

"I don't know if this arm will ever work right again.

But if it don't, I reckon that's a small price to pay for Georgina and the kids comin' through this all right."

Walter came over to them then and looked up at Moss with a solemn expression on his young face.

"I'm sorry, Mr. Moss," he said. "I shouldn't have run out from under the wagon like I did. I thought you were dead and couldn't save my mom and sister, so I figured I'd try to lead those bad men away from them. But I should have known you wouldn't let anything happen to them."

"I sure wouldn't," Moss agreed, "but I was layin' there all bloody and passed out, so you didn't have any way of knowin' I *wasn't* dead. I'm not holdin' any grudges against you, Walt, that's for sure."

A smile lit up the youngster's face. Georgina followed him over to the wagon, along with little Sadie. Georgina said, "Walter, don't pester Mr. Moss. He's been hurt."

"Aw, Walt could never pester me," Moss protested. "And I'm just fine. A little light-headed, maybe, from so much of my blood spillin' out, but nothin' to worry about."

He started to slide off the tailgate and stand up, but as soon as his feet hit the ground, he reeled and would have fallen if Breckinridge hadn't been right there to grab him. Georgina got hold of Moss's other arm, and with Breck's help, she got him back on the tailgate.

"You sit right there and don't try to get up again," she told him sternly. "I'm going to clean and bandage that wound."

"I wouldn't argue with her," Breckinridge advised. "She looks like she means business."

"I ain't arguin'," Moss said. "No, sirree."

Breckinridge looked around for Shaftel, nodded to the captain, and said, "We'd best check around and see if we can find one of the varmints still drawin' breath."

"And I need to see what our casualties are," Shaftel said.

They set out on those errands. A number of people from the wagon train were wounded, they discovered, but surprisingly—and thankfully—only one man had been killed.

The two men Breckinridge had grabbed by the necks and slammed their heads together were dead, their skulls shattered. Another man who had been shot in the leg and body was still alive, although he appeared to be in bad shape. Some of the immigrants had pulled him over next to a wagon wheel, propped him up, and tied his arms to the wheel. His head drooped forward. Breck put a hand under his chin and tipped it up. The man blinked at him but couldn't focus.

Breckinridge drew his knife and held the blade in front of the man's eyes.

"If you can't answer my questions, mister, you ain't a bit of good to me and I might as well cut your throat now and get it over with. You understand that?"

That got the wounded outlaw's attention, but he wasn't in the mood to cooperate. His lips drew back from his teeth in a snarl and he cursed bitterly at Breckinridge, concluding by saying, "You can just go to hell!"

"You'll get there before me," Breckinridge said. "But not too soon."

He lowered the knife, rested the flat of the blade on the grisly wound in the man's thigh, and pressed hard. The man's head jerked back against the wagon wheel as he screamed.

"I can make it hurt mighty bad," Breckinridge went on. "Bad enough you'll wish those shots had killed you right then and there. You can make it a lot easier on yourself just by tellin' me a few things."

The man just glared at him, so Breckinridge bore down on the knife again, this time angling the blade enough so the edge cut into raw flesh.

The scream that came from the man's throat was pretty raw, too.

Behind Breckinridge, Otis Shaftel cleared his throat. Breck looked back at him. Shaftel said, "I was going to ask if this is, ah, absolutely necessary, but I suppose it is or you wouldn't be doing it. You've earned the benefit of the doubt from all of us, Breckinridge. Carry on."

Breckinridge nodded and said, "I figure to." He looked at the wounded outlaw again. "Were you and the fellas with you the same bunch that wiped out some teamsters back along the trail and stole their wagons?"

The man gasped, "You can . . . go to—" He caught his breath as Breckinridge started to press on the knife again. "All right, all right! I'll tell you! Yes, it was us. We ambushed those freight wagons, damn you!"

"There were two people travelin' with them. A short, broad fella with a long beard and a good-lookin' young blond woman—"

"C-Carnahan . . . and his whore."

Breckinridge leaned forward with an intent frown on his face.

"Carnahan," he repeated. "You know his name?"

"I . . . ought to. I was there . . . when our boss made the deal with him . . . at Bent's Fort."

"The boss of your gang, you mean?"

The man nodded weakly and said, "Yeah. We were there . . . scoutin' around for some job we could pull . . . and Carnahan said he could help us . . . grab those freight wagons. He said he'd give us a signal . . . when he was on guard duty . . . and we could jump the teamsters . . . without any warnin'. It worked . . ."

The man's head drooped again, then snapped up when Breckinridge put more pressure on the knife.

"So the attack was Carnahan's idea?" That wouldn't surprise Breckinridge in the least, but he wanted to be sure.

"Y-yeah . . . he got a good cut . . . of the loot. I reckon we might have . . . tried to double-cross him . . . but he was too damn . . . crazy. We didn't want to . . . take a chance . . ."

"He wasn't killed, then."

"No. He took his share . . . and the girl . . . and left . . . Said they were still going on . . . to Santa Fe—"

This time when the wounded bandit abruptly stopped talking, it wasn't just his head that sagged. His whole body went limp. Breckinridge took hold of his chin and yanked his head up again. The man's still-open eyes stared sightlessly at him.

Breckinridge grunted and said, "Reckon he must've been hit worse than anybody figured. Probably bleedin' inside somewhere. One way or another, it was enough."

"He's dead?" Shaftel asked.

"Yep," Breckinridge said as he came to his feet. "And no great loss, either. I found out what I needed to know."

* * *

Charlie Moss was still pale and not completely up to snuff the next morning, so he rode on the wagon seat with Georgina instead of riding with Breckinridge and Captain Shaftel. His saddle mount was tied on to the back of the wagon. Breck had a hunch that was the way Moss would travel the rest of the way to Santa Fe.

And although he would be sad to lose such a staunch ally, he thought it would be a good idea if Moss stayed with the Shaftels to recuperate from his injury. If he did, there was a good chance he would wind up marrying Georgina and being the new pa to those kids, and Breckinridge thought that would be a fine thing. Moss wasn't young anymore, and it didn't make sense for him to keep tramping around the wilderness in search of beaver pelts when he could have a lot of good years with a pretty wife and a couple of fine young 'uns. Not that Breck would be interested in such a thing himself, but then, he was still young, despite the past troubles that sometimes made him feel a hundred years old.

If Breckinridge's hunch came true, he would have to go after Jud Carnahan alone once he reached Santa Fe, assuming Carnahan was still there. That was all right. Enough people had been hurt already because of this war between Breck and Carnahan. He wanted to get Carnahan away from everybody else so they finally could have it out between them, alone, with no one else at risk.

Moss's shoulder was heavily bandaged and he had his left arm in a sling as he rode on the wagon seat next to Georgina. Breckinridge ambled alongside on his horse.

"Ought to be easy travelin' the rest of the way into Santa Fe," he commented. "All them bandits are dead, and I don't think we're gonna run into any Indian trouble all the way down here."

"Mr. Kanigher told my father we might still encounter some Navajo," Georgina said.

"Could be. I don't know near as much about the tribes down this way. But I know most Indians will steer clear of a large, well-armed bunch like this one, and if it comes to a fight, well, you folks have been blooded. You'll put up a good battle. I'm bettin' the Navajo will know that and decide it's too much trouble to bother you."

"I hope so," Moss said. "I need to heal up a mite more before I'll be ready for any Indian-fightin'."

"I don't want *any* fighting," Georgina said. "We've had enough of that. I just want to settle down and have a little farm where I can raise my children."

"That sounds mighty nice," Moss said.

She smiled over at him.

"It does, doesn't it? Have you ever thought any about farming, Charles?"

And that's how it gets started, Breckinridge thought with a grin as he heeled his horse into a faster pace and left his friend sitting there on the wagon, looking tongue-tied and uncomfortable but also very interested in whatever Georgina had to say.

St. Louis was the biggest city Breckinridge had ever seen, but Santa Fe was probably the second biggest. It was for sure the oldest, having been founded by the Spanish almost two centuries earlier, according to what Otis Shaftel told Breck. He liked the looks of the place, with its Spanish architecture featuring thick adobe walls and red tile roofs, its narrow, twisting streets, its sprawling array of colors spread across the valley with the majestic Sangre de Cristos rising to the west. Santa Fe had an air of sheer foreignness to it that greatly appealed to Breck, who had always liked seeing and experiencing new things. He doubted if anybody had ever referred to this picturesque place by a name like Damnation Valley.

Although damnation could be found anywhere, he supposed . . .

Otis Shaftel led the wagon train to the big plaza in the middle of town where the governor's palace and all the territorial offices were located. He would have to notify the authorities that the wagons had arrived. They would remain in Santa Fe for a few days and replenish their supplies before beginning the last short leg of the trip, which would take them to the farmland along the Rio Grande where the immigrants would establish their new homes.

While Shaftel was doing that, Breckinridge tied his horse at one of the hitch racks and walked over to the wagon where Charlie Moss stood with Georgina. Moss looked like he wanted to put his arm around her shoulders but couldn't quite bring himself to do that out here in broad daylight.

"I'll get my gear together, Breck," Moss said. "I was just fixin' to tell Georgina and the young 'uns so long—"

"What in blazes are you talkin' about?" Breckinridge broke in. "Where do you think you're goin', Charlie?"

Moss frowned and said, "Why, with you, of course."

Breckinridge shook his head. "No, you ain't. After

we went to as much trouble as we did makin' sure these pilgrims got where they were goin', you think I'd let you run off and leave 'em high and dry when they're this close? Not hardly. You're gonna stay with 'em until they get to those farms they've been talkin' about."

"Now, that just ain't necessary," Moss argued stubbornly. "It'll only take 'em another day or two—"

"A day or two where anything could happen! No, I just wouldn't feel right about it if they didn't have you along to look out for 'em, Charlie. I'm sure the cap'n and Miss Georgina and all the other folks feel the same way."

"We do," Georgina said as she looked up at Moss. "I know you'd be making a sacrifice . . . I mean, another day on this jolting wagon instead of spending the night in an actual bed and sitting in comfortable chairs . . . but if you could see your way clear to do it, Charles . . ."

"Blast it! You know I can't say no to you, Georgina," Moss muttered, chewed his grayish-blond mustache for a second, and then said to Breckinridge, "If you're sure it's all right with you—"

"I'm the one who suggested it, ain't I?" Breckinridge clapped a hand on Moss's uninjured shoulder. "Lookin' out for these folks is your business now, Charlie. You tend to that, and I'll tend to mine."

"Findin' Jud Carnahan," Moss said grimly.

"That's why I came all this way."

"How are you gonna do that?"

"I figure to start askin' around in all the taverns and saloons," Breckinridge said. He would have added something about the whorehouses, since it was likely Carnahan might want to put Ophelia Garwood to work again, but Georgina was standing right there and the two Shaftel youngsters were in the back of the wagon, hanging over the seat and listening.

"Well . . . good luck to you," Moss said, extending his hand. "And if you wind up needin' help, you come find me, hear?"

"I sure will," Breckinridge promised, even though he had no intention of ever doing so.

This was his fight now, his and his alone, and that was how he intended to finish it.

Chapter 29

Santa Fe was a revelation to Breckinridge. He'd heard Spanish being spoken before, but never so much of it, flowing musically around him like a river. It was a lot more soothing than the often guttural languages of the various Indian tribes he'd been around. He didn't understand much of it, so what the folks in Santa Fe were actually saying was mostly a mystery to him, but it sure sounded nice.

He hoped that when he walked past, they weren't saying *Look at the big, dumb American.*

He didn't believe that was what the gals were saying, not with the way they smiled at him but shyly shielded those smiles with the little fans they carried, all the while cutting their eyes around and giggling with their friends. They seemed quite taken with him, enough so that some of their male companions scowled and fingered the handles of the knives thrust behind the fancy sashes they wore around their waists.

Breckinridge hoped that none of them tried to go to carving on him with those pigstickers. The ensuing fight would draw attention to him, and he didn't want that while he was still looking for Jud Carnahan. It wouldn't do for Carnahan to hear gossip about some huge, redheaded gringo getting into a fracas and laying waste to the crowd in the plaza.

He didn't want to get in trouble with the authorities, either. The Mexican soldiers in their fancy uniforms already eyed him suspiciously when he walked past them.

He didn't know any way to get a clue as to Carnahan's whereabouts other than asking questions. He started in a saloon that appeared to be patronized mostly by Americans, judging by the men going in and out of it. Breckinridge joined them.

From the outside, the place looked like a typical cantina, with thick adobe walls and an arched front door. The entrance had batwings across it, though, like an American saloon, and inside the walls were decorated with old wagon wheels and the stuffed heads of bears and deer. The heads were moldering a mite, since whoever stuffed them hadn't done a very good job. The smell they gave off was masked by the mingled odors of beer, whiskey, piss, vomit, and long-unwashed human flesh. The miasma was pretty potent, but certainly nothing Breckinridge hadn't encountered many times before.

Despite the fact that it was the middle of the day, the saloon was pretty busy. Men lined the bar on the left-hand wall and sat at tables scattered across the big room. Card games went on at a couple of the tables, but mostly the men were drinking, talking, laughing, fondling the sultry, brown-skinned serving girls, and watching a girl dance at the back of the room, accompanied by two middle-aged Mexican men with guitars.

The dancer sported a wild mane of curly, midnight

black hair that she tossed back and forth as she whirled and gyrated. Her white blouse was a stark contrast to her brown skin, and it was cut so low it seemed that her exertions were going to make her ample breasts pop out of it at any second. She whipped her multicolored skirt back and forth and lifted it enough to expose bare feet and equally bare, flashing brown legs.

Breckinridge wasn't sure if the short, heavyset, dark-haired man behind the bar was Mexican or gringo. He could have been either. But there was a friendly smile on his round face when Breck made his way up to the bar.

"What can I do for you, mister?"

"Beer," Breckinridge said.

"Sure you wouldn't rather have tequila? Or maybe pulque? I've got a jug that's just about down to the worm."

Breckinridge didn't have any idea what the fella was talking about. He said, "Just the beer."

"Of course. Every man has a right to name his own poison."

While the bartender was getting the beer, Breckinridge turned his head to look at the dancer. He couldn't help but admire the effort she was making. A fine sheen of sweat covered her face. From time to time, a big enough drop of the moisture collected to fall from her chin into the dark valley of her breasts. Breck had to swallow hard when he noticed that.

"Lupe is spectacular, isn't she?" the bartender asked as he placed a wooden bucket of beer in front of Breckinridge.

"She sure is." Breckinridge forced himself to turn back to the bar. He lifted the bucket with both hands and took a deep swig from it.

"She's not for sale, though. None of the girls who work here are. I don't mind if the customers' hands stray. That's only to be expected. But anybody who wants more than that can go to the Black Bull or one of the other houses."

Breckinridge licked warm beer suds off his upper lip and said, "The Black Bull?"

"El Toro Negro, it used to be called when old Hernandez owned it. On account of the big, black wooden bull he used as a sign. But since that gringo bought it, folks have started using the gringo name."

Breckinridge found that interesting, but before he could ask any more questions, an angry voice spat a loud curse that went through the whole room, then the same man said, "Damn it, I've told you before, you can't bring that redskin in here! Greasers are one thing, but a savage is another!"

Breckinridge turned his head to look toward the entrance. The guitar music had fallen silent. The dancer stood with her braceleted arms hanging at her sides as her impressive chest rose and fell with her breathing. The men at the tables and the bar were looking around as well.

An Indian stood just inside the batwings. He was tall and broad-shouldered, a very impressive physical specimen despite the fact that he was well into middle age. His hawkish face was completely impassive. Slowly, he lifted brawny arms and crossed them over his chest, making the long fringes on the sleeves of his buckskin shirt sway. Breckinridge recognized him as a Crow and figured it was probably unusual to see a member of that tribe this far south.

As the expectant silence hung in the room, the Indian said in a deep voice, "Umm."

"As my friend has just demonstrated with that eloquent comment, he is hardly a savage. Though he lacks a formal education, due to the circumstances of his birth, he is in many ways the most learned man I know."

That comment, also in a powerful voice, seemed to come out of nowhere. Breckinridge frowned in confusion, unable to figure out who had spoken.

A man had risen to his feet at one of the tables. He was an American, wearing rough town clothes, which led Breckinridge to figure he worked somewhere here in Santa Fe. A big nose and a thick, drooping black mustache dominated his craggy face. He took a step forward and pointed a blunt finger.

"It's bad enough when a freak like you comes in here. I'm not drinking with a heathen around!"

"I daresay he's more spiritual in his own way than you are, so I'd be careful who I was calling a heathen."

Those powerful tones once again seemed to come from empty air.

Then a figure that made Breckinridge's eyes widen in surprise stepped into view.

The man wore buckskins and a broad-brimmed felt hat, carried a pistol and knife at his waist, and had a rifle cradled in the crook of his left arm.

But he was no bigger than a child, and everything from his clothes to his weapons had either been made to fit his size or altered to do so. Like the Crow warrior, he was middle-aged, with a lightly grizzled beard curling on his chin and jaws. He had the arms, shoulders, and torso of a full-grown man, and his legs appeared sturdy, too, just much shorter than normal.

At the sight of the man, something stirred in Breckinridge's memory. He knew he had never seen anybody as distinctive as the little man, but he struck Breck as familiar somehow.

The black-mustached man who was offended by the Indian's presence said, "You're the one who'd better be careful, runt. I'll pick you up and toss you back out in the plaza like a little doll some kid left behind."

The Indian said, "Ummm."

The little man lifted a hand toward his companion and said, "I know, he's quite obnoxious, but we came to Santa Fe on business, not to give ill-mannered louts a lesson on etiquette and civilized behavior. Although I agree with you, he could use one."

The angry man stepped closer and demanded, "Are you callin' me names?"

"Umm," from the Crow.

The little man laughed. "Yes, you're right, Nighthawk. If he possessed even a modicum of intelligence, he'd *know* whether or not he was being called names, wouldn't he?"

"That does it!" the man roared. "I'm gonna twist your head off, you little pip-squeak!"

He started to lunge at the little man. Instantly, the Crow warrior lost his casual pose. He snarled, and his hand plucked a wicked-looking tomahawk from behind his belt. At the same time, the little man drew his pistol with surprising speed.

Neither of them had to use those weapons, though, because as soon as Breckinridge heard the name *Nighthawk*, he had realized how come he seemed to know this unlikely pair. Three long, quick strides while everything else was happening took him across the room. He looped his left arm around the angry man's neck and jerked him back. Breck's right hand held his knife, which he pressed to the man's throat.

"You're a damned fool, mister," he said. "You'd be better off if I cut your throat right now. More than likely, these two would kill you their own selves, but if you got lucky and managed to hurt 'em, you'd have their best friend huntin' you down to settle the score. You know who he is?"

The man made a noise, but he couldn't actually talk with the razor-sharp edge of Breckinridge's knife pressed against his Adam's apple that way. Not without risking the blade slicing into his throat.

"Their friend's name is Preacher," Breckinridge went on. "Does the thought of havin' Preacher after you make somethin' warm run down your leg? It ought to. You see why I said you'd be better off if I cut your throat and got it over with." Breck moved the knife, just a little. "Why don't you say you're sorry, and then maybe you can get outta here without embarrassin' yourself even more."

Breckinridge felt the man swallow hard. Then he said, "I . . . I'm sorry, mister. I didn't realize . . . who you were."

"Yes, because there are so many who resemble my Crow friend and me out here on the frontier," the little man said. "It's easy to see why you would make such a mistake." He looked at Breckinridge and nodded. "You can let him go. He's not going to cause any more difficulty."

Breckinridge lowered his arm. The man stumbled forward a step, short of breath and feeling the strain of coming within a whisker of being killed.

"To show how magnanimous my friend and I are, there are no hard feelings," the little man went on. "Isn't that true, Nighthawk?"

"Umm," the Indian said.

"Yes, such generosity is perhaps more than he deserves, but it's up to us to be *big* about it."

The Crow warrior half turned, pointed at the door, and said, "Umm."

"I'd do what he says, if I were you," the little man added.

The angry man, apparently no longer angry, started to shuffle toward the door. But then he stiffened suddenly and clawed at the pistol at his waist.

The move didn't take Breckinridge by surprise. He still held his knife. Almost faster than the eye could follow, he brought it up and crashed the brass ball at the end of its handle against the back of the man's head. The man's knees buckled and he went down. Breck prodded him in the ribs with a boot toe, maybe a little harder than was absolutely necessary to make sure he was out cold.

The rotund bartender lifted his voice and said, "Some of you boys drag him out and leave him in the alley. Can't have him cluttering up the plaza."

Several of the customers took hold of the unconscious man's arms and legs and lifted him from the floor. As they carried him out, the little man and the Indian came up to Breckinridge, who was sheathing his knife again.

"You have our gratitude, my young, fiery-haired friend," the little man said, "but it really wasn't necessary for you to come to our assistance. Nighthawk and I could have handled that cretin."

"Yeah, I know," Breckinridge said with a grin, "but

he got under my skin." He stuck out his hand. "You'd be Audie, I reckon. My name's Breckinridge Wallace."

The little man cocked his head to the side for a second before he shook Breckinridge's hand. Breck's big paw completely engulfed the smaller hand, but Audie's grip was surprisingly strong.

"Indeed I am, and my companion is Nighthawk, as I surmise you're already aware. From your mention of Preacher, I assume you've made his acquaintance and that's how you know who we are?"

"I ran into him a while back. We were on the same side in a little scrap a long ways north of here. I remember him tellin' me about the two of you. I said then that I'd sure admire to run into you one of these days."

"And now you have, in Santa Fe, of all places. This isn't our usual stomping grounds, but Nighthawk and I, we like to roam far afield from time to time."

"Umm," Nighthawk said.

"Come on over to the bar and have a drink with me," Breckinridge invited.

"It would be my pleasure. Nighthawk, being of the aboriginal persuasion, does not partake."

Breckinridge's grin widened. "Preacher said you used to be a professor and still talked like one."

"A vestige of a previous life," Audie said with a wave of his hand.

One of the serving girls intercepted them and steered them toward a vacant table. She had Breckinridge's unfinished bucket of beer and a cup of wine for Audie. Breck dug into a pocket for a coin so he could pay for the drinks, but behind the bar, the bartender waved off the gesture.

"Mr. Stanton and I are old friends," Audie explained as he and Nighthawk sat down at the table with

Breckinridge. "Despite running a saloon in this largely untamed territory, he's an educated man, and he says that the occasional conversation with me is enough repayment for whatever libations we consume."

"Them are expensive words, I reckon. I don't quite know what all of 'em mean, exactly, but I can figure 'em out."

"That's because you have a keen native intelligence. I can tell." Audie took a sip of his wine, then asked, "What brings you to Santa Fe, Breckinridge?"

Having lifted the bucket of beer, Breckinridge took a healthy swallow from it before answering. Then he lowered the bucket, wiped the back of his hand across his mouth, and said, "I came here to kill a man who's badly in need of killin'."

Chapter 30

That blunt statement didn't seem to surprise either of Breckinridge's companions. Nighthawk had lived his entire life on the frontier, and Audie had been out here for a long time. Both men knew what a harsh, violent, and unforgiving place it could be.

And they knew that, as Breckinridge said, there were some men that just needed killing.

Audie asked, "Who might this man be?"

"A fella name of Jud Carnahan," Breckinridge replied. "I met him in St. Louis last year, but we didn't really have our first run-in until we were both up in the Yellowstone country. Since then he's hurt or killed a whole bunch of folks I care about."

"I see. Do you know for certain that he's here in Santa Fe?"

"I reckon not," Breckinridge admitted. "But I know he was headed here. I've been on his trail for months now, and he's done a lot of wanderin' around, tryin' to throw me off. By now there's a good chance he figures he's given me the slip, so he can afford to stay in one place for a while." Breck paused, then added, "Carnahan's got a girl with him, too."

"Ah," Audie said, raising an eyebrow. "Someone who's special to you?"

"No. There ain't really anybody like that right now. She's just more of a friend. But she don't deserve what he's been doin' with her, neither. Nobody does." Breckinridge's hands clenched into fists. "He was sellin' turns with her to the bullwhackers he traveled with for a while, before he led those fellas into an ambush by a gang of outlaws who wound up murderin' all of 'em."

"Umm," Nighthawk said.

"I agree," Audie said. "This man Carnahan sounds as if he deserves whatever happens to him."

"No doubt in my mind about that."

"Or in mine. What does he look like?"

Breckinridge described Carnahan, then added Ophelia's description, too. Audie and Nighthawk looked at each other, which made Breck lean forward in his chair as excitement sprang to life inside him.

"Do you happen to have seen the varmint?" he asked.

Audie hesitated. Nighthawk said, "Umm," and the little man nodded.

"Nighthawk and I make it a practice to mind our own business," he said, "but he believes, and I concur, that we should share a bit of information with you. Several nights ago, we entered an establishment known as the Black Bull. Are you acquainted with it?"

Breckinridge glanced at the bartender and said, "I've heard of it, but I ain't been there and don't really know anything about it."

"The current proprietor, from what I gather, hasn't owned it for long. We got a good look at him the other night, and he matches your description of Jud Carnahan down to the smallest detail."

"Umm," Nighthawk said again.

"I'm getting to that. I hesitate to say this, Breckinridge, since I'm not certain how deeply it will affect you, but the young woman you mentioned was there, too."

Breckinridge blew out a breath and nodded. "Actually, I reckon it's a relief to know that she's still alive."

"Perhaps. But as far as I could tell, she was serving as the, ah, madam of the place, being in charge of the other . . . young ladies of the evening."

"She's runnin' the whores?"

"To put it bluntly, yes. And Carnahan was working behind the bar, as well as being in overall charge of the place." Audie raised a finger. "You understand, this understanding was gleaned from limited information, because we weren't there for very long. It was a more sordid venue than we tend to frequent, and some of the ladies were quite upset at the prospect of sharing their dubious charms with a native or a person of my, ah, stature. Not that Nighthawk and I had any intention of arranging for their services. It was more of a stray . . . wandering-in, so to speak. We departed as soon as we realized what a wretched hive of scum and villainy it really was."

Breckinridge didn't care whether his two new-found friends had been wanting whores or not. What mattered to him was knowing where he could find Carnahan and Ophelia. He was sad to hear that she had lowered herself to being a madam, but given the ordeal she had been through, he wasn't really surprised.

He put his hands on the table and got ready to push himself to his feet.

"Reckon it's time I go pay a visit to this Black Bull place."

"Hold on a moment," Audie said as he raised a hand. "I should give you a word of warning, Breckinridge. When Nighthawk and I were in there, I saw Carnahan talking in a quite friendly and animated fashion with Captain Armando Consalvo."

"Who?"

"Captain Consalvo is an officer at the Mexican garrison here," Audie explained. "He's very close with the governor, and he's a man you don't want to have for an enemy if you're going to be in Santa Fe for very long. Also, he's a man with very healthy appetites, for young ladies, to be sure, but especially for money and power. Understand, I know him only by reputation. We're not personally acquainted. The captain and I don't travel in the same, ah, circles."

"You're saying he's crooked as a dog's hind leg."

"Not by Mexican government standards. The wheels of their bureaucracy can't turn without considerable greasing, sometimes in the form of favors traded back and forth but often by outright and blatant bribery."

Breckinridge sank back in his chair and frowned in thought.

"You think Carnahan is payin' off this Captain Consalvo to protect him?"

"Paying off . . . or perhaps Consalvo is actually a silent partner in the Black Bull. They had the look of business associates sharing a friendly talk together." Audie laced his fingers together on the table and gave Breckinridge a solemn look. "Either way, the situation is greatly complicated for you. You can't simply go in there and kill Carnahan, as you might be able to get away with it if your enemy was someone not connected with a Mexican official. The laws around here are enforced rather laxly, even the one against murder. It all depends on who you know."

"Umm," Nighthawk said.

"Or who you're willing to pay off—that's exactly right, my friend," Audie said.

"I can't let Carnahan get away with everything he's done," Breckinridge insisted.

"That's not what I'm suggesting. But perhaps you should wait a bit and try to think of a different approach." The two older men traded glances again. "And perhaps Nighthawk and I might be of assistance to you."

Breckinridge shook his head. "I was just thinkin' earlier today that this was my fight, and I needed to handle it alone. You fellas don't even know Carnahan."

"You said you and Preacher fought on the same side, correct?"

"We did," Breckinridge admitted.

"That makes you Preacher's friend, and any friend of Preacher's . . ." Audie smiled and left the rest of it unsaid.

"Well, maybe you're right," Breckinridge allowed. "If Carnahan's bought this whorehouse and got himself tied up with some Mexican official, it ain't likely he plans on leavin' Santa Fe anytime soon."

"Very doubtful that he would," Audie agreed.

"And he don't know I'm in town or even still on his trail. That gives me some time to think about it, like you said. Problem is, I've always been better at fightin' than thinkin'."

"I'm sure there'll be plenty of fighting before this is over."

Nighthawk nodded and said, "Umm."

The air inside the Black Bull was thick with the smells of smoke, liquor, sweat, and lust. Ophelia Garwood picked up a thin black cigar that was smoldering at the edge of the bar and took a deep drag on it, drawing the smoke from the peppery Mexican tobacco into her lungs. A few months ago, she had never smoked a cigar or even dreamed of indulging in such a vice, she thought.

But since then, she had indulged in plenty of vices she had never dreamed of, including some she hadn't even known existed. None of it had been her choice, of course, but she had learned not to worry about that and just survive, even if it meant hardening her heart to a chunk of stone.

Carnahan strolled along the bar and stopped across the hardwood from her. He looked very self-satisfied and smug, as he usually did these days. He had traded in his buckskins for a fine Mexican suit with a lot of velvet trim and fancy embroidery. He poured himself a shot of tequila, threw it back, and said, "You need to speak to the girls. They're taking too much time with their customers."

"Most of them were whoring long before we got here, Jud," Ophelia said. "I think they know their business." She started to lift the cheroot to her lips again.

Carnahan reached across the bar and grabbed her wrist, holding it in a strong enough grip that she winced and almost dropped the cigar.

"Don't try to tell *me* how to run *my* business," he told her, still smiling but with a warning tone of menace in his voice.

"Sorry," she said, trying not to let him hear the pain his grip was causing her.

"We're here to make money, whatever that takes." He let go of her arm. She stepped back a little as he poured himself another drink, then went on, "Speaking of that, Captain Consalvo will be dropping by here tonight. He'll expect to spend some time with you."

"Of course," Ophelia murmured.

She hated the arrogant Mexican officer, but she had to admit, Consalvo wasn't as bad as some of the men Carnahan had forced her to be with. He didn't smell all that bad, especially compared to the men who had taken turns with her when they were traveling with the freight wagons. Bullwhackers, they were called, and they smelled even worse than the bulls they drove with their whips and sticks. Consalvo wasn't as rough with her as Carnahan had been, either, when he'd finally gotten around to raping her. The officer just had an air of casual corruption about him that turned her stomach. Given the chance, she would have gladly cut his throat, just on general principles, because he had allied himself with Carnahan.

It was different with Carnahan. She wouldn't cut his throat . . . not until she had spent hours or even days torturing him for everything he had done, from killing her father to turning her into . . . what she was now.

She turned away from the bar. The long Mexican-style skirt she wore swirled slowly around her legs. She wore the same sort of lightweight, low-cut, off-the-shoulder blouse the Mexican girls wore, too.

The outfit looked good on her, good enough that men overlooked the slight limp she had from the foot that had never healed completely after the long flight away from the trading post had damaged it so badly. She had to bandage it every day and figured she would lose the foot eventually, but she had lost so much more she didn't see how it really mattered.

Her eyes scanned the room as she moved along the bar. She was still pretty new at this, but she had learned a great deal already. She knew how to watch the girls, to watch how they acted with the customers and make sure they weren't trying to set up some rendezvous outside the Black Bull, so they wouldn't have to share the money with Carnahan. Nobody could be trusted less than a whore.

She watched for signs of potential trouble, too, like a man who might get too rough with one of the girls. That was pretty difficult to do, but it *was* possible. Sometimes a man came into the Black Bull looking for a fight, too, and Ophelia thought she spied one of them now. He was standing at the end of the bar, his shoulders hunched, his head down, staring with peculiar intensity at the half-full glass of tequila in front of him. Ophelia saw his lips moving, and as she came closer, she heard him muttering to himself.

Most of the words she could make out were curses. Once such vile language would have shocked her, but she was beyond that. She paid a little more attention, though, when she heard him say, ". . . kill him! Big redheaded son of a . . ."

The voice trailed off into more imprecations. Ophelia glanced around the room, searching for any redheaded men. The mutterer, who had a big nose and an untidy black mustache, might have followed someone in here who he had a grudge against. He could be trying to work up the courage to make a try for that enemy with a gun or blade.

She turned around and went back up the bar. Carnahan still stood where he had been a few minutes earlier.

"Jud, you see that fellow down there with the black mustache, the one who's bent over the bar? He's talking to himself about killing somebody."

Carnahan scowled. "Not in my place, he's not going to. I'll throw him out."

"Wouldn't it be a good idea to find out who he's mad at first? Maybe it's not even anybody here. It might be somebody who's still back wherever he came from, and you'd be running off a paying customer for no good reason."

Carnahan frowned in thought for a couple of seconds, then a grin appeared under his bushy beard.

"You're learning," he said. "You're a smart girl. See, I told you you were cut out for running a whorehouse and a saloon. I'll go talk to that gent."

Ophelia drifted along in front of the bar as Carnahan approached the man at the end.

"You look like you're upset about something, mister," Carnahan said as he rested his hands on the bar in front of the man. "I hope it's not because you haven't been treated right in here."

"What?" The man looked up, seemingly confused. Then he shook his head and went on, "No, it's not anything that happened in here. I had a run-in earlier in another place with some big, no-good bastard. Snuck up behind me and held a knife to my throat, he did, just because I didn't want to drink with a blasted redskin and a litle freak."

"What did he look like?" Ophelia asked abruptly, surprising both Carnahan and the stranger. She had heard the man mention red hair, and a wild thought had just forced itself into her head.

"He was big. Tall as a tree. Shoulders as broad as an ax handle. And he had shaggy red hair."

Carnahan started to breathe harder. He leaned forward with his hands on the bar and asked in a taut voice, "Do you know his name?"

"I didn't at the time, but later, after he'd run me out of the place like I wasn't any better than a blasted dog, I heard somebody say it. They heard him introduce himself to the freak and the Indian. He called himself Breckinridge Wallace."

Chapter 31

Ophelia's heart slugged heavily in her chest. For a moment, she couldn't believe she'd actually heard what the man just said.

Carnahan looked just as shocked as Ophelia felt. And being Jud Carnahan, he reacted violently. He reached across the bar, grabbed the front of the man's shirt, and jerked him forward.

"What did you say?" Carnahan demanded.

The man looked angry and frightened at the same time. He had good reason for the latter, because Carnahan appeared ready to commit murder. After a moment, the man found his voice and was able to say, "Wallace . . . he told the others his name was Breckinridge Wallace."

"You never heard the name before?"

"No. Should I have?"

Carnahan let go of the man. The big, blunt-fingered hands smoothed the man's shirt. Since settling in Santa Fe and buying this brothel, Carnahan had made an effort to become more civilized and act like a businessman, if not actually a respectable one, Ophelia knew. But that was difficult for someone with Carnahan's brutal, impulsive nature.

"Sorry, friend," Carnahan muttered. "You're drinking on the house tonight."

That made the man perk up some. "Thanks," he said, licking his lips.

"You're sure about the name you heard?"

"Yeah. It's not a name you'd easily mistake. Just like anybody who ever saw him before would recognize that big ox." A nervous expression suddenly appeared on the man's face. "Say, Wallace isn't a friend of yours, is he?"

"A friend?" Carnahan grunted and shook his head. "No, he's not a friend. In fact, I'd say he's about as much of an enemy as I've ever had. He's been nothing but a thorn in my side for a long time now!"

A shrewd, calculating smile replaced the apprehensive look on the man's face. He said, "If you ever get ready to pluck that thorn and need a hand doing it, I'd be obliged if you'd think about me. I'd like nothing more than a chance to even the score with Wallace."

That suggestion certainly got Carnahan's interest, Ophelia saw. Carnahan's eyes narrowed as he said, "Is that so? Would you happen to know anybody else who might like to throw in with us?"

"I know several who might be interested . . . if you could sweeten the pot by promising them some time with your girls without having to pay."

"Oh, I can promise that, all right." Carnahan looked at Ophelia. "Isn't that right?"

"Whatever you say, Jud," she replied. She wasn't going to argue with him and risk having his rage directed at her.

At the same time, her heart was still thudding in her chest, and for the first time in months, she was thinking about something other than just surviving to the end of another day. There was only one reason for Breckinridge Wallace being in Santa Fe: he had tracked them here and was still after Carnahan. Although she didn't know the details, she was aware that Breck had had a serious grudge against Carnahan even before the man showed up at the trading post on the Yellowstone. It had to do with the injury to Morgan Baxter and something that had happened with some Indians Breck had spent the previous winter with.

She wondered suddenly if Breckinridge knew she was still with Carnahan. Would it make a difference if he did? Would he want to help her if he got the chance?

After everything that had happened, did it even matter? She couldn't go back to her sisters now, not after all the degrading things that had happened. She was soiled, damaged beyond repair, and always would be. She knew Desdemona and Eugenia loved her and probably would welcome her back, but they would always know what a sordid creature she had become.

Ophelia brushed aside in her mind the fact that none of it had been her fault.

So she couldn't do anything to oppose Carnahan on her own account. But what about for Breckinridge? He had never done anything except try to help her family. He didn't deserve to be murdered, and that was exactly what Carnahan had in mind. She knew that.

"What's your name, mister?" Carnahan was saying to the stranger.

"O'Leary," the man replied. "Terence O'Leary."

Carnahan shook hands with him across the bar and said, "Round up those friends of yours and meet me back here. Where was it you had that trouble with Wallace?"

"A saloon called The Territorial. Used to be El Grande, when a Mex owned it. It's a few blocks from here."

Carnahan nodded. "I've seen the place. Do you think Wallace will still be there?"

"I've no way of knowing," O'Leary said, spreading his hands. "But he might be. If he isn't, maybe somebody there will know where to find him." An ugly grin stretched the man's thin lips under the ragged mustache. "Are you gonna ambush him tonight?"

"There's no point in wasting time. Besides, Wallace would do the same to me, if he had the chance."

"We, ah, haven't talked about money yet."

"If things turn out the way I want, you'll be well paid. You can split it up with your friends however you want, or just let them collect on some favors from my girls if you'd rather do that. Whatever arrangement you make with them is up to you. But don't worry, Terence, I'll take care of you."

When Ophelia heard Carnahan say that, she had a pretty good idea what he meant. Once Breckinridge Wallace was dead, more than likely Carnahan would double-cross O'Leary and kill him, too, to shut him up and to keep from having to pay him. Captain Consalvo would see to it that nothing ever came of that.

O'Leary was eager, though, and none too bright, evidently, because he didn't seem to hear the same hidden threat in Carnahan's voice that Ophelia did. He nodded again and hurried out of the Black Bull.

Carnahan looked at Ophelia and said, "Can you

believe that Wallace is still on our trail after all this time? I thought we'd lost him!"

"He's determined, I suppose."

"A stubborn fool, is more like it. It's time we deal with him, once and for all. Then he'll never bother us again."

From the sound of it, Carnahan was the fool. He had deluded himself into believing that he was her partner, that she wanted Breckinridge disposed of as much as he did.

And yet, as she stood there watching Carnahan smirk in self-satisfaction, she couldn't help but wonder if he was right. Was she going to do anything to stop his plan? She honestly didn't know. It would be simpler to just let things go on as they had been. At least she would know what to expect. If anything happened to Breckinridge, maybe it *was* his fault for being so stubborn. Muleheaded, her father would have called it.

Thinking about her father made Ophelia's breath catch in her throat. What would Absalom Garwood's reaction be if he knew she was considering standing aside and letting a good man be killed? She thought she knew, and that knowledge almost forced a sob out of her.

"What's wrong with you?" Carnahan snapped. "You look like you're about to start crying again, like you used to."

Ophelia shook her head and forced the emotions down.

"No," she said, "don't worry about that. I'm not going to cry."

Never again, she vowed. Tears solved nothing.

But she wasn't going to let Carnahan get away with murdering Breckinridge Wallace, either.

* * *

Audie claimed to know the best place to eat in Santa Fe, so Breckinridge went with him and Nighthawk to a small, hole-in-the-wall café run by a spindly, solemn Mexican man and his much more cheerful and abundantly framed wife. The food was almost spicy enough to make Breck's hair stand up on end, but once he got used to it, he found the various dishes delicious. Tortillas and beans with some sort of sauce Audie called mole rounded things out. Breck was stuffed when they finally left.

"Probably shouldn't have done that," he said as he patted his full belly. "I figured on havin' a look at that Black Bull place this evenin', but if it came down to a fight with Carnahan, I ain't sure I could move fast enough to keep him from killin' me."

"Umm," Nighthawk said.

"There's no need for comments about condemned men and last meals," Audie told the big Crow warrior. "Yes, we ate heartily, that's true, but . . . On the other hand, there *is* that old proverb that says to eat, drink, and be merry, for tomorrow—" He stopped short and waved a hand. "We're getting very far ahead of ourselves here. Breckinridge, I suggest postponing any confrontation with Jud Carnahan and getting a good night's sleep tonight instead. Nighthawk and I are staying at a stable not far from here where our horses are also domiciled. The hotelkeepers hereabouts are loath to allow one of Nighthawk's hue to rent a room, which is ludicrous considering how vermin-infested many of their more highly regarded guests are. I daresay both of us probably bathe more often and subscribe to higher standards of cleanliness than many of the people who pass through Santa Fe, and the local citizens, as well."

"Uh, sure, I can sleep in a stable," Breckinridge said, wondering how Audie packed so dang many words into such a small body. "Slept in lots of worse places, I reckon."

"Actually, it's the hayloft we'll be sleeping in."

"Fine with me."

Audie led the way. Breckinridge realized that between being in a town for a change, instead of out on the trail, and having eaten so much for supper, he wasn't quite as diligent about keeping an eye out behind him as he normally was. But under the circumstances, he didn't think it was likely to hurt anything.

Captain Consalvo showed up early in the evening. Ophelia showed him to a fairly isolated table in a corner of the barroom and said, "I'll fetch you a bottle of wine." She knew his tastes ran to that, rather than tequila or whiskey.

Before she could turn away, Consalvo looped an arm around her waist and pulled her onto his lap. He caressed her blatantly, intimately, through the thin garments as he said, "One of the other girls can bring the wine. You will sit here with me and we will enjoy our time together, eh?"

Ophelia signaled to a girl whose raven hair was so long it hung down below her waist. When she came over, Ophelia told her, "A bottle of wine for *el capitán*."

"Do not try to ply me with too much to drink, *bonita*," the officer said with a chuckle. "I would not want to go to sleep before we have enjoyed all the delicacies the evening has to offer."

Ophelia was glad the candlelight in this corner was rather dim. That made it less likely Consalvo would see her roll her eyes at his smirking comments.

She didn't care for his wandering hands, but since she had endured much worse, she didn't say anything about it. She was glad, though, when the long-haired girl, whose name was Belita, came over with the bottle of wine and two glasses on a tray. Ophelia used that as an excuse to slip off Consalvo's lap.

"We'll drink first, before we go upstairs," she said.

Consalvo shrugged. He looked a little impatient, but not enough to argue.

She poured the wine for them and sat down on one of the other chairs instead of in Consalvo's lap. They could make the bottle last quite a while if she worked at it.

Carnahan came over a few minutes later and greeted Consalvo, saying, "Good evening, Captain. I hope Ophelia is treating you well, as usual."

"But of course," Consalvo replied. "One so charming could never do less."

Ophelia managed to smile at the compliment. Her smile faltered as she spotted Terence O'Leary. The man had just come into the Black Bull and was looking around, no doubt for Carnahan. O'Leary had been here several times since his first conversation with Carnahan that afternoon. On a couple of those occasions, he'd had other men with him . . . large, hard-featured men, some Mexican, some American, but all of them looked like cutthroats to Ophelia. She had figured it was only a matter of time before

Carnahan began putting together a gang to do his criminal bidding, as he had always done in the past, and now the news that Breckinridge Wallace was in Santa Fe had prompted Carnahan to get on with that.

O'Leary saw Carnahan standing next to the table where Ophelia and Consalvo were sitting and started across the room toward them. He came up and said, "I need to talk to you, Mr. Carnahan."

Carnahan was obviously annoyed by the interruption, but he said, "Excuse me, Captain," and turned to grip O'Leary's arm and lead the man several steps away from the table.

O'Leary leaned in and talked quickly. Ophelia couldn't make out many of the words, but she thought she heard O'Leary say, "Found him."

That had to refer to Breckinridge Wallace. Ophelia tensed inside. She had hoped that Carnahan wouldn't get in any hurry to go after Breck, which would give her a chance to find him first and warn him. Fate had dumped a willing and eager accomplice in Carnahan's lap, though, in the form of Terence O'Leary, and Carnahan wanted to take advantage of that stroke of luck.

Which meant that if she was going to help Breckinridge, she would have to do it quickly.

"I'm sorry, Captain, I suddenly don't feel well," she said.

"Oh?" Consalvo didn't look or sound particularly sympathetic. "A shame. You should rest tonight . . . after we have had our visit."

Carnahan turned back to the table and said, "I have to go, Captain."

"Trouble?" Consalvo murmured.

"Nothing you need concern yourself with."

"Be careful, *mi amigo*. Our friendship has been profitable for both of us so far. I would hate for anything to disturb it."

"Nothing will," Carnahan stated bluntly. "I just have to squash a rat, that's all."

"If you need any help with your . . . rat killing . . . my men and I stand ready."

Carnahan shook his head. "*Muchas gracias*, but I can handle it."

He nodded to Consalvo, ignored Ophelia, and strode away with O'Leary. They were on their way to kill Breckinridge, Ophelia thought. She was sure of it.

She slid back her chair and said, "I'm going to get a bottle of whiskey."

"I prefer wine," Consalvo said.

"I need something stronger," she told him, then headed for the bar. She knew he was frowning after her but didn't look back. She wasn't really after whiskey but needed something to allay his suspicions for a few moments.

When she reached the end of the bar, she ducked through the door there into a short rear hall with doors on both sides and at the other end. She hurried to that one and opened it to step out into the alley at the back of the building. Her hastily formed plan was to hurry around to the plaza, follow Carnahan and O'Leary, and hope for a chance to warn Breckinridge, even if it was just a shout.

She had taken only a few limping steps through the thick shadows when a hand closed around her throat with terrific force. Whoever had grabbed her swung her around and slammed her against the building's adobe wall. The back of Ophelia's head struck hard and the impact made her senses reel.

An all-too-familiar voice hissed at her. "Thought you could sneak out and go warn that big bastard, didn't you? I knew you never really came around to being on my side, you bitch." Carnahan slammed her against the wall again. "You turned out to be a pretty good whore, but there are a lot of good whores in the world. Time for you and me to part ways, girl."

Ophelia heard the finality in his voice and knew what he meant by that. She tried to fight him, kicking at him and hammering punches against his head, but Carnahan just laughed off her efforts. She figured he was going to choke her to death, but instead he crashed her head into the adobe . . . again and again . . .

When he finally let go of her, she slid down the wall and wound up in a limp, huddled heap on the filthy, hard-packed dirt of the alley. Carnahan turned and walked away, bound on his errand of vengeance.

He never saw the slender figure that darted out of the shadows and knelt next to Ophelia.

Chapter 32

The big, cavernous stable was constructed of rough planks sawed from logs brought down from the wooded slopes of the Sangre de Cristos, unlike so many of the adobe buildings in Santa Fe. There was a hostler on duty when Breckinridge, Audie, and Nighthawk got there, a friendly young man named Fernando, whose father owned the business. He was more than happy to rent space not only for Breck's horses but also for Breck himself to sleep.

"A good lad, Fernando," Audie commented as they made themselves comfortable in the hayloft. "Smart and ambitious, as well. He'll be one of the town's leading businessmen someday, I expect."

Breckinridge didn't know about that. He was tired enough by now to be a little groggy. He stretched out in the piles of hay, hoped there weren't too many little critters lurking in it to bite him, and fell sound asleep.

It seemed like only minutes had passed when a light touch on his shoulder woke him. Instinct took over, and his earlier weariness vanished in an instant.

In less than the blink of an eye, he was wide awake, sitting up, and ready to fight.

"Easy, my young friend," Audie said quietly in the hayloft's gloom. "Someone is down below talking to Fernando. I thought I heard your name mentioned."

"Who in blazes—"

"It sounded like a woman."

Breckinridge's heart leaped. *Ophelia!* he thought. Somehow, she had found out he was in town, had escaped from Carnahan, and had come to him hoping he would keep her safe and take her back to her sisters.

That was exactly what Breckinridge intended to do . . . but only after he killed Jud Carnahan. If he failed in that, he thought he could count on Audie and Nighthawk to help Ophelia. Even though he had just met the oddly matched pair of mountain men, he could tell they were decent, valiant individuals.

Getting up on his hands and knees, he crawled quickly to the edge of the loft and peered over. He was ready to call down to Ophelia and tell her that he was up here.

Instead, he saw a woman he had never seen before talking to Fernando, who stood holding a lantern in an upraised hand.

She was young, but already well curved and lovely in a low-cut blouse and long skirt. From this angle, Breckinridge had an even better view than Fernando did of the intriguing cleavage between the girl's breasts. Her hair was black as midnight and hung straight down her back to the curve of her hips.

She and Fernando were both speaking Spanish, too fast for Breckinridge to keep up with it. But after a moment he gestured toward the loft with his free hand, and the girl turned her head to gaze upward. Her dark eyes were wide with what Breck suddenly realized was fear.

Something was wrong, and this girl seemed to be looking for him.

That spelled trouble—and trouble was just another name for Jud Carnahan.

"What is it?" Audie asked from behind Breckinridge.

"I don't know, but I'm gonna find out."

He would have climbed down, but before he could do so, the girl ran over to the ladder leading to the loft and ascended it with lithe, swift motions. Breckinridge stood up, having to stoop a little, otherwise his great height would have had his head bumping against the roof, and held out a hand to help her as she reached the top of the ladder.

"Señor Wallace?" she asked breathlessly, then didn't let him answer as she went on, "*Sí*, you must be. No one else could be as big as the señorita said you are."

"What señorita?" Breckinridge asked as a feeling of foreboding began to well up inside him.

"Señorita Ophelia. My, how do you say, boss. My friend."

Despite her age, she was probably a whore at the Black Bull, Breckinridge realized. That was why she'd referred to Ophelia as her boss. Without thinking about what he was doing, he reached out and closed his big hands around her bare upper arms.

"Is she all right?" he asked in a voice made hoarse by emotion. "What's happened? Why are you here?"

"She . . . she sent me to help you if I can. With her dying breath, she asked me—"

She stopped short and cried out as Breckinridge's hands clamped harder on her arms. He realized what he was doing and eased up on his grip as he whispered, "She's dead?"

"*Sí, señor.* I am so sorry. She was a good friend, a good person despite everything that man did to her. She told me some of it. She never wanted to talk much about what had happened, but sometimes it helped."

"Carnahan."

"*Sí.* He is outside now, with some other bad men. One of them saw you, trailed you here, and now he has come to kill you. While they hesitated to make their plans, I slipped in ahead of them to warn you."

Breckinridge stood there, his chest heaving. His hands dropped from the girl's arms and clenched into hamlike fists as they hung at his side. For a moment he couldn't speak, but then he was able to ask, "Did Carnahan kill Ophelia?"

"*Sí.* I saw." She shuddered in the faint glow of lantern light that came from below. "He hit her head many times against the wall of the Black Bull. There was nothing I could do to stop him. She was still alive when I reached her, but she spoke only for a moment before life departed."

"Of course there was nothing you could do to save her, my dear," Audie said in a calm, soothing voice. "If you had tried to intervene, no doubt Carnahan would have killed you, too, and you wouldn't have been able to carry out the lady's last wish and warn Breckinridge. You did the right thing."

"I hope so, señor. But now, they will be here soon. You must hide—"

That was never going to happen. Breckinridge wasn't the sort to hide from trouble. Anyway, there wasn't any time left. Breck heard Fernando shout, and then a pistol cracked down in the main area of the stable, followed instantly by a crash of glass. Breck thought he knew what that meant, and a second later his hunch was confirmed by a burst of garish, flickering light. Horses screamed in their stalls as smoke billowed up. That glass breaking had been Fernando's lantern shattering.

The stable was on fire.

Breckinridge leaped to the edge of the loft and in the nightmarish glare from the already-strong flames, he caught a glimpse of Jud Carnahan, a pistol in each hand, standing near Fernando's crumpled body. Behind Carnahan were a dozen more men, including the one Breck had had the run-in with earlier in the day.

That man shouted, "Up there!" causing Carnahan to jerk his head back and look up at the loft. The un-fired pistol in his left hand streaked up and belched flame and smoke. Breckinridge threw himself backward as the ball whipped in front of his face and smacked through the boards of the roof.

A roar of laughter from Carnahan followed the shot. He bellowed, "Keep them pinned up there until the fire's too big for them to get out! Hey, Wallace! You're gonna burn, you son of a bitch!"

"An old building like this, filled with straw, is going to burn very quickly," Audie said. "It'll be an inferno in a matter of moments, Breckinridge. We need to get out."

Breckinridge had grabbed his rifle and pistols from the floor. He glanced at the girl, who was sobbing in terror.

"Maybe we can fight our way past 'em," he said.

Guns were going off down below as Carnahan and his men backed toward the stable's entrance while the blaze spread. Rifle and pistol balls chewed splinters from the edge of the loft and hummed through the air in the close quarters under the roof.

"We'd have no chance that way!" Audie said.

"Ummm!"

Nighthawk's urgent interjection made Breckinridge and Audie look around. The big Crow warrior was pointing to the door in the wall where hay was lifted and loaded into the loft. It opened onto the alley at the side of the building. Flames were already climbing up the wall on that side and were visible along the edge of the floor.

They had no time to waste on debate. Breckinridge yelled, "Let's go!" and looped his left arm around the startled and frightened girl, lifting her off her feet.

Nighthawk grabbed Audie the same way and threw the door back. He went out first, diving through the opening with a yelling Audie tucked under his arm. Breckinridge followed, not really thinking about what he was doing but trusting to his own strength and agility to make the jump and survive.

One second he was still in the flame-lit loft, the next plummeting through dark, empty air with the girl cradled against his broad chest, both arms around her, rifle clutched tightly in his right hand. The fall seemed to take longer than it really did.

Then his feet hit the ground and he let his momentum carry him into a forward roll, twisting his body as he went down so his shoulder would hit the ground first and buffer the impact for the girl he held. Despite that, she let out a loud "Ooooff!" when they hit.

Breckinridge didn't figure Carnahan and his men

would have heard that over the continuing gunfire. He let go of the girl, pushed himself to his feet, and then reached down to help her up. The light from the fire was spreading into the alley, and in its glare he saw Audie and Nighthawk getting up as well. Both of them appeared to be all right. The drop from the loft had been bone jarring and tooth rattling, but they'd been lucky and hadn't broken anything.

"Run back somewhere safe," Breckinridge told the girl as he rested a hand on one of her bare shoulders. "After tonight, I don't know if you'll have a job at the Black Bull, but you can find something better."

"You are going to kill Señor Carnahan?"

"I derned sure am," Breckinridge said. "Now, get outta here!"

He pushed her toward the back of the alley and sent her fleeing.

Then he, Audie, and Nighthawk headed for the street, where Carnahan and his men had retreated to keep pouring rifle and pistol shots into the burning building. Carnahan was still laughing like he was having the time of his life, Breckinridge saw as he edged a look around the corner. The heat was getting bad here in the alley. Breck and his two newfound friends couldn't stay here much longer.

"Audie, you and Nighthawk don't have to do this," he told them above the crackle of the flames. "I just swore to myself earlier today that I was gonna tackle Carnahan by myself from now on. You two can ske-daddle outta here, and I won't take no offense."

"Your argument is no more compelling now than it was earlier," Audie replied. "Jud Carnahan is the sort of monster Nighthawk and I would feel compelled to exterminate, regardless of whether we had taken a liking to you right away, which we did."

"Umm," Nighthawk agreed emphatically.

"All right, then," Breckinridge said. "Let's go stomp us some snakes."

Chapter 33

The three men checked their weapons and gave one another grim nods. Breckinridge recalled the promise he had made to Wolf Tooth, that Carnahan would die knowing he was being sent to hell for the murder of the chief's son as well as all his other crimes. Breck wasn't sure he would be able to keep that promise, because he intended to put a rifle ball through Carnahan's diseased brain as soon as he stepped around that corner.

It wouldn't be as satisfying as killing Carnahan with his bare hands, but it was time to end this.

Breckinridge took the lead, charging around the corner and lifting his rifle to his shoulder. Audie was to his right, Nighthawk on his left. Breck saw Carnahan standing just in front of the other men, the firelight washing over his face and making him look more demonic than ever.

Breckinridge pressed the trigger.

At just that moment, one of the other men stepped forward, pumped the rifle in his hand over his head, and let out a gleeful whoop at the destruction of the stable. The ball from Breckinridge's rifle struck him just above the left ear and lifted his hat off his head, along with a sizable chunk of skull and brain. Blood splattered across Carnahan's face.

The two mountain men fired a split second after Breckinridge, and two more of Carnahan's men went down. Somebody screamed a curse as the whole bunch wheeled to their left to face this new and unexpected threat.

Breckinridge dropped his empty rifle while the smoke from its discharge was still spreading through the air. He yanked both pistols from behind his belt and charged toward the men with a full-throated war cry echoing from him. The double-shotted, heavily charged pistols boomed like the crash of thunder, scything three more men off their feet. Breck, Audie, and Nighthawk had cut the odds almost in half in little more than the blink of an eye.

Then Breckinridge's long, swift running strides had carried him among his enemies. He dropped the empty pistols and grabbed his knife and tomahawk to go to work with them. Guns continued to go off as Audie and Nighthawk fired their pistols and some of Carnahan's men returned the shots.

Breckinridge wreaked bloody havoc as he whirled through the men, hacking and slashing. He was looking for Carnahan but in the chaos couldn't seem to find him. A pistol went off almost right in his face, blinding and deafening him for a moment, but he kept striking out at the vaguely seen shapes anyway. The small, still-coherent part of his brain hoped that Audie and Nighthawk were staying out of his way, because he was so caught up in the lust of battle that he couldn't really tell friend from foe.

Gore smeared his hands and sleeves up to the elbows and dripped from knife and tomahawk by the time a strong hand caught his arm and someone shouted in a deep, powerful voice, "Breckinridge, stop! They're all dead! Stop fighting!"

Breckinridge stood there, muscles still trembling from the urge to strike out. It was Nighthawk who had hold of him, he realized as the Crow said, "Umm," and Audie who had shouted at him to break through his blind rage. Breck could see and hear again, and as he drew in a deep breath, he smelled powder smoke and the coppery tang of freshly spilled blood—a lot of it.

He looked around, blinking eyes that stung from the smoke, and saw the corpses heaped around him in the street. The man he had tussled with earlier in the day was there, his head still attached to his body only by a stringy clump of neck gristle. Breckinridge vaguely recalled taking a swing at the man with his tomahawk. Obviously, that near-decapitation was the result.

The one thing he didn't see was Jud Carnahan's body.

"Where—" he began, but he was too hoarse to go on. He had to try again. "Where's Carnahan?"

"I caught a glimpse of him fleeing, but I was unable to stop him," Audie said. The little mountain man's face was grimy from burned powder, and the tomahawk in his hand was bloody, too. Nighthawk looked much the same. Hard to tell if they were wounded, but Breckinridge hoped none of the blood splattered on them was theirs.

"The Black Bull," Breckinridge rasped. "That's

where he has to be headed." He glanced around at the carnage again. The streets in this part of town were empty at the moment because everybody had scurried for cover when the shooting started. But they wouldn't stay that way. Folks would hurry out to see what had happened and also to make sure the fire didn't spread. An adobe building stood on one side of the stable, an empty lot on the other, so the odds of that were small, but no one on the frontier wanted to take any chances with fire.

Some of the soldiers from the garrison would be coming to investigate the ruckus, too, maybe even Captain Consalvo himself.

"Let's get out of here," Breckinridge said. "You two lay low. I'm headed for the Black Bull."

"We can come with you—" Audie began.

Breckinridge shook his head and said, "Nope, this is down to just Carnahan and me. Reckon that was the way it always had to be."

He found his rifle and pistols where he had dropped them but didn't take the time to reload as he loped off into the darkness. Audie and Nighthawk went the other way. Breckinridge figured there was a chance they would circle around and follow him to the Black Bull anyway, but he'd done what he could to stop them.

He had a showdown calling him now.

It was easy for a fella to get turned around in Santa Fe, especially when he had been in town less than a day and had to stick to the shadows so he wouldn't be noticed. The crowds he had expected to see rushing toward the burning stable showed up, all right, forcing him to take to the back alleys. The town was full of hullabaloo tonight, a situation which he'd added to considerably.

Eventually he found his way back to the plaza, though, and from there it was easy to find the Black Bull. Every lamp in the place was lit, from the looks of it. Breckinridge paused for a moment, across from the entrance, and loaded his pistols. He stuck them behind his belt and left his rifle leaning against the wall of another building. He could retrieve it later, if he was still alive.

While he was doing that, he watched the Black Bull. Nobody was going in and out right now. He wondered if all the customers had gone to see what the commotion was. It didn't matter, he decided. Anybody who was inside, he would just run them out at gunpoint before he confronted Carnahan.

Gripping his pistols, Breckinridge strode across to the door and kicked it open. He went in fast, the pistols tracking back and forth as he searched for enemies.

"You won't need those," a familiar voice said. "It's just you and me, Wallace. I sent everyone else away. I knew you'd be coming. It's time we finish this, you and me."

Jud Carnahan stood in front of the bar. He had a glass in his hand, half-full of nearly colorless liquid. Probably some of that tequila, Breckinridge thought. Carnahan threw back the drink and thumped the empty glass on the bar. A pistol lay on the hardwood within easy reach, but he didn't make a move for it.

Breckinridge hated to take his eyes off his mortal enemy, but he glanced around the room to make sure Carnahan was telling the truth. The Black Bull seemed to be empty, all right.

But then he caught a flicker of movement in the shadows at the top of the stairs leading to the second-floor hall where the soiled doves had their rooms. His first impulse was to jerk up his right-hand pistol and fire at whoever it was, but he controlled that urge. It didn't surprise him in the least that Carnahan would try some sort of trick.

A second later, he was glad he hadn't fired, because a woman's voice called from the top of the stairs, "The end of the bar!"

Breckinridge reacted, swiveling in that direction as a man leaped into the open with a double-barreled shotgun in his hands. Breck fired first as smoke gushed from the pistol in his left hand. The ball slammed into the shotgunner's chest and knocked him back as he jerked the triggers of both barrels. The weapon thundered as it discharged its double load of buckshot into the ceiling.

Breckinridge started to turn back to Carnahan, who had snatched up the pistol from the bar. The gun blasted and Breck felt the shock of the ball. The impact turned him slightly but didn't knock him off his feet. He thrust out the right-hand pistol and fired at Carnahan. Carnahan rocked back against the bar and dropped his empty pistol, but he caught his balance a second later and charged at Breck, bellowing like the bull on the sign outside might have.

Breckinridge saw blood on Carnahan's shirt, but the wound didn't slow the man down, any more than Breck's injury affected him in this moment. A year of deep, smoldering hate fueled both men. They came together with a resounding crash.

Breckinridge was a head taller than Carnahan, but

Carnahan weighed as much or more. They were both incredibly strong. Locked together in a death struggle, they swayed and staggered back and forth as they fought for the upper hand that neither seemed able to gain. They crashed into chairs and tables, upsetting the furniture.

Then Breckinridge stumbled over a chair leg, and Carnahan instantly seized the chance to drive into him and knock him off-balance. Breck went over backward.

But as he fell, he got a desperately outflung hand under Carnahan's beard and locked around his throat. Both men toppled to the floor and rolled over and over as they battled.

When they came to a stop, Breckinridge was on top. He ignored the tremendous blows that Carnahan hammered into his head and body, absorbing that punishment as he clamped his other hand around Carnahan's throat as well. Breck's fingers tightened.

It was like trying to choke a tree trunk to death, but if anyone could accomplish that, it was Breckinridge Wallace. The muscles in his arms and shoulders bunched under the buckskin as he applied more and more pressure to Carnahan's throat. Carnahan kept fighting, but his struggles began to weaken.

Breckinridge leaned closer. His lips drew back from his teeth in a grimace as he snarled, "This is for Dawn Wind! For Rock Against the Sky, the son of Wolf Tooth! For what you did to Morgan! For Absalom Garwood and . . . and for Ophelia!" His face was only inches from Carnahan's face now. "And for me, you evil son of a bitch! Die! Die!"

Carnahan's mouth opened. An ugly gurgling sound came out. His face was purple, and his eyes protruded so much it seemed they were about to burst from their sockets. A stench rose around Breckinridge, and he knew Carnahan's bowels and bladder were emptying as death claimed him. Carnahan's eyes rolled up and began to turn glassy.

He was dead, but Breckinridge held on for another two minutes anyway, just to be sure.

Then, with his heart pounding so hard that his pulse sounded like peals of thunder inside his skull, he slumped forward. He caught himself and started to crawl off Carnahan's corpse.

He heard a shout in Spanish, followed by the blast of a gunshot. Wearily, almost in slow motion, he turned his head to peer over his shoulder.

The girl with the long black hair was halfway down the stairs, holding a pistol from which smoke still curled. On his knees on the floor near the entrance, a pistol lying in front of him where he had dropped it, was Captain Consalvo. Blood stained the front of his fancy uniform jacket. His mouth opened and closed and opened again to let more crimson well out. Then he pitched forward onto his face and didn't move again.

"He was going to shoot you," the girl said to Breckinridge.

"Yeah, I . . . I'm obliged to you." The titanic struggle against Carnahan had exhausted Breckinridge, but he had a nearly endless supply of strength, and vigor was beginning to flow back into him. He staggered to his feet and looked down at his left side, where Carnahan's shot had creased him. It hurt like blazes and was bleeding some, but he knew neither of those things would slow him down.

With Consalvo dead, the Mexican authorities

would be looking for somebody to hang. Breckinridge met the girl at the foot of the stairs and took the pistol away from her.

"Get out of here," he told her.

"You are hurt!"

"I'll be fine. Anyway, it won't matter much. I reckon they'll be stringin' me up for killin' the cap'n."

"No! I shot him—"

More footsteps sounded, this time from the back of the room.

"No one is getting strung up," Audie said as he beckoned to Breckinridge. "Nighthawk and I have horses out back, ready to ride. You can be out of Santa Fe before the confusion subsides."

"What about you two?" Breckinridge asked. "Somebody might've seen you with me."

Audie smiled. "We'll be heading for the tall and uncut, too, as Preacher would say. Civilization is a fine thing for most people, but men such as Nighthawk and myself have to take it in small doses."

Breckinridge knew he was right. He had done what he set out to do—Jud Carnahan was dead—and if settling that debt cost him his life, Breck would have been fine with that.

But there was still a narrow opportunity to escape, and Breckinridge realized he still had some living to do. There were a whole heap of places out here on the frontier that he hadn't seen yet.

As he took a step toward Audie, though, his knees threatened to buckle. The girl gasped and caught hold of his arm.

Bracing himself, Breckinridge told her, "You ain't near big enough to hold me up, darlin', but I appreciate the thought."

"I can care for your wound," she said. "If I go with you."

"Not the worst idea I ever heard," Audie said. "But time is fleeting, Breckinridge."

He nodded, took the girl's hand, and said, "Come on."

He hadn't really thought this through . . . but thinking things through had never been his strong suit, anyway.

The three of them hurried out into the alley, where Nighthawk waited with Breckinridge's saddle mount and the packhorse. Breck paused long enough to say to Audie, "Somebody needs to see to poor Ophelia."

"I have friends here I can trust," the little man said. "I'll leave money with them and make sure that she's laid to rest properly."

"And her sisters and Morgan need to know what happened. It'll break their hearts, but that's better than never knowin'."

"You say the trading post is on the Yellowstone River?"

"Yeah." In just a few words, Breckinridge described how to find it.

"Don't worry, we'll see to that, as well," Audie promised.

"Umm," Nighthawk added.

Breckinridge took the reins from the big Crow warrior and swung up into the saddle. He looked down at the girl for a moment, then held out his hand to her. She grasped it, and he lifted her easily and set her in front of him.

"Where are you going, Breckinridge?" Audie asked.

"Someplace I ain't been before."

He rode away without looking back.

* * *

They paused on a ridge outside of town. Breckinridge turned the horses for a moment so they could look back. A faint orange glow rose into the sky where the stable was still burning. He was sorry about what had happened to Fernando. Death and destruction seemed to follow in his wake, Breck mused, but maybe now that Carnahan was dead, that would stop . . . for a while, anyway.

He couldn't smell the smoke anymore, but the girl's long hair felt good as she sat close against him on the horse's back. He said, "What in tarnation is your name?"

She turned her head to look at him and said, "I am called Belita."

Breckinridge pulled the horses around, nudged them into motion headed east through the night, and said, "Well, Belita, let's go find out what folks are up to in the Republic of Texas."

Chapter 1

"It's a good thing I decided to check," John Gates said to Sonny Rice, who was sitting in the wagon loaded with supplies. They had just come from Henderson's General Store, and John wanted to stop by the telegraph office on the chance Perley might have sent word.

Sonny was immediately attentive. "Did he send a telegram? Where is he?"

"He's in Deadwood, South Dakota," John answered. "He said he's on his way home."

"Did he say if he found your grandpa?"

"He said he found him, but Grandpa's dead, said he'd explain it all when he gets back."

"Well, I'll be . . ." Sonny drew out. "Ol' Perley found him. I figured he would, he usually does what he sets out to do."

John couldn't disagree. His younger brother was always one to follow a trail to its end, even though it often led him to something he would have been better served to avoid. He laughed when he thought about what his older brother, Rubin, said about

Perley. "If there ain't but one cow pie between here and the Red River, Perley will most likely step in it." It was a joke, of course, but it did seem that trouble had a way of finding Perley. This was true, even though he would go to any lengths to avoid it.

"We might as well go by the diner and see if Beulah's cooked anything fit to eat," John casually declared, knowing that was what Sonny was hoping to hear. "Might even stop by Patton's afterward and get a shot of whiskey. That all right with you?" He could tell by the grin on the young ranch hand's face that he knew he was being japed. As a rule, Sonny didn't drink very often, but he would imbibe on some occasions. John nudged the big gray gelding toward the small plain building at the end of the street that proclaimed itself to be the Paris Diner. He was glad he had thought to check by the telegraph office. It was good news to hear that Perley was on his way home to Texas. He had a long way to travel from the Black Hills, so it was hard to say when to expect him to show up at the Triple-G. His mother and his brother, Rubin, would be really happy to hear about the telegram. Perley had been gone a long time on his quest to find their grandpa. His mother had been greatly concerned when Perley didn't return with his brothers after the cattle were delivered to the buyers in Ogallala. These were the thoughts running through John's mind when he reined the gray to a halt at the hitching rail in front of the diner, then waited while Sonny pulled up in the wagon.

"Well, I was beginning to wonder if the Triple-G had closed down," Lucy Tate sang out when she saw them walk in.

"Howdy, Lucy," John returned. "It has been a while

since we've been in town. At least, it has been for me. I don't know if any of the other boys have been in." He gave her a big smile. "I thought you mighta got yourself married by now," he joked, knowing what a notorious flirt she was.

She waited for them to sit down before replying. "I've had some offers, but I'm waiting to see if that wife of yours is gonna kick you out."

"She's threatened to more than once," he said, "but she knows there's a line of women hopin' that'll happen."

She laughed. "I'm gonna ask Martha about that if you ever bring her in here to eat." Without asking if they wanted coffee, she filled two cups. "Beulah's got chicken and dumplin's, or beef stew. Whaddle-it-be?"

"Give me the chicken and dumplin's," John said. "I get enough beef every day. How 'bout you, Sonny?"

"I'll take the chicken, too," Sonny replied, his eyes never having left the saucy waitress.

Noticing it, John couldn't resist japing him. "How 'bout Sonny, here? He ain't married and he's got a steady job."

She chuckled delightedly and reached over to tweak Sonny's cheek. "You're awful sweet, but still a little young. I'll keep my eye on you, though." She went to the kitchen to get their food, leaving a blushing young ranch hand to recover.

"She's something, ain't she?" John asked after seeing Sonny's embarrassment. "Can't take a thing she says seriously." He thought at once of Perley, who had made that mistake and suffered his disappointment. Further thoughts on the subject were interrupted when Becky Morris came in from the kitchen.

"Afternoon, John," Becky greeted him. "Lucy said

you were here." She greeted Sonny as well, but she didn't know his name. "It's been a while since any of the Triple-G men have stopped in. Perley used to come by every time he was in town, but I haven't seen him in a long time now. Is he all right?"

"Perley's been gone for a good while now," John answered. "I just got a telegram from him this mornin', from Dakota Territory, said he's on his way home."

"Oh, well maybe he'll come in to see us when he gets back," Becky said.

"I'm sure he will," John replied. He couldn't help wondering if Perley had taken proper notice of Becky Morris. Shy and gentle, unlike Lucy Tate, Becky looked more the woman a man should invest his life with. And he might be wrong, but he suspected he detected a wistful tone in her voice when she asked about Perley.

Before they were finished, Beulah Walsh came out to visit. John assured her that her reputation as a cook was still deserved, as far as he was concerned. He paid for his and Sonny's meal, and got up to leave. "We've gotta stop by Patton's before we go back to the ranch," he said. "Sonny's gotta have a shot of that rot-gut whiskey before he leaves town."

"I never said that," Sonny insisted. "You were the one that said we'd go to the saloon."

"Don't let him bother you, sweetie," Lucy said and gave him another tweak on his cheek. "I know how you heavy drinkers need a little shooter after you eat."

"What did you tell her that for?" Sonny asked as soon as they were outside. "Now she thinks I'm a drunk."

"I doubt it," John replied.

* * *

Moving back down the short street to Patton's Saloon, they tied the horses to the rail and went inside. Benny Grimes, the bartender, called out a "Howdy" as soon as they walked in the door. "John Gates, I swear, I thought you mighta gave up drinkin' for good."

"How do, Benny?" John greeted him. "Might as well have, we ain't had much time to get into town lately. Ain't that right, Sonny?"

"That's a fact," Sonny agreed and picked up the shot glass Benny slid over to him. He raised it, turned toward John, and said, "Here's hopin' Perley has a safe trip home." He downed it with a quick toss, anxious to get it over with. He was not a drinker by habit and took a drink of whiskey now and then only to avoid having to explain why he didn't care for it.

"Well, I'll sure drink to that," John said and raised his glass.

"Me, too," Benny said and poured himself one. After they tossed the whiskey down, he asked, "Where is he?"

"Way up in Dakota Territory," John said, "and we just got word he's on his way home, so we need to let the folks hear the news." He had one more drink, then they headed back to the Triple-G.

The man John Gates had wished a safe trip home earlier in the day was seated a few yards from a crystal-clear waterfall. It was a good bit off the trail he had been following, but he had a feeling the busy stream he had crossed might lead to a waterfall. As high up as he was on the mountain, it stood to reason the stream would soon come to a cliff. It pleased him to find out he had been right, and it had been worth his while to have seen it. It was a trait that Perley Gates had undoubtedly inherited from his grandfather, an obsession for seeing what might lie on the other side of the mountain. And it was the reason he found himself in the Black Hills of Dakota Territory on this late summer day—that and the fact that he was not married and his brothers were. That meant it didn't matter if he rode all the way to hell and who knows where. There wasn't any wife waiting for him to come home, so he had been the obvious pick to go in search of his grandfather.

His grandfather, for whom he was named, was buried here in these dark mountains, not far from where Perley now sat, drinking the stout black coffee he favored. He felt a strong kinship with him, even though he had not really known the man, having never met him until a short time before he passed away. Even so, that was enough time for the old man to determine that he was proud to have his young grandson wear his name, Perley Gates. The old man had been one of the lucky ones who struck it rich in the Black Hills gold rush before an outlaw's bullet brought his life to an end. Determined to make restitution to his family for having abandoned them, he hung on long enough to extract a promise from his grandson to take his gold back to Texas.

The gold dust had been right where his grandfather had said it would be, and Perley recovered four canvas sacks from under a huge rock before he was satisfied there were no more. With no scales to weigh the sacks, he guessed it to be ten pounds per sack. At the present time, gold was selling in Deadwood at a little over three hundred and thirty dollars a pound.

If his calculations were correct, he was saddled with a responsibility to deliver over thirteen thousand dollars in gold dust to Texas, more than eight hundred miles away. It was not a task he looked forward to. The gold rush had brought every robber and dry-gulcher west of Omaha to Deadwood Gulch, all with an eye toward preying on those who had worked to bring the gold out of the streams. Perley's problem was how to transport his treasure without attracting the watchful eye of the outlaws. It would be easier to convert the dust to paper money, but he was not confident he would get a fair exchange from the bank in Deadwood, because of the inflation there.

To add to his concerns, he had accumulated five extra horses during his time in the Black Hills and he didn't want the bother of driving them all the way to Texas with no one to help him. With forty pounds of dust to carry, he decided to keep one of the horses to use as a second packhorse. His packhorse could carry the load along with his supplies, but with the load divided onto two horses, he could move a lot faster in the event he had to. His choice of the extra horses would have to be the paint gelding that his grandfather had ridden. The old man loved that horse, maybe as much as Perley loved Buck, so he wouldn't feel right about selling it. With Custer City and Hill City reduced almost to ghost towns, he decided to ride back to Deadwood to see if he could sell the other four. Deadwood wasn't a good market for selling horses. Cheyenne would be a better bet, or maybe Hat Creek Station, for that matter, but he figured he hadn't paid anything for them, so he might as well let them go cheap. With that settled, he packed up and started back to Deadwood.

* * *

"Evenin'. Looks like you're needin' to stable some horses," Franklin Todd greeted Perley when he drew up before his place of business.

"Evenin'," Perley returned. "Matter of fact, I'm lookin' to sell four of 'em, if I can get a reasonable price. I'm fixin' to head back to Texas, and I don't wanna have to lead a bunch of horses back with me."

Todd was at once alerted to the prospects of acquiring four horses at little cost, but he hesitated for a moment, stroking his chin as if undecided. "Which four?" He finally asked. Perley indicated the four and Todd paused to think some more. "I really ain't buyin' no horses right now, but I'll take a look at 'em." He took his time examining the four horses, then finally made an offer of ten dollars each. Perley wasn't really surprised by the low offer and countered with a price of fifty dollars for all four. Todd didn't hesitate to agree. "These horses ain't stolen, are they?" He asked as he weighed out the payment.

"Not till now," Perley answered.

With an eye toward disguising four sacks of gold dust, he left Todd's and walked his horses past a saloon to a general merchandise establishment. "Can I help you with something?" the owner asked when Perley walked in.

"I'm just lookin' to see if there's anything I need," Perley answered and quickly scanned the counters and shelves while taking frequent glances out the door at his horses at the rail. In the process of trying to keep an eye on his horses, his attention was drawn to several large sacks stacked near the door. "What's in those sacks?" He pointed to them.

"Probably nothing you'd be looking for," the owner replied. "Something I didn't order. Came in with a load of merchandise from Pierre. It's about four hundred pounds of seed corn. I don't know where it was supposed to go, but it sure as hell wasn't Deadwood. There ain't a level piece of ground anywhere in the Black Hills for farming. I tried to sell it to Franklin Todd at the stable for horse feed. Even he didn't want it."

Perley walked over to an open bag and looked inside. "I might could use some of it. Whaddaya askin' for it?"

Too surprised to respond right away, the owner hesitated before asking, "How much are you thinking about?" When Perley said he could use a hundred pounds of it, the owner shrugged and replied, "I don't know—two dollars?"

"I could use some smaller canvas bags, too, four of 'em. You got anything like that?"

With both merchant and customer satisfied they had made a good deal, Perley threw his hundred-pound sack of seed corn across the back of one of his packhorses and started back toward Custer City. Although already late in the afternoon, he preferred to camp in the hills outside of Deadwood, considering what he carried on his packhorses. So he rode for a good nine or ten miles before stopping. When he made camp that night, he placed a ten-pound sack of gold dust in each of the twenty-five-pound sacks he had just bought, and filled in around it with seed corn. When he finished, he was satisfied that his dust was disguised about as well as he could hope for, and the corn didn't add a lot of weight with the amount necessary to fill the sacks.

He downed the last gulp of coffee from his cup and

got to his feet. "Well, I can't sit here and worry about it all night," he announced to Buck, the big bay gelding grazing nosily a few yards away. "You don't give a damn, do ya?"

"That horse ever answer you back?"

Perley, startled, stepped away from the fire, grabbing his rifle as he dived for cover behind a tree, searching frantically for where the voice had come. It didn't sound very far away.

"Whoa! Hold on a minute, feller," the voice exclaimed. "Ain't no need for that there rifle."

"I'll decide that after you come outta your hidin' place," Perley responded and cranked a cartridge into the cylinder of the Winchester.

"Hold on," the voice came back again. "I didn't mean to surprise you like that. I shoulda sang out a little sooner. I was just passin' by on the trail up there on the ridge and I saw your fire, so I thought I'd stop and say howdy." A short pause followed, then he said, "It always pays to be careful to see what kinda camp you're lookin' at before you come a-ridin' in. I'm comin' out, so don't take a shot at me, all right?"

"All right," Perley answered. "Come on out." He watched cautiously as his visitor emerged from the darkness of the trees above the creek, alert for any sign of movement that might indicate there were others with him. When he felt sure the man was alone, he eased the hammer back down, but still held the rifle ready to fire. Leading a dun gelding, with a mule following on a rope, his surprise guest approached the fire. "You're travelin' these back trails pretty late at night, ain'tcha?" Perley asked.

"Reckon so," he replied, "but with all the outlaws ridin' these trails, lookin' for somebody to rob, it pays

for a man alone to travel some at night." He looked
around at the loaded packs and the horses grazing
close by. "Looks like you're gettin' ready to travel, too,
from the looks of your camp. I smelled your fire from
the ridge back there. Thought maybe I might get a
cup of coffee, but I see you're 'bout ready to pack up."

"I was thinkin' about it," Perley said. "Where you
headin', Deadwood?"

"Nope, the other way," he answered. "I've seen Deadwood, I'm ready to go back to Cheyenne."

Perley studied the young man carefully for a few
moments. A young man, close to his own age, he figured. There was nothing unusual about him, unless
you counted the baggy britches he wore, that looked
to be a couple of inches short, and the shirt that
looked a size too big. Perley decided he was no threat.
"Well, I've got plenty of coffee, so I reckon I can fix
you up with a cup. What about supper? You had anything to eat?"

"As a matter of fact, I ain't," he said. "I had that
thought in mind when I caught sight of your camp.
I'd be much obliged. My name's Billy Tuttle."

"Perley Gates," Perley replied and waited for him to
ask the name again, which was the usual response.
When he didn't, Perley said, "Take care of your animals and I'll make us a pot of coffee. It's kinda late to
go any farther tonight, anyway, so I think I'll just stay
here. You like venison? 'Cause that's what I'm cookin'
for supper." Billy said that would suit him just fine.
He'd been living on sowbelly and little else for the
past couple of days.

Perley soon decided there was nothing to fear from
his surprise guest. As he had said, he was focused on
getting back to his home in Cheyenne and he guessed

the young man was short on supplies. "You any kin to Tom Tuttle there in Cheyenne?" he asked.

"He's my pa," Billy replied. "You know him?"

"I've done some business with your pa," Perley answered. "Matter of fact, I sold him a couple of horses when I stopped at his stable one time. He's a good man." It didn't take long before Billy told the story of his attempt to make his fortune in Deadwood Gulch, a story that left him headed for home with empty pockets. It was a story all too common in boomtowns like Deadwood and Custer City. "So you partnered up with a couple of fellows and they ran off with all the gold the three of you found?" Perley summed up.

"That's a fact," Billy confirmed. "It wasn't but about four hundred dollars' worth. Wouldn't paid us much when we split it three ways, but it was still a helluva lot more than I came out here with."

"I swear," Perley commented. "That's tough luck, all right. Did you know these two fellows before you partnered up with 'em?"

"No, I just ran up on 'em one mornin' and they looked like they could use a hand, so I went to work with 'em, building a sluice box. Wasn't long before we started strikin' color, and it wasn't long after that when I woke up one mornin' and they was gone, cleared out while I was asleep."

It was hard for Perley not to feel sympathy for the unfortunate young man. He couldn't help thinking that Billy's experience sounded like the kind of fix that he carried a reputation for. He thought of his brother Rubin saying, *If there wasn't but one cow pie on the whole damn ranch, Perley would step in it.* Perley had to admit that sometimes it seemed to be true. Maybe he and Billy had that in common. "So whaddaya plan on doin' now? Go back and help your pa in the stable?"

"I reckon," Billy replied, then hesitated before going on. "Pa ain't gonna be too happy to see me come home. I think he was hopin' I'd stay on out here in the Black Hills."

That was surprising to Perley. "Why is that?" Tom Tuttle impressed him as a solid family man. He had to admit, however, that he had only a brief acquaintance with him.

"The woman Pa's married to ain't my mama," Billy said. "Pa married her when my mama died of consumption. She's my step-mother and she's got a son of her own about my age. She's talked Pa into turnin' his business over to her son when Pa gets too old to run it, and I reckon I'm just in the way."

Perley didn't know what to say. In the short time he had dealings with Tom Tuttle, he would not have thought him to be the type to abandon his own son. He had compassion for Billy, but all he could offer him was common courtesy. "Well, I'm sorry to hear you have troubles with your pa, but if it'll help, you're welcome to ride along with me till we get to Cheyenne. I'm guessin' you ain't fixed too good for supplies."

"You guessed right," Billy responded at once. "And I surely appreciate it. I won't be no bother a'tall. I'm used to hard work, and I'll do my share of the chores."

"Good," Perley said, with as much enthusiasm as he could muster. Truth be told, a stranger as a traveling companion was close to the last thing he wanted, considering what he was carrying on his packhorses. He didn't intend to get careless, even though Billy seemed forthright and harmless. Close to Perley's age, Billy

might come in handy if they were unfortunate enough
to encounter outlaws on the road to Cheyenne.

After the horses and Billy's mule were taken care
of, the two travelers ate supper, planning to get an
early start in the morning. "Here," Billy insisted, "I'll
clean up the cups and fryin' pan. I've got to earn my
keep," he added cheerfully. After everything was done
they both spread their bedrolls close to the fire and
turned in.

Perley was awake at first light after having slept fit-
fully, due to a natural tendency to sleep with one eye
open, even though he felt he had nothing to fear
from Billy. He revived the fire and started coffee
before Billy woke up. "Here I am lyin' in bed while
you're already at it," Billy said as he rolled out of his
blankets. "Whatcha want me to do?"

"Just pack up your possibles and throw a saddle on
your horse," Perley said. "We'll have a cup of coffee
before we get started, eat breakfast when we rest the
horses."

It didn't take long for Billy to load the few items he
owned on the mule, so when he finished, he came to
help Perley. "What's in the sacks?" Billy asked when he
saw Perley tying two twenty-five-pound sacks on each
of his packhorses.

"Kansas seed corn," Perley answered casually. "I
found a store in Deadwood that had about four hundred pounds of it. Ain't nobody in Deadwood wantin'
seed corn, so I bought a hundred pounds of it at a
damn good price. Gonna take it back to Texas and
start me a corn patch. If I'd had a couple more horses,
I'da bought all he had." He made a point then of

opening one of the sacks and taking out a handful to show Billy. "You can't get corn like this in Texas." Billy nodded his head politely, but was obviously unimpressed, which was the reaction Perley hoped for. Packed up and ready to go, they started the first day of their journey together, following the road back toward Custer City, heading south.

The second night's camp was made by a busy stream halfway between Hill City and Custer. By this time, Perley's supply of smoked venison was down to only enough for another meal or two. Then it would be back to sowbelly, unless they were lucky enough to find some game to shoot. Perley was not inclined to tarry, considering the gold he was transporting. As somewhat of a surprise to him, he found Billy just as eager to put the Black Hills behind them, considering what he had said about his father. Curious, Perley asked him, "What are you aimin' to do when you get back to Cheyenne? You think your pa really won't be happy to see you back?" He couldn't believe that Tom Tuttle would kick his son out.

"Oh, I ain't worried about that. I don't wanna work in the damn stable, anyway. I've got a few ideas I'm thinkin' about."

"What kinda ideas?" Perley asked.

"Yeah, what kinda ideas?" The voice came from the darkness behind them. "Maybe stealin' gold from your partners, stuff like that, huh Billy?"

"Don't even think about it," another voice warned when Perley started to react. He had no choice but to remain seated by the fire. "Come on in, Jeb. I've got 'em both covered."

A tall, gangly man stepped into the circle of firelight. He was grinning as he held a double-barreled shotgun on them. In another second, he was joined by a second man, this one a bull-like brute of a man. "Hello, Billy," he said. "I see you got you another partner already. It took me and Luke a while before we tracked you down. Seems like you took off so quick, you must notta realized you took all the gold, instead of just your share."

"Whoa, now, Jeb," Billy exclaimed. "You know I wouldn'ta done nothin' like that. Luke musta buried it somewhere else and forgot where he put it." He looked at the lanky man with the shotgun. "What about it, Luke? Ain't that what musta happened? You were awful drunk that night."

His question caused Luke to laugh. "I gotta give you credit, Billy, you can make up the damnedest stories I've ever heard."

Jeb, who was obviously the boss, said, "We'll see soon enough when we take a look at the packs on that mule." He stared hard at Perley then. "Who's this feller?"

"His name's Perley Gates," Billy said, causing both of the outlaws to laugh.

"Pearly Gates," Luke echoed. "Well, ain't that somethin'? Looks to me like he's carryin' a helluva lot more than you are. Maybe ol' Pearly struck it rich back there in the gulch and now he's packin' it all outta here."

"If I had," Perley spoke then, "I reckon I'd still be back there in the gulch, lookin' for more." Angry that he had been taken so completely by surprise, it didn't help to learn that Billy had fooled him, too. Not only was he a thief, he had brought his troubles to roost with him.

"Damn, he talks," Luke mocked. "We'll take a look in them packs, too."

"You're makin' a mistake, Jeb," Billy said. "Pearly ain't got nothin' in them packs, but supplies and some kinda fancy seed corn he's fixin' to plant. If you think I stole your gold dust, then go ahead and look through my packs."

"Oh, I will," Jeb replied, "you sneakin' rat. Luke, go through the packs on that damn mule. There's five pounds of dust in 'em somewhere. That oughta be easy to find." When Billy started to get up, Jeb aimed his pistol at him. "You just set right there and keep your hands where I can see 'em."

Caught in a helpless situation, there was nothing Perley could do but sit there while Luke rifled through Billy's packs. When he glanced at Billy, he saw no sign of concern in his face. Maybe he really hadn't stolen their gold, but it sure seemed like his former partners were convinced that he had. "Ain't no need to make a mess of my stuff just 'cause you was wrong," Billy complained when Luke started throwing his possessions around in frustration.

"Shut your mouth!" Jeb yelled at Billy. "Look in his saddle bags," he said to Luke then.

"I told you I ain't got your gold," Billy argued. "Looks to me like maybe you oughta be askin' Luke where that dust is. All I wanted was to get the hell outta that creek after you shot that feller. I figured you and Luke could have my share."

Jeb shifted a suspicious eye in Luke's direction. "I don't reckon somethin' like that mighta happened, could it, Luke? I mean, we was all drinkin' kinda heavy that night. Last thing I remember before I passed out was you holdin' that sack of dust and talkin' about what you was gonna buy with your share. When I woke up the next mornin', you was already up and Billy was gone."

"Hold on a minute!" Luke blurted out. "You're lettin' that lyin' son of a bitch put crazy ideas in your head. Me and you been ridin' together long enough for you to know I wouldn't do nothin' like that."

"You looked through all his packs and there weren't no sack of gold dust," Jeb reminded him. "Whaddaya suppose happened to it?"

"How the hell do I know?" Luke shot back, then nodded toward Perley, who was still a spectator at this point. "Most likely it's in his stuff. Billy musta put it on one of his packhorses." He turned and started toward Perley's belongings, stacked beside his bedroll.

"This has gone as far as it's goin'," Perley said, getting to his feet. "You've got no call to go plunderin' through my things like you did with Billy's. Billy just hooked up with me last night and he wouldn't likely just hand over five pounds of gold dust for me to tote for him, would he? You can take a look at what I'm carryin', but I'll help you do it, so you don't go tearin' up my packs like you did with Billy's."

His statement caused them both to hesitate for a moment, surprised by his audacity. Then they both laughed at his obvious stupidity. "Mister," Jeb informed him, "you ain't got no say in what we'll do. It was bad luck for you when you joined up with Billy Tuttle. I'm tired of jawin' with both of you." Then, without warning, he said, "Shoot 'em both, Luke."

"My pleasure," Luke said and raised his shotgun to fire. Before he could cock the hammers back, he was doubled over by a .44 slug from Perley's Colt. Jeb's reaction was swift, but not fast enough to draw his pistol before Perley's second shot slammed into his chest. He was already dead when his weapon cleared the holster and fired one wayward shot in Billy's direction.

Billy howled, grabbed his leg, and started limping around in a circle. "Damn, damn, damn . . ." He muttered over and over as he clutched his baggy trouser leg with both hands.

Perley holstered his .44 and moved quickly to help him. "How bad is it? Let me give you a hand."

"It ain't bad," Billy insisted. "I can take care of it. You make sure them two are dead. I'll take care of my leg."

"They're both dead," Perley said. "Now sit down and I'll take a look at that wound." He paused then when a peculiar sight caught his eye. "What tha—" was as far as he got when he saw a tiny stream of dust spraying on the toe of Billy's boot, not understanding at once what he was seeing. When he realized what it was, he looked up to meet Billy's gaze.

"Looks like I sprung a leak," Billy said, smiling sheepishly. "The son of a bitch shot a hole in my britches." When Perley said nothing, but continued to stare in disbelief, Billy tried to divert his attention. "Man, you're fast as greased lightning. You saved both our lives. I ain't never seen anybody that fast with a handgun."

Perley's gaze was still captured by a little pile of gold dust forming on the toe of Billy's boot, with Billy hesitant to move his foot for fear of causing the gold to mix in the dirt beneath it. "You caused me to kill two men you stole gold from," he said, not at all pleased by the fact.

A little more apprehensive now that he had seen Perley's skill with a gun, Billy countered. "Let's not forget that they was fixin' to shoot us. There weren't no doubt about that. I saw 'em shoot a man at a placer mine and take that little five pound sack of dust. That's when I decided that weren't no partnership for me."

"So you cut out and took the gold with you," Perley reminded him. "Looks to me like they had good reason to come after you."

"Well, they didn't have no right to the gold," Billy said, "'specially after they killed him for it." When it was obvious that Perley was far from casual when it came to the taking of a man's life, Billy tried to change his focus. "I reckon you've earned a share of the gold and I don't mind givin' it to you. I figure I've got about sixteen hundred dollars' worth. That'ud make your share about eight hundred." When there was still no positive reaction from Perley, he tried to make light of the situation. "And that ain't countin' the dust runnin' outta my britches leg." He hesitated to make a move, still not sure what Perley had in mind. "All right if I see if I can fix it?"

"I reckon you might as well," Perley finally said, not really sure what he should do about the situation he found himself in. He was still feeling the heavy responsibility for having killed two men, even knowing he had been given no choice. The one called Luke was preparing to empty both barrels of that shotgun. There was no time to think. "I don't want any share in your gold," he said. "Go ahead and take care of it."

Billy's expression was enough to indicate that he was more than happy to hear that. He immediately unbuckled his belt and dropped his britches to reveal two cotton bags, one hanging beside each leg from a length of clothesline tied around his waist. Perley could hardly believe what he saw. Jeb's wild shot had drilled a hole straight through Billy's trouser leg and the cotton bag hanging inside. "What about their horses and guns?" Billy asked as he transferred the remaining dust in the damaged bag into the other one.

"What about 'em?" Perley responded, still undecided what he should do with Billy.

"I mean, hell, you killed 'em, both of 'em, so I reckon you'd be right in claimin' you own all their belongin's." He glanced up quickly. "I sure as hell ain't gonna give you no argument."

Perley took an extra few minutes to think it over while Billy was busy trying to recover every grain of dust that had poured through the hole. He had to admit that he didn't know what to do about it—a thief stealing from another thief. The part that worried him was the killings he had been forced to commit and he blamed Billy for causing it. One thing he knew for sure was that he'd had enough of Billy Tuttle, so when he made his decision, he told Billy. "I ain't ever operated outside the law, and I don't reckon I'll start now. Those two fellows were outlaws and you were ridin' with 'em, so I reckon whatever they done, you were part of it. So you're sure as hell an outlaw, too. I reckon this is where you and I part ways. You take your gold and the horses, and anything else on those two. If your daddy wasn't Tom Tuttle, I might be inclined to turn you over to the sheriff back in Deadwood. But your pa doesn't need to know you got on the wrong side of the law, so if you'll go on back to Cheyenne and start livin' an honest life, he'll never hear about you bein' mixed up with these outlaws from me. We'll go our separate ways and forget about what happened here. Can I have your promise on that?"

"Yessir, you sure do," Billy answered in his most contrite manner. "I 'preciate the chance to get myself right with the law. I've sure as hell learned my lesson. If it weren't for you, I'd most likely be dead right now, so you have my promise." He hesitated for a few moments, then said, "I don't see no use in us splittin' up, though. It looks to me like it'd be better for both of us to travel together for protection. Whaddaya say?"

"I don't think so, Billy," Perley answered. "At least for me, I'll be better alone. Good luck to you, though."